THE JOURNEYS OF MCGILL FEIGHAN combines the epic sweep of *The Lord of the Rings* and the tight suspense of the *Dune* trilogy with the wry humor and techno–fantastic imagination of *Stranger in a Strange Land*...

Book One: CAVERNS

Welcome to a world of unlimited possibilities, in a universe of no escape!

Beginning a new Series by
KEVIN O'DONNELL, Jr.
Author of MAYFLIES

The Journeys of McGill Feighan, Book I

CAVERNS

KEVIN O'DONNELL, JR.

BERKLEY BOOKS, NEW YORK

CAVERNS

A Berkley Book / published by arrangement with
the author

PRINTING HISTORY
Berkley edition / April 1981

ISBN: 0-425-04730-X

A BERKLEY BOOK® TM 757,375

PRINTED IN THE UNITED STATES OF AMERICA

I'd like to thank some people who helped me during the writing of this book: Al Sirois, Victoria Schochet, Cherry Weiner, Mark J. McGarry, and of course my wife, Kim Tchang. Their advice and support made all the difference.

To Margaret Ann O'Donnell,
who taught me to speak, to read, to write,
and to dare to do all three well,
I dedicate this book with love.

▪ **Chapter I** ▪

Despite the arrow-tipped winter winds, the giant gastropod form-flowed out of sheer enjoyment. On its home planet, in weather like this, it would be hibernating, but here the food supply didn't hide from the cold. What wonderful availability! Even halfway to the rocky island, it could break a tendril through the ice and pull seaweed from the bottom. Delicious!

It had no idea why the Far Being Retzglaran had sent it on its journey, but it didn't regret not asking for an explanation (its master being notoriously unable to abide inquisitive courtiers). Not that it cared. From budhood it had wanted to travel to the pinpricks of light that burst through the night sky, and now it had the opportunity.

Much opportunity, in fact, for the Far Being had sponsored a Galactic Grand Tour. Thirty-eight planets, so far, and the thirty-ninth was coming up, a new net node called Sol III. What an excursion! Twenty-six local days wandering in the undeveloped hinterlands of each planet, looking, smelling, nibbling on the local flora (unless the guidebooks said it was intelligent), and finding intimacy with the earth. It bore no responsibilities, except on the thirty-ninth planet, where a detailed schedule had been arranged. The itinerary was strange indeed, but the gastropod was not one to question a benefactor. After all, *it* wasn't paying for this trip, and if the Far Being wanted it to run an errand on the side, well, that was fine and dandy, no problem, no problem.

Snow crunched and compressed as it oozed up the ramp to

1

the Customs Building, where a bored functionary coded its passchip and reminded it to change its local currency into FNC's before it left. Throngorn II money was valueless anywhere but T-II itself. Even there, most natives ignored it, preferring to trade in the decorated shells they'd trusted for millennia.

Once inside the spacious Flinger Building, it swallowed its passchip into the appropriate stomach, searched out the second most recently activated file, and erased the visa from Delurc, its previous stopover. Just as its master had ordered.

The authorities thought civilians couldn't alter the card-sized passchips, for one entered date into them by realigning the molecular structure of their visa-files, but the authorities hadn't taken into account sentient metallurgical laboratories that could work on the subatomic level.

Exuding puffs of diluted fluorocarbons, it slithered to the Ticket Booth, a lashed-together grillwork of polished sticks. There sat a furry, big-eared Trainee Flinger, proud of her lustrous tunic. The gastropod squashed itself down to display its communication membrane. Across the membrane it wrote, in passable Throngornian, "A one-way ticket to Sol III, New York City, please."

Due to the atmosphere, and the distance from its primary, wintertime Throngorn II was noted for dimness. Thus the Trainee's eyes were naturally huge, and it would be unfair to say that they widened with surprise. They did, however, bulge. "I apologize, honored sir," she said hesitantly, "but you are much too heavy to cast. There is a weight limit—"

"Mistake mine," it scribbled. "Apologies also mine. Will return." Rippling into reverse, it backed out of the building, slipping down the ramp into a snow-crusted field of boulders. With regret over its waste of valuable nutrients, it flushed all the rock and metal out of its system. It shrank as the pile beneath it rose; it squatted on 300 tonnes of stone like a mad brooding hen. But still it was some 87,000 kilograms overweight.

Sighing inside, it drained from its storage cells 99.5% of their fluids . . . steam rose on the winter wind, and ice crystallized almost audibly under the slag heap. Vacuoles vanished, cell walls contracted; layers of spongy flesh thinned and hardened. An hour later, the gastropod—now a quadruped with a coffin-shaped body that was almost all dry, dormant storage meat—tottered up the ramp and again requested a ticket.

The Trainee nodded her approval. "Fifty FNC's, please."

Elevating a forelimb with a hole in its end, the gastropod spat forth a single orange-white bill. After sucking up its change, it headed for Fling Booth 9, as the Trainee had indicated.

When it was inside, the Flinger on duty peered through the glass window. "Are you ready?" he called out.

The gastropod, so bulkless as to be sapped of energy, darkened with irritation as it showed the Flinger its membrane. "Yes," it scrawled abruptly.

"Brace yourself."

PING

Transition was always a time of frozen terror. One minute the gleaming white tiles of the Fling Booth surrounded one; the next, utter blackness dropped. It was true blackness, the absence of light (and the gastropod, sensitive to both infrared and ultraviolet, was perhaps more oppressed by this deprivation than most). Following hard on darkness' heels thundered contradiction: the traveler was growing, swelling, inflating beyond the galaxy's limits; at the same instant, it deflated, shrank, dwindled down to subatomic size. For a tenth of a pulse it was both infinitely large and infinitely small— and then came the tearing. It felt like the very molecules of its body had rebelled, half straining to speed off in one direction, the rest tugging in another. That lasted till the universe died of old age, though the gastropod was certain (having been reassured by no less an expert than the Far Being itself) that it was actually of no duration at all. Then tearing became healing; its cells sang the joys of re-union. The contradiction resolved itself with a return to normal size. Blackness fled from the gleaming white tiles of a Flop Booth. Through the glass window in the ceiling peeped a smooth, hairless face, one with two probable eyes, one bi-holed protrusion, one orifice—

"You okay?" called a voice in Terran.

Feebly, it tilted its forward end to the ceiling. "Yes," it wrote on its translucent membrane, "I fine am. Much thank. Need water."

"Restroom's to your right as you leave the Booth, then follow the signs to the Customs area." With a friendly salute, it disappeared.

The gastropod creaked out the door, found the lavatory, and turned on the faucet not a moment too soon. It was already collapsing from thirst as the first drops of water dampened its forelimb. It sucked. And grew enough to reach another sink. It gulped. It grew. Before too long, water splashed in every basin while the being lay on the dirty floor and distended like a sausage skin being stuffed.

Eighty-seven thousand kilograms of water later, it burped, shut off the taps, and wriggled out of the restroom. Six aliens waited angrily outside; two had embarrassed themselves because they hadn't been able to get in. "Apologies," it flashed, "death/life at stake." And it flowed past, ignoring their attempts to continue the dispute.

Down the hall, it submitted to a full-body scan, and cleared Customs with minimal trouble. In exchange for a 50 FNC deposit, a guarantee that it had a ticket off Earth, the Immigrations official affixed a visa to its passchip. When the last strand of red tape had fallen away and freed it, it snaked outside and emptied a passing garbage truck. Then it consulted the road map in the memory molecule its master had provided.

Unsure of how to begin, it waved an ochre pseudohand at a gesticulating biped, one whose starred cap and three-meter height suggested authority. Five minutes elapsed before it realized the biped was a computer-generated simulacrum. Then, locating the sensors in the generator pedestal, it pressed its membrane against a camera to ask, "Way which to Van Wyck Expressway?"

"Where are you headed?" monotoned the light sculpture.

"Cleveland," it replied, in boldface Gothic type. "Take I Van Wyck to Cross-Bronx to Interstate 80, correct?"

"Correct, but—" The police-sim delineated the height and breadth requirements for highway travelers, which the alien far exceeded. "You're too wide!"

"Problem no," it flashed. "Watch!" After a touch of tinkering, it had shortened and narrowed itself, although the redistributed flesh lengthened it to a good twenty meters. It would grow some more once it got some food in its belly. "Okay is?"

"What about your speed? The law sets a 60 kph minimum."

"Can do." More bioengineering produced 15 pair of two-meter high wheels, as well as a waver in the cop-sim while the computer searched for the appropriate program. "Side by side me," it wrote, "and measure."

The simulacrum, now fuzzy around the edges, simply waved a hand and said, "I believe you. Take off. Have a nice trip, and welcome to New York City."

It set out at once.

The 800-odd kilometers to Cleveland were among the smoothest of its recent excursions. It covered them in just over twelve hours, though the Pennsylvania hillsides tempted it with spring. For a while it weighed rumbling off the road and disappearing into the forests, where delicate buds fattened on the branches, but it had its mission. The Far Being had specified how it should spend its time on this planet, minute for minute almost, and what the master wanted, the master got. It contented itself with licking the dust off the highway, and found it nutritious, if bland.

The hovercars that howled past flashed windows full of gaping faces, but it didn't mind. It had been traveling now for some five years (in its own reckoning), and for that long it had been drawing stare-equivalents. In some places the inhabitants pointed; in others, they averted their buttocks; in still others, they writhed in the dusty sand until acrid crystals coated every square centimeter of their hides—but in each case, the notion behind the gesture was the same. Surprise—astonishment—and closer inspection of the odd being.

So it wheeled toward the heartland, splashing here and there through icy puddles of melting snow, especially in the higher regions of Pennsylvania. Smelling the air of forest and city, it watched the colors flash by—the greens of plants, the browns of treetrunks and soil, the variegated rusts, tans, and blacks of rock outcroppings . . . it stored these impressions like a squirrel its nuts, preserved them for later winters on its home planet, when there'd be little else to do but lie in a frozen burrow and untangle its chromosomes for the spring fission.

Turning off 80 onto 71, it rode that north into downtown Cleveland. The ancient Memorial Shoreway amused it, for a while, until it found its bearings and the off-ramp, and exited two blocks from Lakewood Hospital.

Yes, exactly as instructed. It was nighttime, and lights shone with awesome profligacy, lights and crowds and crawling traffic that slowed even further when the gastropod cruised past like a float in search of the Rose Bowl Parade. A policewoman flagged it down. After pointing out that it lacked a driver's license, registration, and license plates, she ordered it to follow her to the station. Demurring, it presented its passchip, in which the visa declared that self-propelled beings needed no such documentation.

The cop scratched her helmeted head, sighed at the size of

the traffic jam accumulating, and waved it on.

So into the hospital parking lot it rolled, the overhead lights gleaming off its ochre skin. The building matched the Far Being's description brick for brick. Trundling around to the far side, it snuggled against the foundations. The ivy it crushed tasted delicious; well-tended gardens were always more savory than wildlife.

Soaking up the building's vented heat, it extruded, from the middle of its back, a pseudopod that became an Indian fakir's rope that became a periscope. Up it went, and up, and up, until it peered through the windows of the maternity ward. Fat women here, a skinny exhausted one there, white-clad nurses, next room, ah, yes, the children, row upon cribbed row of them.

The pseudopod flattened against the glass of the window, dimpled up a thousand tiny suckers, and heaved! The frame ripped out of the wall with a rending crash. A nurse screamed. An orderly dropped a tray, spun on his heel, and clattered away.

It gently set the window on the asphalt and returned to the breached wall. Again the pseudopod reshaped itself, this time into an elephant's trunk. It entered the gaping hole. What was the number? Four.

It counted down from the near wall. One, two, three— ah, four. The limb-tip poured over the baby in the crib, coating him like pancake batter. After a few seconds, it hardened, and slurped! When it raised itself, the infant was gone.

The clipboard at the end of the crib, swaying in the fresh spring breeze, said, "Baby Boy Feighan."

It was April 1, 2083.

Downstairs, people had begun to cluster around the giant ochre flanks. They were curious, mostly; a lot of aliens lived in Cleveland, but nothing—*nothing*—like this had been seen before. White-jacketed orderlies, under the direction of an elderly security guard, tried to keep the surging crowds back. They continued to advance, although their high tides fell a dozen meters short, as if it exerted two forces on them: one that drew them close, and another that kept them from coming too close.

The newspeople had arrived, too, and they were different. Unaware as yet of what it had done, they scampered between its wheels, thrust microphones under its ends (they couldn't figure out which was the talking and which was the, uh, other end), snapped holos of it from every angle, flipped through paperback copies of Audobon's Guide to Intelligent Extraterrestrials, hollered questions at it, and, in general, tried to work up front page articles.

At this moment, an elderly nurse leaned out a fourth-floor window and gave them their headline: "The monster ate a baby!" he shouted. "It ate a baby!"

The gastropod was vastly entertained by all these comings and goings. Having slithered the baby down the appropriate tubes, it now shifted the sac containing it to its outer side, where it transparented the skin so that the crowds could see the child. Across its membrane it wrote, "Will not harm baby, I; please provide proper nutrition in slot marked X." A smile spread across its front end, and above it appeared the letter "X" in violent violet. Then, perhaps sensing that the mood of the masses had soured suddenly, it triggered the biochemical thaumaturgy that rendered its hide invulnerable to just about every assault an intelligent entity could devise.

Such self-shelling had its disadvantages, it admitted. For one thing, motion was impossible. It couldn't even turn its head, not that it had one. It couldn't extrude pseudopods, couldn't spin its wheels, couldn't do a thing except sit tight, scrawl on its membrane, and wait for the fullness of time to remedy the situation, as the master had promised it would.

Police swarmed over the grounds like mosquitoes over a swamp, blowing their whistles, screeching their sirens, and shouting exasperated commands. Their weapons ranged from night sticks to automatic cannons; some carried shields, others staggered under the weight of bulky flak jackets. Their captain approached.

"Give him back!" he bellowed.

The translucent patch warped itself to focus on him; letters crawled across it: "Of course. In 71.4 hours, local time."

"Now!"

"No!"

"What are you doing with him?"

"Examining, as by Far Being Retzglaran ordered."

"Who?"

"Mind never. Please in slot marked X provide proper nutrition. Will not harm baby, I. Okay is all. 71.4 hours." With that, it fell silent, and remained that way for the next three days, despite the impassioned pleas of doctors, nurses, policemen, orderlies, clergymen, the Feighan family, and a twelve-legged, blue-shelled baseball fan from Cygnus XII which, passing through town, had been drafted to help solve the problem.

For seventy-two hours it lay like a stone sphinx, displaying the baby through the window in its skin (a burly, thirty-eight-year veteran of the CPD said, "Damn slug's holding him as a hostage." A frail, sallow xenobiologist retorted, "Nonsense. It's studying him, as it said, but it's showing the boy to us as a sign, as proof, that it's not hurting him. And let's have no ethnic slurs, bohunk"). Impervious to assault (Army demolition men summoned to blow it open gave up in disgust when they couldn't slice even a piece of it loose, no matter how much power they pumped into their lasers), uncaring about trespassers (the director of the hospital, studying both the alien and the next year's budget, considered roping it off and charging five or ten bucks a head for the privilege of crawling on it; he was overruled by the Cleveland chapter of the Society for the Prevention of Cruelty to Extraterrestrials), it lay like so much breathing concrete until the time was up.

Then, on April 4, 2083, the epidermis split, top to bottom, like the temple in Jerusalem, and a moving slab of flesh thrust Baby Boy Feighan into the open air. He weighed ten pounds, four ounces; naked and clean and sweet-smelling, he had a smile on his miniature lips and a twinkle in his eyes. His mother, Nicole Buongiorno, heavily perfumed with rum, snatched him off the shelf and clutched him to her bosom. For a moment she stood dazed and red-eyed. Then she ran weeping for the family car in the north parking lot, looking back often, as though convinced the beast would change its mind and steal him again.

Flashing, "It's been wonderful, but I really must leave," on its forehead, the gastropod rearranged its body chemistry and revved its wheels. The crowd scattered. An irate policeman (due to start his vacation on the 2nd, he'd been called back for extra duty; his wife had gone on the trip without him but not, he was sure, alone) leveled his automatic rifle and fired a 200-round burst into its side.

It felt rain on its flanks, heard noisy chattering, smelled a peculiar acridity, and absorbed a bit of kinetic energy. Popping open a visual orifice, it studied the cop, who was inserting a metal cube into the shoulder end of his stick-weapon. The alien chuckled to itself. Silly thing, to think he could hurt it with that.

The patrolman ripped off another full burst and hastily reloaded.

Although unscathed by the 400 bullets that had zipped through its body, the being's feelings were hurt. It didn't like entities that became so angry that they wanted to kill. It didn't like hate.

Its spirits, however, were boosted by the onlookers, who seemed not to agree with the cop. Many were shouting at him to stop; some even attempted to disarm him. A few ran up to it and asked if it were wounded.

"No," it wrote, "but for asking many thanksyous. I really must go. My timetable quite tight is." It rolled forward, through the path the crowd had made for it, reached the highway in minutes, and sped back to the New York City Flinger Building.

Before departure, in accord with the instructions of the Far Being, it established a $10,000,000 (US) trust fund, the interest on which was to be applied to expenses incurred by the Feighan family in attempting to cope with the trauma they had undoubtedly suffered. That pleased it. It wouldn't want to think that its master was unfeeling.

Then, properly shrunk, it staggered to the Fling Booth. Its sole regret as it left the Earth was that it hadn't had time to go wandering through the wilderness.

The hospital staff reclaimed the baby from its distraught parents and quarantined it at once. They felt they had to: the child did not move. Initial tests suggested that his paralysis, if it were such, was not of physical origin. They imputed it to hysteria.

Medical experts from the world over descended upon Cleveland in such droves that car rental agencies ran out of luxury models, hotel rooms were as available as free consultations (desk clerks willing to relinquish the reserved suites obtained all the medical advice they needed, *gratis*), and half a dozen country clubs canceled guest privileges because their own members couldn't get onto the courses.

Each doctor had his own theory, and his optimum means of proving it. Some wanted blood samples; others, bone fragments. Some yearned to scan, others to skin. Biopsies were demanded a hundred times an hour. The baby (now named

McGill no-middle-name Feighan) had his fingers pricked so often that he couldn't have sucked his thumb even if he could have moved it to his mouth.

The researchers requested so much material from McGill that a hospital intern, not entirely facetiously, suggested that they sacrifice and quick-freeze him, then take as many cross-sections as possible. It was a sign of scientific frenzy that the motion was voted down 1307–1211 . . .

The psychologists and psychiatrists, there to cure his hysteria, fought for their share of experimentation. Roughly half wanted to put him in an isolation cell and observe him till he reached puberty; the others opted for the age of twenty-one.

Six weeks after the alien had left, Patrick Sean Feighan, the baby's almost-forgotten father, stormed into the hospital, raving that he'd have his son or the heads of those who got in his way. A bull of a man, an erstwhile professional football player who worked out regularly and whose shoulders were so broad he had to go through most doors sideways, he got attention.

"Mr. Feighan," said the receptionist, "I'm afraid the doctor's in conference right now, if you'll take a seat—"

"I'll just pop in, won't be a minute, it's the release, you know, it must be signed." Pulling a cookie from his pocket—snacks helped him cope—he headed for the varnished oak door.

The nurse shrugged to herself, and pressed the disguised button that activated the door's electro-lock. "Mr. Feighan," she said, swiveling her chair around, "really, the doctor is very busy, and he'll see you as soon—"

"He'll see me now," bit off Feighan, "or— hunh. Locked, is it? Well now, what can we—" He wrapped his fingers around the handle and pressed his shoulder to the wood. "—do about that, I wonder?" Grunting, he heaved forward, as though it were some damn fool trying to protect his quarterback.

Like most blockers who'd confronted him during his career, it yielded. He smiled into the doctor's plushly carpeted office, shook his head, and said, "It's the humidity that warps it, sir, and it's the warp that sticks it to its frame. Ah, they just don't make things like they used to, now do they?" Still smiling, he rested the unhinged door against an inner wall. The lock plate lost its charge and fell to the floor. "It's my son I've come about," he said, sauntering up to the doctor's glossy desk. His ankles swished through blue wool. He curled his knuckles into his palm, rested them on the desk, and leaned forward. "You won't be causing the mother of my son any more heartache by being stubborn about his release, now, will you?"

Two security guards, alerted by the receptionist, burst into the room. The senior said, "All right, Mr. Feighan, let's just leave quietly, all right?"

Feighan had been feeling feisty since he'd rolled out of bed, so he turned and said, "As quietly as a lamb, my boys. The instant my son is placed in my own two arms. It's home I'll be taking him."

The doctor shook his head. "Throw him out," he ordered the guards.

They approached with exaggerated wariness, remembering, perhaps, Super Bowl CXII, in which he'd thrown a 280-pound tackle over the goalpost.

Feighan beamed. "What great good fortune," he told them. "The ambulance boys won't have so far to wheel you to the Emergency Room."

The guards stopped, thought it over, and smiled to the doctor. "Nice visiting with you, doc," said one. "Mr. Feighan, if I could get your autograph? It's for my son, he's a wowser fan of yours."

By this time, the Feighan family lawyer had arrived, and presented the doctor with a summons ordering him to show cause why he should not be indicted for kidnapping.

Reluctantly, the doctor signed the discharge papers.

· Chapter II ·

In a windowless room on the far side of the Moon, Milford Hommroummy prowled like a spider tugging the strands of its web: a man in Rio, a woman in Hong Kong, a machine in Zurich...all fed him what his appetites demanded. Forty-seven years old, he wore a six-pleat poncho with Syra-quartz buttons and a Rigelian bat-snake belt. On his head, a horseshoe of harsh black bristles held out against baldness. The furry brows over his adamantine eyes were his softest facial features. First in his class at Harvard Law School, he had a predator's instinct for vulnerability, but was kind to cats. Brilliantly ruthless, he ran the Terran arm of The Organization, the interstellar crime syndicate. Wealth dripped from it like rain from a cloud, but for Hommroummy, there was never enough. He spun his schemes to gather up more.

His view of the universe was distinctly his own. As he saw it, every civilization extended into a dimension that transcended the apparent, the tangible; there it occupied a volume defined by the culture's age, population, and geographic distribution. Expand as it would, though, no people could ever completely fill its sphere—because its persons were unique, almost random, while its growth pattern was determined by its mean ability to perceive, to describe, and to deal with reality without destroying it: senses, language, technology and mores, in other words. But the space not filled by the society was not, could not be, empty. There lived the anticultures, the *yins* to the primary's *yang*.

The Organization was a very large anticulture. A parasite, if you will. It could exist only because its hosts left room for it, and food, and members. It could prosper only by drawing more food, room, and members, but that was dangerous: if it milked too much, it could starve its host to death. Yet if it took too little, it would disintegrate into a swarm of leaderless fleas. It was Hommroummy's duty to strike the balance.

That was not an easy assignment. Earth reacted to parasites as an animal would: that which perceptibly annoyed it was attacked, unless Terran civilization itself sheltered it, as a dog's belly does a worm.

So part of his job was to minimize the pain The Organization caused Earth, to make it invisible. He reined in his subordinates, forced them to lead lives that casual observers would find unremarkable. His Number Three, for example, administered an operation that satisfied 150,000,000 addicts daily— but the strongest drugs in Number Three's own cabinet were caffeine and aspirin. Similar rules held for everyone, and ignoring them meant death.

Another part of it was to evolve a symbiotic interface between The Organization and Earth—to raise a two-faced layer of cells, as it were, white on one side and black on the other. The cells on the skin of a culture, those whose actions help determine the shape of a society, are those responsible for defending that civilization. Policemen, judges, legislators, executives, ministers, media personnel—once recruited by Hommroummy and subsumed into The Organization, they couldn't jeopardize it without endangering themselves. He gave them roles in the night that they could do well because of what they did in the light.

But his main task was to make his branch office profitable. As The Organization operated on 693 worlds, each having from one to one hundred eighty-three legal systems, it was complex to the point of self-contradiction. On Auxytrgn III, for example, the natives would sell their grandmothers for contraband Terran beer. Literally. But dealing in those grandmothers was a losing proposition because there was no market for them, not even on Markurilla V, where private zookeepers would pay dearly for smuggled grandmothers from anywhere *but* Auxytrgn III . . . cold and analytical, Hommroummy knew this, for he understood profitable crime as a scorpion knows the desert. He insulated himself with layers of fall-takers, yet planned their moves like a drillmaster. Inhumanly sensitive to new opportunities, he always wrote his bottom lines in black.

Now, looking into a glass-walled cube filled with 1000 cubic meters of blue and gold gases, he wondered again why they wouldn't mix. He also wondered if the container held Gryll, the alien which claimed to live inside it. He was talking to a transceiver mounted on its side, but that meant nothing. Organization toppos liked to play games. *How would Gryll react if, next time, when the curtain of its tank whispers into the wall, it finds itself staring at an identical tank, and barking at an identical transceiver?*

A disciplined man, he returned his attention to the matter at hand. "No, sir," he said, consulting his notes, "it wouldn't be worth our while to smuggle Furthten mugger fish onto Terra. They're legal here."

"Just a thought," crackled the speakers. "This morning's paper. McGill Feighan. Young child swallowed by ochre alien. Discharged from hospital yesterday. Bring him here."

"May I ask why?" He spoke the name to his legal pad.

"Alien stooge of Far Being Retzglaran. Never met, but destinies have intersected. Paid heavy price. Will intersect again, could cost more. Must be prepared. If FBR interested by Feighan, must be interested also. Bring him here."

"Who is this Far Being Retzglaran?" Crossing his legs, he squinted into the gases for some sign of Gryll. His superior sounded flustered, and that was rare enough to merit investigation.

"Do not know. Origin a mystery. Home planet a mystery. Present location a mystery. Detect only through effects of subordinate's actions. Like studying pebble-thrower by examining ripples in pond. Two centuries ago, one ripple closed four branch offices. FBR is enemy. Bring Feighan here."

"Dead or alive?" he asked idly.

"Alive," snapped the speakers. "And quickly."

Hommroummy nodded, rose, and, after the ritual bow, sauntered out of the underground room. It shouldn't be difficult to find and snatch a newly born child. He'd give the job to The Nurse.

Early in June of 2083, The Nurse approached the modest two-story home of Patrick Sean Feighan and Nicole Buongiorno. The Nurse was a 190 cm. Korean-American with black belts in more martial arts than there are arts on Mars. Her trade name came from the first-aid kit she carried everywhere. In that line of work, it was useful.

Her subdued tweed suit shortened her steps; the genuine leather briefcase, a legacy from her grandfather, bumped the outside of her powerful right thigh. She took good care of the briefcase. It gave her an authentic look. And the kit fit neatly inside it.

At her side strode sharp-nosed Taddeucz, who would have been a race-pilot if The Organization hadn't persuaded him to drive its hovercars. Though disinclined to engage in hand-to-hand combat, he was reasonably competent with the semi-automatic needler under his left armpit.

"Cover the back," she told him, as she turned up the walk to the door.

"I've got a better idea," he said. "I'll cover the front. You go in through the back."

"You always have to change my plans, don't you?" she complained. "Why is your way better?"

"Because the car's out front, and if you flee, you'd best have me out front with it. Comprende?"

"Oh, all right." She walked around the side of the cream-painted house. Glancing at the windows was futile; the faded olive drapes were closed. A buckeye tree cast its shade on the south face of the house, and its bark everywhere. She turned up her nose at the shrubbery—scraggly and unpruned, it needed weeding, and a thick mulch.

At the back door she knocked, waited, and rapped again. Eventually a black-haired, brown-eyed woman appeared. "Ms. Buongiorno?" she asked, remembering her sketchy briefing.

"Why, yes," said the woman, drying her hands on a dish-towel. "What can I do for you?"

"Ms. Chan, from the World Health Organization." She unlatched her briefcase and rummaged in it, as if for identification. "I've been sent here to examine your son; apparently there is concern that he has contracted an alien disease which could spread if—"

Buongiorno frowned and held up a silencing hand. "Put your thumb in the ID slot," she said.

The Nurse froze. She hadn't expected *this*. While her eyes fell to the small electronic box by her right hand, she thought furiously. Then she drew herself up and said haughtily, "I will not. It is against my religion."

Puzzlement wrinkled Buongiorno's face. "All right," she

said. "Your choice." She stepped back and began to close the door.

"I say!" bit off The Nurse. "Open this at once!"

"No."

"I have, in my briefcase, a court order compelling you to permit me to inspect your son. Do you wish to be held in contempt of court?"

Worry ruffled Buongiorno's fatigue, but disappeared. "So sue me."

It was more than The Nurse could stand. Setting herself, she kicked her booted foot through the screen door. Wire twanged with irritation. Buongiorno jumped into the shadows of the kitchen and shouted, "Pat!"

So her husband's home, thought The Nurse, as she shook her leg free of the entangling screens. Entering, she looked quickly around. A standard kitchen. Neat, though. Very neat. No handy pepper pots, no cups of steaming coffee, nothing boiling on the stove. Good. The woman wouldn't be able to throw things at her while her husband was getting his ass—

A man drifted in through the swinging door at the far end. For an instant, as he stood under the lintel like a portrait in a frame, she almost laughed. This little runt was going to protect his son? He'd be laid out in no time fl— then her eyes adjusted. The door was half a meter taller than average, and a full meter wider. The guy was no runt. He was, in fact, one of the largest men she'd ever seen.

"Well now, darling," he said, smiling at The Nurse yet offering warmth only to his wife, "what is it that's raised your voice?"

"Her." Buongiorno's voice quavered. Her finger, as it pointed first to The Nurse and then to the mangled screens, trembled like a hummingbird's beak.

"Ah." He seemed to notice the wreckage for the first time. "It's a proper mess she's made, isn't it?"

"She kicked it in. She wants McGill. She says she's World Health Organization, but wouldn't thumb the ID slot." Shivering, she backed to the safety of her husband's side. "Pat, I'm scared."

The Nurse had had enough familial byplay. Balancing herself on the balls of her feet, she said, "Gimme the kid or I take him."

"Well now, miss," said the man she was facing, "since we

won't give, you'll have to take, won't you?"

His eyes were a deep, unflecked blue. They saw her without acknowledging her. Uneasy, she stared into them, challenging them to show feeling or concern. Still they lay on her as though she were a wall, or a dead rat. For a moment she tried to recall whose eyes they reminded her of. Then she remembered: her own.

The time for words was past. Any second the woman would leap for the phone and call the police. She had to act, and now! The briefcase, dropped, thudded on the speckled vinyl tile.

A step forward, and a feint with the stiffened hands. She saw his own rising to parry them, and knew then that she could take him, she could break him. Jubilantly she swung up her foot, blurring the boot at his balls. To her astonishment he pivoted, caught her heel, and twisted it.

She rolled with the torque. Turning her upper body, outstretching her arms to bear her weight, she whipped the other foot off the floor and snapped it at his head. That should— it missed! But at least he'd released her right foot. She scrambled away and bounced up.

A pleased smile played about Feighan's mouth, but it came nowhere near his eyes. That ran sweat down her back—*she* was supposed to be enjoying this, not him. He ambled toward her, as flat-footed as a bear, and damn near as big.

With a shout she launched another attack, a flurry of chops and kicks and punches. Half missed entirely. The others thwacked into slabs of muscle without provoking even a grunt. She retreated a meter and studied him.

His sandy hair was tousled and his blue workshirt torn. His only expression was the remnant of his smile. His breath came soft and easy.

Fear slipped into her, then, bubbled up her spine and sizzled in her brain. This wasn't at all what she'd been expecting. She should have been warned! The guy was a killer. He'd taken her best shot and hadn't even *tried* to reply in kind.

Uh-uh, she decided abruptly, *Hommroummy wants the kid, Hommroummy can snatch him himself*. She spun and dove for the door. Before she could reach it, the ceiling fell in. The floor slapped her face. Huge hands clutched her wrists and tugged them behind her back without even noticing her resistance. Then—she was so insulted she could have screamed— *one* of them fettered *both* her hands while the other slid under her belly and hoisted her to her feet.

"Do you want me to call the police, Pat?" she heard Buongiorno say.

"Of course not," replied the incongruously cheery voice. The bastard *still* wasn't breathing hard. "The police would come and take her away with all due respect for her civil rights to silence. It's a fine thing indeed, this respect, because the innocent do contrive to have themselves arrested—but it's not for this little lady. This little lady wants to talk."

"Bullshit," she spat out. "You're not getting anything from me."

"Boil me some water, Nicky."

"Pat!" Horror infused Buongiorno's exclamation.

"And isn't it your son she came to steal?"

"One kettle or two?"

"That's my little Nicky." He said it with genuine affection. *Dammit*, she thought. Soft footsteps sounded in the front hall. She drew in breath to scream: "TAD! HELP!" She'd barely uttered the second word before a hard blow knocked the light out of her eyes. As she crumpled to the floor, clinging desperately to consciousness, she heard a familiar sportshover engine roar into life. Turbofans shrieked. The sound faded in the distance. Night guillotined down.

Fifteen minutes later, when Feighan was about to awaken the would-be kidnapper with a pitcher of ice water, the phone rang. "I'm nearer," he called, and stretched to set the jug on the counter below the wall phone. Not once did his eyes leave the unconscious Nurse. *A true she-devil*, he thought, remembering her slashing hands and feet. *It's close I should watch her, very close. Ah, but it felt good* . . . "Hello?"

"Mr. Feighan, I presume?" The voice was chilly; its words, clipped.

"None other," he said.

"We have your child, you have our agent. If—"

"Who are you?" he demanded. His fingers tightened on the receiver.

"If she survives, McGill does. Call—"

"What is it you want, man?" Nicole pushed through the swinging doors. so he waved her over and mouthed, "Find McGill."

"Call the police and your boy dies. I'll get back to you."

A metallic click severed the connection.

Feighan stood motionless, staring at the phone with numb anger. The house around him was silent, except for Nicole's scampering feet. Outside a car raced its fans, and the buckeye rustled its leaves in the wind. Somewhere a child laughed, but it wasn't his.

"Pat!" shrieked Nicole. "He's gone, McGill's gone!"

"I know," he said softly, not speaking to her, or to anyone. In a moment he'd hold her, and comfort her, as she would him. In a moment. But now . . . tendons bulged on the back of his hand. The receiver snapped. "I know."

Hommroummy paced the length of a small, bare room lasered out of the Moon's bedrock. Its gray walls were rough, and streaked with shininess where mineral veins had been cross-sectioned. It contained only one item of furniture: a crib. On its satin-covered mattress breathed a two-month-old child, blue-eyed and dark-haired. His arms were at his sides; his legs lay flat, with the toes leaning outward. He hadn't moved since he'd been put there, and that made Hommroummy wary. Kids were supposed to flap their hands, flop their heads, and make noise. Kittens did. This one hadn't done a thing.

He stopped pacing and leaned over the crib. The baby's skin was soft, clear, milky-white. His eyes were flecked with brown, and full of . . . *fear?* he marveled. *What's he afraid of? How does he know to be afraid?*

A young, frizzy-haired doctor entered without knocking, started at Hommroummy's presence, and immediately bowed. "Please allow me to present my deepest apologies, sir," he began, running his words into a singsong chant, "but I have been instructed, by a party which wishes to remain anonymous, to take skin and blood samples from the infant for a detailed laboratory analysis. Although my instructions do specify promptness, if you wish to spend a few—"

Hommroummy's upraised hand cut off the flow of verbiage like a dam. "If Gryll sent you," he said, "go ahead."

"Ah," said the doctor, a beam washing over his dusky face, "my gratitude knows no bounds, sir, and if you will just step to one side and draw this mask—" A square of sterile filter-plas appeared in his hand as suddenly as if he'd created it. "—over your mouth and nose, I can begin."

Complying, he stood at the head of the crib and watched

delicate dark fingers wield tiny scalpels and miniature needles. Snip. Pop. Slice. Poke. The child's eyes widened and his face reddened, but his mouth would not gape, nor would he cry. He didn't even twitch when the doctor swabbed out a throat sample.

Gutsy kid, thought Hommroummy, as the medic departed. *Or retarded.*

The ceiling speaker awoke with a yawn of static. Gryll's odd intonations filled the room and echoed off the stone walls. "Return him. Retrieve Nurse. Execute her immediately. Know where child is at all times. Be prepared to seize him again."

"I don't understand, sir," said Hommroummy, "why—"

"Job is to do, not to understand. Obey."

"Yes, sir." He sighed, and shook his head. It was bad enough that he had to kill one of his best operatives, but to remain ignorant was worse. Knowledge is money, and money, power. Though he wanted to resist, to refuse—that would be futile. His predecessor had tried it, once, ten minutes before he'd died. Gryll did not permit disobedience.

Heels crunching gravel, he left the room to issue the proper instructions.

Feighan was biting into his third ham and cheese on rye when the back doorbell chimed its two-note refrain. His head jerked up; bread crumbs scattered on the checked tablecloth. "Who is it?" he called harshly, wiping mustard off his lips.

"Delivery," returned a high, sharp voice. "Exchange some merchandise?"

"Just a minute." As insurance, he waved Nicole into the broom closet and handed her the new telephone. Once the interior lock had snapped into place, he opened the lavatory door and hauled The Nurse out. Clothesline tied her hands behind her back; electric wire lashed her ankles together. The gag between her teeth had been a cleaning rag, and soap bubbles foamed the corners of her mouth. Dropping her in the middle of the kitchen, and resting his right foot on her neck, he said, "Come in."

The repaired screen door creaked. A thin, short man inched into the room, holding an airlines pet crate in one hand and a cruel-angled gun in the other. His nose was as pointed as a mosquito's. Nervously, he smiled. "Good morning, Mr. Feighan," he said, chattering away as though afraid of silence, "it's an honor to meet anyone who can best our Nurse in hand-to-hand, or in anything for that matter. Impressive, quite impressive." Gently lowering the dog carrier to the floor, he nudged it toward Feighan with the toe of his boot. "I believe you will find everything in order."

Feighan glanced from the gun to the aluminum crate. Pine-scented cologne drifted over to him. In the closet, a cork popped; liquid gurgled. He growled, "It better be," and bent to open the meshwork door.

"Ah, sir, my colleague?" Taddeucz gestured at The Nurse with his automatic. "We would like to be on our way."

"Once my own eyes have seen for themselves that my son is in health." He pulled the baby out by his blankets, peeled back the blue flannel, and looked into familiar miniature features. Tickling McGill under the chin, he said, "You're home now, boy, and everything will be fine."

"May I take—"

"What's this scar?" Feighan rasped suddenly. His large finger shook as it pointed out a dark-scabbed line above McGill's right ear. "What have you done to him?"

"Mr. Feighan—" Reddening, Taddeucz tweaked the tip of his nose. "—I must apologize for that. When I tossed your son into my car the other day—"

"It was you?" Feighan seemed to swell, to grow 20 cm. in seconds.

"—he received a paper cut, from a newspaper. A doctor has treated it, and—" With his free hand, he fumbled in his coat pocket for a memo, which he thrust at Feighan. "—here are the doctor's instructions."

Good, stiff paper, it crackled when Feighan unfolded it. He looked for a name, or an address, but there was neither. His eyes skimmed the text, touching on "Date," and "Nature of wound," and "Treatment applied," and "Treatment prescribed," which said, "Do not bandage, but keep clean. If redness, tenderness, or swelling develops, a physician's attention is indicated. Otherwise, the scab should disappear within a week."

"All right," he said, as he hooked his foot underneath The Nurse's belly. "Take her." He grunted, and swung his leg up. The huge, bound woman flew toward Taddeucz, who collapsed under her weight. "Take her and be gone."

"Yes, sir." He didn't bother untying her. Rolling her over

his shoulders into a modified fireman's carry, he staggered out the back door and gasped his way around the side of the house.

Feighan waited till he heard the hovercar start up and glide away. "You can come out now, darling," he said to the closet door.

From within sounded a plastic thud, and a *ding* as the phone hit the floor; breaking glass; fumbled bolts; Italian cursing. After a few minutes the lock finally lost, and Nicole stumbled into the kitchen, wincing at the change of light. With her came the aroma of bourbon, thick clouds of it. "Hic," she said. Her eyebrows lifted, then she squinted. "Mc-hic-Gill!" A loose, uncertain smile spread across her face. "Gi-hic give him to me." She held out her arms.

"Careful, now." He kissed her on the forehead. At her nearness, love flared, as it always did. Beaming, he eased their baby into her waiting hands.

Just as he let go, Nicole hiccuped again. Her entire body jerked and her shoulders heaved. McGill seemed to slip through her fingers.

"Dammit, woman!" roared Feighan. His hands flashed to become a safety net.

She had already recovered her aplomb. "You'll scare the baby, shouting like that," she scolded, as she cradled him in her left arm and stroked his forehead. "What got you so upset?"

Feighan scratched his jaw as he studied his wife and child. The two together was a sight happy enough to weaken his knees. "I thought—" He shook his head. "My apologies, darling. I thought you'd dropped him."

"Me?" She brushed back a strand of shining black hair, and held McGill tightly while she hiccuped again. "Why would I want to drop our son?"

"I—" Fondness was so full in him that he could do nothing but smile and shrug. "Sure and it must have been the tension, Nicky. I'm sorry for raising my voice and scaring the bejesus out of the both of you. Is there any of that cake left, do you know? I'm of a mind to snack a bit."

"In the breadbox." Carefully, she pinched the budlike red cheek. "Mommy's got you, McGill. Mommy's got you."

"All you do," the white-smocked programmer was saying at that moment, "is type 'MONITOR: FEIGHAN.' The computer will tell you—on the screen here, or from that speaker, or whatever—where he is. If he's in any of the one hundred largest US cities or their suburbs, it'll give you a street address as well, and tell you inside, out front, or out back. If he's traveling, it'll give you the speed, the direction, the street or highway, and the crosstreets ahead and behind. Unless he's on a plane or a train, in which case it'll print out the flight number, his ticketed destination, intermediate stopovers, estimated time of arrival, and the like. Is that what you wanted?"

Hommroummy, leaning on the terminal, examined the screen. The room smelled of plastic, metal, and coffee. "Yes," he said at last, "except for one thing: program it to alert me if he goes more than, say, fifty kilometers away from his home. Can you do it?"

"Can you find loopholes in tax law?" retorted the programmer. "What kind of alert do you prefer: bell, buzzer, seductive voice in your ear, what?"

"Bell," said Hommroummy. "No, wait—route it through my pocket telephone, have that ring, and the voice tell me, when I answer, where he's going."

"Sure." The programmer lowered himself into the seat in front of the terminal. "Anything else?"

"How long will that battery last?"

"In the implant-trans?"

"Yes."

"No idea, it's not my job." He turned to the computer and typed "REF: ? LIFE SPAN BATTERY OF IMPLANT-TRANS #—" He swiveled his head. "Do you know the number on that?"

"The model number?"

"Yes."

"It doesn't have one."

"Oh." He thought a moment, then tapped in, "ORGANIZATION STANDARD."

The screen blinked: "INDEFINITE. MELANIN ACTIVATED."

"There you have it," said the programmer. "As long as the kid gets some sunlight now and then, the battery stays alive, and the computer keeps track of him. Good enough?"

"That's excellent," said Hommroummy. "Thank you." And he left.

Ice cubes clinked when Nicole lifted her glass, then they slid down its side to rap her teeth. It was empty. The last sip must have finished it. As she stubbed out her cigarette, she tried to recall if they had another bottle of bourbon. It seemed to her that there should be one, ah, in the linen closet? No . . . under the sink.

She started to rise from the living room sofa, but there was a weight on her lap. She looked down and, with difficulty, focused her eyes. It was one-year-old McGill, staring up at her. *How'd he get here?* From the smell of him, he needed fresh diapers. *He's sopping; my skirt— Pat! Again!*

Chuckling, she hugged her child and stood. If that wasn't just like Patrick Sean Feighan, to pick up the kid, see he'd dirtied himself, and then slip him onto her lap when she wasn't looking. She'd have to tease him about that—he'd probably spent longer waiting for her to glance away than he would have needed to change McGill.

Balancing herself on chair arms, she made her way to the kitchen, where Pat pretty much lived these days. The door swung open in front of her, and there he sat, legs spread, elbows on the table, gut hanging over his belt, stuffing a greasy chicken leg into his mouth.

"Afraid changing him would spoil your appetite?" she asked, then frowned at the echoes of her tone. She hadn't meant to sound accusatory—she'd just wanted to needle him.

He looked up. "Is he needing it?"

Her tongue turned sour without permission, and drew words from a bitter well she'd tried to cover with her lightness. "You knew damn well he needed it when you dumped him on my lap." Good humor gone, she plopped into the other chair and scowled at her husband.

His blue eyes were guilelessly puzzled. "Not tonight," he said. "I haven't been in to see him in . . . two hours? Three? Maybe . . ." His face darkened. Lowering his head, he bit into the drumstick, ostentatiously dropping the subject.

Rigid she sat, while alternate waves of fear and anger flushed love from her heart. She couldn't have blacked out, not again. She'd been careful about . . . that, since the last time. She had. And the self, which would rather look through a magnifier than into a mirror, focused her attention on her partner, where it found cause for enough indignation to blot out her worries about herself.

Who was he to accuse her of drinking, him with his blubber and the case of peanuts he kept under the bed, "In case I feel the need at night, darling," fat slob, her mother had warned her athletes turned to jelly when they stopped working out, and much as she hated to admit it, it looked like Mama was right for once.

She hadn't blacked out. She could remember every minute, relaxing there in the living room after a miserable day, reading the newspaper article about . . . about . . . well what the hell did it matter if she could remember the subject or not, it wasn't important, what was important was that she *hadn't* blacked out, *please God, I couldn't have, not again, please, he'll leave me, please, I love him I don't want to be a drunk, please . . .*

"This is the weirdest thing I've ever seen," said the programmer.

"I don't care what you've seen," snapped Hommroummy. "I want that fixed and fixed fast."

"I don't think the problem's here," insisted the computer man. "Really. It's got to be in the implant-trans. Or maybe in the triangulators; those receivers are tricky, you know. If you don't wire them just right, hell, an airliner passing overhead gives you a blip."

"This is more than a simple blip." He fought for self-control, and settled for a fast pace up and down the room. "When your machine tells me that that child travels nine meters, northwest to southeast, in a straight line, dropping three meters as he moves, and does it all *instantaneously*—" He didn't finish the sentence. He didn't need to. The programmer knew what happened to members of The Organization who didn't do their jobs right.

· Chapter III ·

At a few minutes to midnight, a gray man awoke in a piss-stunk alley. Above his head glimmered a strip of stars, broken bottles catching headlights on a highway. They were old friends; he'd Flung himself to many of them—once upon a time—when he'd been young and strong—when laughter had been as natural as breathing. That was before he'd retired, before he'd become so Sensitive.

Voices and music and glass clatter tumbled through the nearby bar's back door; he sat up, coughing and hawking in unison with a rummy impatient to take his nest among the garbage cans.

His name was Jose Schwedeker; he was sixty-three years old, a retired Flinger, and rich, by normal standards. By the standards of his needs, he was desperately poor. And desperately competing with an emaciated man named Mort Tobbins, who was, he knew, Searching for the same surcease he was. Old Mort. They never had been friends. Fitting that in this June of 2088, their rivalry was less diminished than they.

The derelict's face hung above his, like a bewhiskered moon studying its reflection in a pond. Their mingled odors were worse than the alley's. "Take it," he grunted, crawling out of the bed of rags and crashing over a dented can in the process. For a moment he heard a bell, soft and distant and silver, and he started toward it, aching for its peace, but then a buzz saw rasped in his brain and chewed his hangover into separate but equal tormentors. The broken asphalt was wet beneath his dirty palms; he pushed himself to his feet and stumbled toward the back entrance of the bar.

"No' friendly i' there," wheezed the rummy. Bottle uptilted, he gurgled cheap wine through the gaps in his teeth. "No credit—no work—no–thing." His legs gave way and he sat down abruptly.

"'sokay," said Schwedeker, waving a hand and almost losing his own balance. He grabbed at the doorframe to steady himself, to gather the strength and the courage he needed to enter. Termites tunneled through his gray cells, but their sound was that of a wolfpack shredding a carcass.

His change-ringer, gray-haired Anita Nkame, once the best of the Movers, had tried to tell him how age would mock him. "Your body, Jose, he weakens," his mentor said. They'd been hiding from the winter in his father's paneled basement. He'd been shooting pool; mischievously, she'd goosed the cue ball with her telekinesis. "Your eyes, mon, be blurred by all the fogs you ever walked through. Your honds be rusty claws; your knees, broken hinges. And when you make love..." She'd shaken her head. "You fall asleep right after."

He'd hooted, made his shot, and asked about the Sensitivity.

"A church burns in your head," she'd answered dolefully. "Every mon, woman, and child be a tongue of flame, growling and crackling, and it hurts like you'd never believe. The rum I drank to quiet it...inside it all, you can hear the heat tolling the bells..." She'd made the cue ball jump, then, winked at him. "Die young, mon. Die young or ring your changes quick."

But he hadn't done either, and now was paying the price. He jiggled the locked door. A broad, squat dishroom man approached and began to speak. Though Schwedeker could see his thick lips move, he couldn't distinguish a single syllable. The noise in his head garbled the connection between his ears and his mind. It drowned the chiming of the bell, masked the whereabouts of Tobbins.

With a disgusted wrinkle of his broken nose, the man unlocked the door, leaned close to Schwedeker's head, and shouted, "No freebies! Get lost!"

A swimmer struggling in a riptide, he swayed erect and did his best to enunciate: "If it is after midnight, there is money in my account. Lead me to a bank."

"Whaddayou, nuts?" His hands started for Schwedeker's

shoulders, but stopped in midflight, as if their destination were too dirty even for them. A tattooed rose budded inside his right wrist.

"No, I—" It was much too difficult to explain, especially in his condition, so he let his buttonless coat fall open and speak for him.

The dishroom man stared at the shimmering tunic. A glitter in his dark-brown eyes mirrored the woven patterns of coherent energy.

The tunic, once Schwedeker's pride, was now his pain. At fifteen, when they'd implanted the activator cell keyed to his individual brainwave pattern, he'd vowed never to cloak that marvelous meshwork. At sixty, he'd learned that Sensitivity-sapped Flingers get mugged. Seemed all the street creeps knew about the trust funds; too few understood that the interest, paid daily, was spent before it could accumulate any of its own. So he wore the coat, the gift of a horn-tooting Salvation Army Major, and sweltered in the summer because it was the only way to keep safe.

"A Flinger?" the man asked, contempt melting out of his battered features.

"Uh-huh." Between his ears a hyena howled. He stiffened, and clamped his scraped palms to his temples. "Seven years retired. Getting more Sensitive every day."

"Poor bastard." Indecisive, now, he stepped forward, then back. "It's after midnight—you sure you got money?"

"Pos. I. Tive." Three words—that's how bad off he was.

"It's the Occleftian you want, right?"

"Please." It was halfway between a request and a shriek. He was rolling his head around, as if the motion could dislodge the monsters, could bring back the bell.

"All right, big boy." The man made up his mind. With an apology to his food-spattered white jacket, he bent forward and tipped Schwedeker over his shoulder. He straightened easily, though he growled at the stench, and said, "Take you up the back way; no sense making the customers puke. The bug's got a bank up there anyway."

Blood pooled in Schwedeker's head, blood and ache and tearing sound. Though he wanted to resent his helplessness, his repulsiveness, he could only be grateful. This dish machine technician could have called the cops, who would have prolonged his agony for unendurable hours. Yet he hadn't.

The broad shoulder pressed his stomach to his spine; his head and free arm bounced and swayed with every step up the metal grate stairs. Their single Shiva-shadow shortened gradually into sharper focus, tightened into a multilimbed puddle at the man's feet, then preceded them down the narrow corridor. Knuckles on plastic added their rap-tap to the inner din. Another few jounces and his feet hit hard floor.

A high buzzing sound, like a mosquito chorus, said, "Beefo. One carries this kind *out*. Not in."

"He's a Flinger." He braced Schwedeker against the rough, unfinished wall. "Says he's got money." His scarred hands parted the grimy coat to reveal the tunic. "I got to get back to work."

"I see," whirred the voice. "Thank you. Leave him."

"Right." The door closed and an electro-lock hummed to life.

Schwedeker forced himself upright, and squinted at the pearl-gray alien. A man-sized millipede, it smelled like a damp library. Two of its faceted red eyes scrutinized him; the other two guided the arms that were lifting the bank-plate. Schwedeker licked his thumb, wiped it on the front of his coat, and held it ready. "What's your fee?" he croaked.

"One hundred," replied the Occleftian. "No haggling."

"All right, all right!" He jabbed his thumb at the shiny plate. At contact, he said, "Debit me one hundred dollars; credit them to—"

"—Arkorninu X83," finished the millipede. When the green light glowed to indicate completion of the transaction, it shimmied its mid-legs in the gesture of mild surprise. Not astonishment—it had lived in Cleveland too many years to be astonished by anything a Terran did. "Please," it said, more polite now that it had been paid, "be seated."

Turning around, Schwedeker slumped to the bare concrete floor and put his head between his knees. Dozens of tiny pincers pulled his coat down his back, then reached through the tunic to massage his spine. Others fastened onto his neck; still others nibbled on his skull. He closed his eyes. For the five thousandth time, desensitization began.

First came the colors, sheets of vivid translucence flaring behind his eyelids. Red rivers; orange aurorae. Forks of yellow lightning slashed diagonally and their afterimages faded slowly. Green mountains humped up from the flame-burnt ground. Blue grass sprouted on their rugged slopes, flourished, and deepened into indigo when night pulled a violet blanket over everything.

"Aaaaahhhh," said Schwedeker.

"Yess," hissed Arkorninu X83, digging its hundreds of digits into his slack skin, "yess, yess."

Smells percolated through his nostrils, first the real ones, his own rankness, the Occleftian's mildew, then the memories, of lemons and ozone and voluptuous women and early morning mists when the factories forgot their pollution-control equipment and the acid reek burned through choking throats. Fresh fish and soy sauce and ketchup on a charcoal-grilled steak...

"Ohhhh," he moaned.

"Jussst ssso," soothed the alien. "Relax, relax, re..."

And then silence blew in to clear out the noise like the wind cleans dead leaves off a lawn. Buzz saws sputtered to a halt. The hyena slunk into the night. Police sirens dopplered down the road. The hurricane, moving out to sea, let the breakers fall into a gentle susurrus. Audiences hushed.

"God, that feels good," he breathed.

"Doesn't it, though?" The Occleftian claws left his skin, tugged his coat back over his shoulders.

Schwedeker sat up and pressed his elbows against the chilly wall. He didn't dare move, not yet. His legs couldn't support him. "I needed that."

"I know. You're very Sensitive. You must need it twice a day."

"Used to get it, too, till you all raised your prices." He said it without rancor. "Now I can only afford one."

"Supply and demand, my dear." It raised a gentle claw to stroke the stubble on Schwedeker's cheeks. "Until we recover from the plague..." It lifted his chin, brought up a specialized limb, and began to shave him. Another limb, a hollow one, sucked up the whiskers. "You're new in town."

"I'm Searching. Got in from Cincinnati last night." *Half a step ahead of Tobbins the ubiquitous*, he thought. *Have to get there first!*

"You must have met my podder, Arkorninu B212." It combed his hair and trimmed it. "B212 must have been very busy to send you out so shaggy."

"No, it wanted to, but I heard the bell." *And staggered into the night*, he remembered, *trying to get a fix on it, listening*

*to it recede to the northeast, probably up 71, limpracing to
the bus depot, fuming, pacing, extorting cigarettes from
strangers by the implicit threat of standing next to them if they
wouldn't hand them over ... then sitting alone in the back, still
hearing, far ahead, the long-lived echoes, the haunting rever-
berations ... and far behind, the sullen untuned clunk of Tobbins on the trail ...*

"Bronze?" asked X83.

He shook his head. "Silver." Honesty made him add, "I
think."

"I would have heard if they'd found it here," buzzed the
alien. "Are you sure it hasn't moved on? Silvers are generally
loud."

"I know, I know." Fear caught at him, made him hug himself for safety. If Tobbins rang its changes first— but no, he
couldn't think that way. When sanity depends on being the
first to flush the ghost of a promise in the night, one can't
afford to contemplate coming in second. "It was small, though.
And—"

"And you're inordinately Sensitive. What a Flinger you
must have been!" Patting him on the head, it offered its car-
apace as a handhold, so he could pull himself to his feet. "You
really must go now, dear. I have other customers."

He dug his knuckles into his eyes until the itch went away.
"Thanks," he said, reaching for the door.

"One question, Searcher," called the alien.

"What's that?"

"Do you Search for the reward, the reponsibility, or the
peace?" Its eyes framed him in ten thousand ruby octagons.

Schewedeker paused to marshal his thoughts. "All of the
above, some of the above, and none of the above," he said at
last. "The reward's nice, the responsibility's good for a guy
who's got nothing to do, and the peace ... God, the peace!"
He shook his head and dragged a dirty hand across his mouth.
"But for why I'm Searching—ask an iron filing why it flies
to the magnet. I have to go; good-bye."

As he clattered down the metal stairs, he knew X83 had
been hurt by his reply, had thought it to be unnecessarily
cryptic. It wasn't, though. It was the simple truth. One answered the bell because one needed to, not because one chose
to, or wanted to. Like using the power while one could—it
was just something one had to do. People thought it was the

chance to see the moons of Throngorn, or to wallow in the clay pools of Mellna, but they were wrong. The wielding was the reward, and nothing else mattered. He waved his thanks to Beefo the dishroom man and stepped into the night.

He heard it again, a distance-muted ringing, pure and tuned and compelling. It was off to the west, far off, probably one of the suburbs. Through shadows he moved to Euclid Avenue, where he found a bus stop. The area was almost lifeless. Discarded newspapers somersaulted down the sidewalk, slapping at his ankles as they passed. The sign said a bus would be along in twenty or thirty minutes. His luck had turned: that would be the last of the evening.

It would be easier if he could Fling himself out there, if he could home in on the bell and appear at its side. But he couldn't. He'd never been in Cleveland before; he didn't know the feel of its street corners, or the flanks of its contours. It can be painful to materialize in front of a taxi cab; explosive, to teleport into a hillside.

He thanked God for the Occleftian silence, the stillness that squelched the incomplete and the crippled so that full health stood alone. The bell was clear and alluring, now, though its timbre . . . he'd thought it to be silver, but now he wasn't sure— Maybe— no. He couldn't let himself hope for gold.

It was young, too. Very young. It had to be, to have gone undetected. An older one would have had its changes rung long ago. Probably asleep, then, and potent only in its dreams. That was how Anita had found him, when he was—four? Six?

Boy or girl? Couldn't tell, couldn't ever tell, not from the chimes. He hoped for a boy—parents got antsy about a ringer's responsibility in crossgender situations.

Ironic about the reward—if he earned it, he wouldn't need it. If he didn't earn it, he would need it. Bureaucracy. One million for a silver-ringer, when the peace, and the fulfillment of need, would be enough.

The bus braked in front of him; air escaped its plastic skirts to blow dust across his tattered shoes. He disliked buses, especially at night. They weren't friendly. Boarding, he thrust his thumb into the fare box and waited for the green light. The only passenger, he sat behind the driver, who groaned and said, "Can't you find another seat, man?"

"Sorry," he said, frowning as Tobbins' dissonance distressed the background, "but I'm a Searcher, and I might need to get off in a hurry."

"A Searcher? You?" The driver's blue eyes, drilling into the overhead mirror, plucked at Schwedeker's rags. "And your niece is the President, right?"

He let his coat fall open; its brilliance filled the front of the bus. "Now you believe me?"

"Shit, yeah." His tone was awestruck. "Never had a Flinger on my run before—hey," he said, suddenly suspicious, "you're a Flinger, how come you're riding? How come you don't just teleport—"

"Don't know the town," he said shortly. "Besides . . . I'm retired."

"So what's that got to do with it?" He took a right onto Lorain Road; the darkened shopfronts, for lack of better entertainment, watched them pass.

"You lose it," he explained. He hunched over and rested his elbows on his knees. Two bells tolled in the back of his mind, one louder at each stroke, the other, softer. His heart was running fast. "Not the power, you've got that forever. Just the, ah, the fine tuning. Set a passenger down above the floor, instead of on it. Or against a wall, instead of in the middle of the room. That's the memory, fraying at the edges, not holding the destination pattern sharp and tight, like it should. They start watching you when that happens . . . the next thing that goes, the thing they retire you for, is momentum maladjustment."

"Wha?" asked the driver, as the bus hissed across the bridge.

"Angular momentum, from the way the planets spin. When you Fling something, you've got to compensate for the difference. There's a . . . a place," he decided, "where we can go to dump some, or to pick up—"

"The Energy Dimension?" The driver, looking into the mirror, shrugged back at Schwedeker. "That's a name I got from the papers."

"That's what they call it. But you've got to do it right, and when your Sensitivity's stuffing your head with static—" He leaped to his feet, gaped out the far window, and said, "Hey! Stop! This is it."

"I can't—" oh, hell, screw the company." The bus whined to a halt; he manipulated the door lever. "Good luck, huh?"

"Yeah, thanks." He jumped from the top step to the sidewalk, stumbling a bit, and caught his balance as the bus whooshed away. The bell was much louder now, but it had been stronger back...there. Maybe down that sidestreet? Damn! Tobbins was coming, too.

He started walking, briskly, clutching his coat closed, feeling his pulse hammer in his ears. Dreamlike, the sidewalk seemed a treadmill, he was shuffling down flypaper streets, stride, stride, stride, but he couldn't go anywhere, he was stuck in the same place, trapped in the dappled shadows cast by streetlights shining through treetops.

Louder it rang, and louder. He turned the corner, broke into a half run, wheezing and gasping while his chest tightened and his shins griped. This house? No, further, a little further, just a—

"Hold it right there, old man," barked a cold voice.

He spun around. Two cops were easing out of their cruiser, their eyes never leaving him, their fingers fumbling with holster snaps. He groaned. "Good— good evening, officers. What can I do for you?"

"Come over here," said the one on the near side, "come over real slow, and lean against the car, and assume the position."

He started, reluctantly, to obey, but he heard— the high triumphant peal of a baby gold! And, even as the smile broke dawnlike on his seamed cheeks, the second sound came in: the offkey clang of a discarded bronze. Tobbins. Tobbins was *here*, on this street. Going for the gold himself.

"I'm a Searcher," he babbled, "I hear the bell, it's right in that house there, I've got to get in quick—"

Disbelieving scowls washed across the patrolmen's faces; the nearer took a menacing step towards him. "Gedover here," he snarled.

He glanced over his shoulder. Yes. It *had* to be that house. He couldn't let Tobbins do him out of it, he couldn't let the cops delay him; damn the risks, the frazzled reflexes—

PING

He was pressed against the plateglass picture window, peeping through a crack in the draperies, hearing the cops shout, "HEY!" while their racing feet scuffed concrete and grass.

PING

Stubbing his toe on the mahogany coffee table, groping

through the shadows for the staircase because the bell was upstairs, and a pounding rattled the front door, and a sleepy angry voice from above said, "Who the hell—"

But the mutter gave him the direction and he was rushing up the stairs on all fours and the cops were bellowing a siren split the distance a hoarse, befuddled woman said, "Pat, shome-body's in the housh!"

"We'll see about that—"

"No, don't, shtay!"

"—somebody breaks into my house, break his damn neck, besides the boy's alone, could be another—"

"Be careful!"

Scrambling across the green-carpeted landing; three doors, all ajar, all dark within; voices there; this, a push, a john dammit; *that* one! Swing it open, stagger through it, kid on a bed. A kid who didn't move, who didn't even turn his head at the intrusion.

When Schwedeker went to him, stood above him looking, the boy's eyes grew. And grew. The bell's echoes shivered down into silence. It was a warm, loving silence, and it embraced Schwedeker like a long-lost brother. *Peace*, he thought, *protection*.

He dropped to his knees by the side of the bed, dropped to his knees and raised his hands high, so the furious father, bursting into the room, throwing on the light, would see that he was no threat.

The kid had black hair and brown eyes. His skin was soft; his cheeks were pinched. Under the blanket, his five-year-old arms and legs were sticks. He did not speak, except with his eyes.

The father, huge and grossly fat, grabbed Schwedeker's collar. The coat flew off; the tunic spattered rainbows on the cowboy-covered wallpaper. "What the hell?"

"I'm a Flinger," he said, rising, turning, but keeping his hands above his head, palms open. "Jose Schwedeker, retired. Your son's a Flinger, too. I've just rung his changes. He's the strongest I've ever met." A thundering crash from the first floor made him wince. "The cops," he explained. "They just kicked in your front door. Don't worry about it, though. I'll buy you a new one." Relief was on him; he couldn't help but laugh. "Two new doors." The laughs dipped deeper and deeper into his belly. His knees gave way, sprawled him on the bare wood floor. "A hundred new ones, with what I save in Oc-cleftian fees. Oh, God, I've found it!"

And then the cops were there, their guns drawn, the barrels glued to Schwedeker's light show. Behind them stood a third man, a gray man, with hollow cheeks and pain-racked eyes. "Hello, Jose," he said over the blue shoulders.

"Mort." He giggled. "Mort, I've change-rung a gold!"

"Uh-huh." He grimaced. "I heard."

"Somebody tell me what's going on here," demanded one cop. The other seconded his motion with a brusque nod.

The father was dazed. Dropping onto the bed next to the boy, he looked up, and choked out, "My son—my son's a Flinger. McGill. He's a Flinger!"

"So you *are* a Searcher," said the cop, nudging Schwedeker with the point of his shoe.

Schwedeker grinned, for maybe the first time since he'd retired. "Was," he told him. He got to his hands and knees and crawled to the foot of McGill's bed. "I *was* a Searcher. Not any more. I don't need to. I'm a change-ringer, now." As the cops left, he spread his coat on the floor and curled into it. "I'll sleep here, okay?" he asked the father.

"Sure," said Feighan. Repeatedly, he tapped the heel of his palm above his right ear, as though to knock dust off his brain. "Sure, it's a fine warm spot and there's a soft quilt for your mattress. But McGill—" Rising, he walked to the window overlooking the front yard, and watched the bantering patrol-men saunter back to their cruiser. Tobbins drifted after them like a leaf caught in a tractor-trailer's slipstream. "But you're wasting your time, you are. The boy's a paralytic, always has been. Five years and two months old; hasn't moved a finger or made a sound since..." His hand found a can of roasted peanuts in his bathrobe pocket. He shook a quarter of the can into his mouth and chewed noisily. His jowls jiggled.

A grenade of sick disappointment burst in Schwedeker's belly. Paralyzed? Mute? All those years of Searching, all the pain and loneliness and derision, was it to end in this? Because the peace was there. The boy McGill was a latent Flinger. The reward would be his, the protection would be his, but the rest—the caring, the coaching, the camaraderie—how could he possibly find that with a child who was almost a vegetable?

What a lousy, rotten way to go out—nursemaid to a cab-bage. Staring at the floor, he cursed. A tear of self-pity trickled down his cheek.

"Whoozhis bum?" asked an intoxicated woman.

He lifted his eyes. Standing—leaning—in the doorway was a pale, red-nosed woman in a dirty nylon nightgown. Her long black hair was snarled and dead. She blinked and squinted at him. "Jose Schwedeker," he said dully. "Flinger, retired. I've just rung your son's changes."

"Him?" An exaggerated expression of disbelief contorted her face as she waved vaguely at McGill. She staggered, and caught the doorjamb for support. "A Flingersh shomebody who—" She raised a finger and belched. "Who can jump from plaish to plaish without moving, right?" Widening her eyes, she gaped owlishly at Schwedeker. "Right?"

"That's right," he said, "but—"

"Boy, thash a relief." She giggled; her eyelids inched shut.

"Pardon?" he asked after a few moments.

"You shtill here?"

"Why is it a relief?"

"'cause I thought—" She half-turned to face her husband, and had to spread her legs to keep from falling. "—an' *he* thought, too, that I wash—" She frowned at herself. "—was blacking out alla time, 'cause I'd find *him*—" She pointed at the bed. "—next to me, or in my lap, or whatever . . . boy, thash a relief. Bet I shleep good tonight. Ta-ta." Pivoting awkwardly, she stumbled out into the hallway.

Schwedeker looked at Feighan curiously. "What's she talking about?"

"She's drunk," said Feighan, with sad simplicity.

"I know that, but what was she talking about?"

"Ah—" He scowled at the empty doorway, but there was pain in the frown, and unsundered love. "—it's her contention that she's forever finding the boy somewhere he wasn't put. She blames me for it. To her way of thinking, it's a grand, cunning scheme to convince her she's crazy, so she'll put herself away. But I ask you, why should I go to all that bother, when I could just as easily walk out of here tomorrow and be divorced the day after?"

Schwedeker hauled himself to his feet and peered into McGill's deep, dark eyes. He could *feel* the power in the boy, feel it as though it were a warm spring breeze. So much strength for such a little child . . . he straightened up with a groan and an ache in his lower back. "She finds him where he wasn't put?"

"So she says, but it's a miracle she can say anything at all these days, given the ungodly speed with which she drains a bottle. A lesser tongue would have been pickled solid by now. Would you say that makes her a trustworthy witness? Or would you say rather that it's touched her in the memory, and inclined her to forgetting just exactly what she *did* do with the child?" The can of peanuts was empty. He eyed it as though it were a friend who had betrayed him, then crumpled it in his massive fist and dropped the wad of aluminum into his pocket. "I wouldn't be trusting her testimony if I were you."

Schwedeker's disappointment was gone, replaced by a pulse-stirring eagerness. He raised his face to the light fixture in the ceiling like a man letting the sun's heat creep into his bones. "Did you," he asked, "ever stop to think that she's the way she is because of what your boy's been doing?"

"Huh?"

He turned and spread his arms. "If you were sober and found an elephant in your icebox, wouldn't you think you were crazy?"

"It'd be a terrible temptation," agreed Feighan.

"But if you saw it when you were drunk—"

"Ah!" He nodded forcefully. "Sure, and you'd have to think it was the alcohol in your brain that was making you see it."

"Exactly!" He spun on his heel and walked back to McGill. "Kid," he said, "if you can teleport around this house, you can sure as hell walk. And talk. And by damn—" He leaned over to touch him on the nose. "—I'm gonna make sure you learn how."

McGill blinked, and stroked Schwedeker with his peace.

It was the only way he had of saying, "Thanks."

· Chapter IV ·

Milford Hommroummy had a problem. The host organism was getting ready to scratch itself in a way that would seriously disrupt the interface he'd been cultivating. He scowled at the computer, which had just announced that the Justice Department was beginning to backtrack the bank records, tax returns, and cash purchases of nearly one thousand Americans. One hundred twelve of them were his people. Almost all held positions of high influence. It would take years to replace any of them. "Repeat your estimate," he said. "Ignore the outsiders—but of our agents, how many will be lost?"

"Five to ten unshakable convictions," it replied, "fifteen to twenty convictions overturned on appeal, thirty to thirty-five acquittals, and thirty to forty additional indictments that will never come to trial. On the other hand, five to ten will escape notice all together."

"We can't afford to have any of them tainted." A button-push spun the chair around, and he got up to pace. The air smelled stale, much more so than usual. Despite the optimism—and, perhaps, technical accuracy—of the Chief of Maintenance, the ventilation system couldn't handle the extra load imposed on it by the new floor, the one they'd opened the preceding week. At least not and keep air quality at the level Hommroummy demanded. "Instruct Barbieri to purchase the new unit," he said to his machine.

"Yes, sir."

Ringed Saturn floated in the disp-screen on the wall. It was an image he liked—sometimes. "And change the picture to, ah, Ginkakuji. That planet's begun to resemble a child's toy."

"Yes, sir." The gas giant faded into the serenity of the Silver Pavilion. Hommroummy had visited it eighteen times, and would meditate before it again in a month, if he could clear the mess up.

"How do I handle this?" he muttered to himself, wiping the moisture of his fingers on the wall's blue velvet. The parasite had angered the host, which shouldn't have happened. Someone must have stepped out of the shadows and drawn its attention ... attention ... unaware, now, of how quickly he was pacing, Hommroummy seized that idea and fondled it. Attention. If he could divert it long enough for some of his technical experts to tap into Justice's Computer Center and reprogram a few machines ... he had it.

The Organization wasn't the only anticulture in existence. There were thousands of them: local clubs, regional groups, even worldwide associations. Diabolists and prohibitionists, royalists and anarchists, antitechs and eetie-haters ... their common gene was their willingness, their eagerness, to deviate from majority opinion. That's what made them anticultures. And that's why one of them would be useful to Hommroummy.

At the point where a civilization ends and a countersociety begins, lies an area of irritation. The majority doesn't like to have its views flouted. Unless restrained by the shape of the culture, it will quash the minority—and even inhibited majorities will slap down deviates if the culture has evolved a mechanism for unleashing itself in times of danger.

So if he could get the host organism more worried about another parasite ... "How many anti-Flinger movements are centered in the Cleveland area?"

"None, sir." The machine's voice was smooth but unaccented.

"Damn. Ah ... how many antialien groups, then?"

"Six."

"Any with a history of violence?"

"Noisy demonstrations, sir."

That would have to do. The majority always wants to believe the worst of the minority, anyway. "Get me Orloffski, and also, give him the names of the noisemakers."

"Yes, sir." The disp-screen flickered. The pine-flanked pond shimmered into the bushy red and gray beard of Nathan

Orloffski, one of Hommroummy's better trouble-shooters.

"Nathan."

"Mr. H, good mornink. What can I do today for you?"

"Kidnap a boy named McGill Feighan; the computer knows his location. Do not harm him: Gryll wants him kept safe. Bring him here. Send the authorities a communiqué claiming responsibility; sign it as whatever Cleveland anti-eetie group seems most suitable. Take a teleport with you to get you all back here. An alien teleport. We don't want to blow anyone's cover. Draft whomever you need for this. Any questions?"

Orloffski seemed troubled. "Taddeucz, he has told us about the boy's father, a fightink machine—"

"Nathan. Are you saying you can't handle an ex-football player?"

"No, sir, but—"

"Avoid him, or use anesthetic darts. Remember. No connection with us. All responsibility goes to the—" He checked the printout. "—Cuyahoga County Coalition to Keep Out Freaks. Or one of its fellows. Do you understand?"

"Yes, sir." He nodded.

"Report back to me when you've finished." He ended the call, and was satisfied. If anything should pull the Justice Department away from its computers for a couple of days, it would be the kidnapping of a very valuable boy by a very disreputable extremist group.

And once the reprogramming had been accomplished, he could have that police captain of his "find" little Feighan, neatly bolstering his image, while virtually convicting the CCCKOF.

The enemy of my enemy, he paraphrased, *is my fall-guy*.

▪ Chapter V ▪

April 1, 2090, marked McGill Feighan's seventh birthday. He took pride in that. It was a rare and wonderful thing to be seven years old; the chance came but once in a lifetime and he was seizing it, doing it, being it! More important, though, he was celebrating a *normal* birthday, his first ever. His own feet were moving him, just like his own hands had dressed him. And he wouldn't have to see the doctor for another two weeks. That was good. He was tired of doctors.

"Not bad progress for twenty months, hey kid?" Jose had said that morning. "What say we stash the wheelchair in the basement so it'll be out of our ways until it's *my* turn to need it?"

McGill had helped, and that had felt good, too. But the best part was not being afraid any more. He wrinkled his nose, which already promised to grow into an impressive beak. Well, not *too* afraid. Not like before Jose.

The weather was moping again. He and Jose had left home under blue skies crowned with a benevolent sun, but shortly after they'd gotten to the zoo, when they'd just reached the veldt enclosure to watch giraffes nibble leaves from the middle of young trees, the wind had blown in a raft of clouds from the west. The clouds were ungrateful visitors. Like many of the zoo goers, they promptly littered the area—with sleet.

They took refuge in the snake house. McGill looked through the large glass walls, into the cold glittering eyes, and shivered. He'd seen things like them in some of his dreams—the bad ones. "Are they really slimy?"

Jose laughed. "Not in the least." He bent down to speak into McGill's ear. "They're dry, and their skin is— well, not soft, maybe, but not rough or scratchy, either. They're just as warm as the air is, or a degree or two warmer. And they can be interesting pets."

"Who'd want to keep a snake?" The idea made his stomach queasy. Partly it was their slithering, and stabbing the air with their tongues; partly it was the building's stink, like their basement last summer, when the sewers had backed up and drowned a rat under the stairs; partly it was something he half-remembered, but wouldn't let into the light.

"I had a snake, when I was a little older than you. Uh, twelve? Thirteen? It was a boa."

"What happened—did it try to squeeze you to death and eat you?" For a minute or two, Jose was an entirely different person: like someone McGill had just been introduced to, and wasn't sure he approved of. That was the problem with adults. You kept finding out new things. Sometimes they were really neat, like when Daddy'd gotten in shape, and showed him how to punt, and kicked the football halfway down the street. Then you walked around glowing because you knew somebody so special. But other times, they were icky, and you didn't know what you were supposed to think. Being friends with kids was easier. They didn't have so many pasts. You could keep up with what they were doing, and depending on how you felt, you could get closer, or drift away. "Did the police come?"

"It wasn't *that* big." He glanced around the reptile room, crowded with others caught by the same sudden storm. "The boa cage's over there; let's see if they've got one about the same size."

McGill was usually a nose-against-glass person—when he waited for Mommy to come home, for example, he always pushed right up to the front window, with his breath fogging the pane until he had to move—but here, in this smelly place . . . he kept his distance.

There must have been a dozen brown-and-white snakes inside, lying on each other, curled around dead sticks, sliding from near end to far . . . one was staring right at him, and he edged closer to Jose.

"That one," said Jose, pointing to a thick, sleepy-looking boa with a bulge in its midsection. It was about a meter and a half long. "That's just about the size of the one I had."

"That's bigger than I am!" yelped McGill.

"Nah—what are you, 140? 145?"

"One hundred forty-five point four centimeters," replied McGill. "They measured me last week—you knew that."

"If I didn't, I should have," apologized Jose. "Now, that one there might be a couple centimeters longer than you are tall—but see how tiny it is compared with, oh, your waist?"

He looked from one to the other, and reluctantly conceded Jose's point. "So what happened to yours?"

"Well, it's a very sad story. I was feeding it one day—"

"What'd it eat?"

"Mice. White ones. Oh, it'd eat any kind you cared to feed it, but there was a laboratory supply house up the street from me, and they sold white mice pretty cheap. So that's what I fed it. And I really liked it, and I wanted it to eat well so it'd get big and strong, but . . ." He shrugged, and walked away from the exhibit, hand on McGill's shoulder to guide him. "One day I put in more than it could handle, so it ate what it wanted, and left the last mouse alone. Now, snakes like to nap a little after dinner—"

"Like Dad, huh?"

"Sort of, yeah. Want some popcorn?" He gestured to the concession stand under the building's front eaves.

"When we leave. Go on. Tell me about the snake that fell asleep."

"Well . . . the mouse was unhappy about sharing the cage with Elmer—that's what I called my snake—because it knew that as soon as Elmer woke up, he'd want breakfast. It also knew what the breakfast would be."

"Itself, huh?"

"You got it, kid. So . . . while Elmer was sleeping, the mouse worked up its courage and *jumped* on him, and bit him, and . . . killed him. And that was the end of Elmer."

"Oh." He thought a moment. It was supposed to be sad, but *he* didn't feel unhappy. Maybe you had to be there. "What happened to the mouse?"

"I gave it to my cat for a Christmas present."

"I don't think I like that story," McGill decided. "It's not very nice. You should have given it a reward."

"But why?" Jose looked surprised. "The snake was my friend, and the mouse was my friend's enemy."

"Boy, I couldn't ever be friends with that." He trembled.

Part of the motion was thee-at-tricks, which Daddy kidded him about, but the rest of it was real. Flickering forked tongues: ugh!

"Well, you know," said Jose, "some day you're going to have to work with people who are a lot like snakes. I mean, that's not what they are, but they uh . . . well, they look like snakes, but they're as smart as we are. You don't have to be friends with them, but you can't shiver every time you see them, either. Not and be a good Flinger."

"I don't wanna do *that*," he complained. "Why do I hafta?"

"Because not all people look like us."

"I know that," he said with a trace of disgust. "There's blacks like Daddy's friend Preacher, and there's whites, and—"

"Oh, I'm not talking color, kid—although some eeties are different colors, too—I'm talking size, and shape, and how many fingers they have, and if they have legs or wings or fins . . . there are 693 inhabited worlds, and nobody out there is exactly like us."

"Are eeties people, too?" he asked.

"Sure. They're different, but they're people."

"When am I gonna be old enough to Fling?" He peeked out the door; the sleet was still slanting down and everything seemed dead except for a couple of people running to the parking lot with newspapers over their heads. "I wanna meet some of these eeties."

"You will, you will," promised Jose. "You'll meet a lot of them."

"When, though?" he persisted.

"When you're ready." Before McGill could blurt out the next logical question, he added, "And I can't say when that will be. It comes at a different time, a different age, for everybody. You, for example, started Flinging yourself around the house when you were just a baby. Remember?"

McGill closed his face. "Uh-uh," he said, as he shied away from memories of shadowy, fear-filled years. A distant voice, hollow like a drum, said, *Don't ever move,* and another one, his mother's without the music, screeched, *You! You monster!* and a deep daddy-voice boomed from its cave, *Ah hush with the howling and bring me the baby to eat.* He shook his head and clenched his fists. "I don't 'member nothing. I can't do it no more, either. How old were you?"

"I was, uh—" A memory of his own flicked his face with

a scorpion tail. "—uh, fifteen. That's when they implanted my tunic. And you'll *know*, yourself, when you're ready."

"How?"

"Because you'll—" He suddenly became engrossed in a large monitor lizard. Swishing its scaly tail, it hissed at its dinner, a fright-frozen hamster. "You'll just use it," he said softly, over his shoulder. "And then you'll know."

"Uh-huh." McGill had gotten bored; he didn't like to talk about things all at once, and forever. Especially not dangerous things. He liked to ask a safe question, and drop the subject for a while while he turned the answer over in his head, over and over like a piece from a jigsaw puzzle, until he found how its uneven edges fit into something he already knew, and then, when it had been tapped neatly into place, he was ready to come back and query again. So he pointed out the door. "It's stopped raining and you said I could have some popcorn."

"Sure." With a smile, he nodded to the busy concession stand. They walked over to it together. "Your treat or mine, kid?" he asked.

McGill scowled up at him. "You know I don't have any money, 'cept in my coin collection. If I put my thumb in there, I'll get a red light. And that's *embarrassing*." It had happened to him last winter, when he and Jose were going to the movies. Grandly had he led the way to the ticket box, saying in his haughtiest manner, "It's on me." He'd stuck his thumb into the slot— and not only had the light burned cherry red, but a buzzer had stuck out its tongue and given him a raspberry and everybody else in line had laughed at him, and...he'd learned a lesson, there, and wasn't about to repeat the experience. "I'll pay you back later," he promised.

"You will, huh?" Jose chuckled.

"You bet." He scratched his nose and made a face. "Sooner or later."

That drew a full-sized laugh from Jose, and McGill beamed. It was a with-laugh, not an at-laugh, and when he could make an adult bellow out a with-laugh he felt very good indeed. For a minute he could step out of his little body, and out of the relationship that always puts a child and a grown-up on different rungs of a ladder. For that minute, he was an equal. He liked it.

Collecting their popcorn—Jose wanted salt only, but McGill wanted lots of butter, too—they strolled off to give some to the polar bears. The zoo was empty, now. People who would have come, hadn't, because of the rain, and many of those caught in the storm were leaving while they had the chance. It was a relief. In front of each exhibit stood a talking box, to describe the animals beyond the moat and to answer any questions you had, but when dozens of kids clustered around it and hurled question after question at it, sometimes not even waiting their turns, the box got confused, and started babbling. And of course the kids gabbed among themselves anyway, so you couldn't hear, and...all in all, McGill liked the zoo better empty.

When they rounded the corner, shadow-striped by the bud-tipped branches of a pin oak whose acorns were still crunchy underfoot, four men and an alien were waiting for them. It was a neat eetie, McGill thought. It had purple skin, four eyes, and tiny squiggly things on its head instead of hair. It looked funny in Earth clothes. "What kind is it?" he whispered to Jose.

"It's a Dirdrixian," replied Jose, whose face had gone stiff and odd. "Look," he said, without glancing down, because his eyes were moving back and forth across the five beings ahead, "let's see the polar bears some other time, I think it—"

"No," he protested, "I wanna see 'em—"

"C'mon, kid, we'd better—"

"Hold it," said the man in the middle of the path. He was thin and short, not much taller than McGill, although he had a kinky beard that was half red and half gray, like a new scouring pad. His voice was flat and dull. He stepped toward them.

"What do you want?" demanded Jose. His voice was flat, too, and hard in a way that McGill had never heard before.

"You know what we want, Gramps." Brillo Beard's hands gestured. Obediently, his human companions hurried to McGill and Jose's sides. Two of them resembled Tweedledum and Tweedledee from the Alice book. The eetie stayed where it was, watching them through all its matte-finish eyes. "We're takink the kid, and you're not goink to put up a fuss. You hear me?"

McGill froze. Deep in his mind, ugly memories awoke; he didn't want to feel them. They were going to take *him?* Where? Why? He tugged at Jose's sleeve, trying to control his voice as he asked, "Jose—"

"Sshh," said the old man, drawing his coat around him as

though he were cold. "You stay quiet, McGill. Everything'll be okay."

"B-b-but—" He looked around. Tweedledum held a gun, and poked it into Jose's ribs. It probably hurt: Jose's face twisted. McGill was scared enough to cry, now, because the third man, whose right hand was big on his small shoulder, had a gun, too. He bit his teeth together and squeezed his lips hard. He couldn't cry. He wouldn't move. He— he couldn't see the alien. He craned his neck to spot it, but the man touching him said, "Keep still. I'd rather not use this."

He tilted his head back and stared into the man's face. It was long and narrow, and had a big nose that came to a sharp point. He hadn't shaved very well; patches of black bristle clung to his neck. His cologne smelled like a Christmas tree. "Please, mister," he said, "don't hurt me."

"I've no intention of doing so needlessly. Be a good boy and don't provoke me." Impatiently, Needlenose glanced at the other two and scraped his foot across cracked acorns.

While Tweedledum kept his gun in Jose's side, Tweedledee was tying the old man's hands behind his back. He tested the knot with a hooked finger; Jose grunted in pain. "Shut up," Tweedledee snapped, reaching into his pocket for a roll of tape and a handkerchief.

The hand on McGill's shoulder lifted. For a moment he almost ran—he could call the police—but, *no*, he thought, *no, these guys have guns and Jose'll get hurt and I better do just what they tell me* . . . his legs quivered, but he gave a sidelong glance to see where Needlenose's gun was pointing. His eyes roamed around and around without finding anybody. So he lifted his head. Only two men were left, the two concentrating on Jose. The alien, Brillo Beard, Needlenose— they must have gone on ahead or something.

And then, even as he watched, Tweedledum disappeared. One second he was there, the next he wasn't. Gone without a trace. Tweedledee, who was taping Jose's mouth, didn't notice. Not at first, anyway. But then he said, "Here, Tim, hold this," and held out the roll of tape. Impatiently, still glaring into Jose's tired old face, he waved the hand. Then he said dammit and turned his head. His eyes widened. He stepped back. Dropping the tape, he fumbled in his pocket for the gun that bulged it and—

He vanished. Completely. McGill blinked and rubbed his

eyes. But Tweedledee was still gone.

"Mrmrmrmrmrmrm," said Jose, bending down, and waggling his head at McGill. He was very pale. Sweat dripped from his forehead.

"You want me to take the tape off?" he asked.

Jose nodded, and made more funny noises.

He wasn't afraid any more, which made him feel silly. For a minute he wanted to say, "Say please," but he had a feeling that if he did, he might not be able to sit down in the car home. He reached for a corner of the tape. "Fast?"

Jose nodded, and shut his eyes tight.

He ripped the tape away, and winced as Jose shouted "ARR!" Then, since the old man was coughing, trying to spit the handkerchief from his mouth, McGill reached up and tugged it out. It was soggy. He dropped it at once. "You okay?" he asked.

"Yeah, I guess so." He shrugged, which wasn't easy, since his hands were still tied. "Wanna cut me loose?"

"I don't have a knife."

"I do. In my coat pocket, right-hand side. Be careful with it, it's a souvenir from Noxtrimml."

He reached into Jose's pocket. A round, warm smoothness brushed his fingers. When he pulled it out, it glowed green in the April sunlight. "Is this it?" he asked, juggling it. His hand still shook. "It doesn't look like a knife."

"That's it," answered Jose. "Hold it very carefully, like a baseball, and turn it around until all your fingers are on the buttons. Make sure the hole shows between your thumb and forefinger."

He spun it around until it looked right. Just to be safe, he showed it to Jose. Then he pressed his thumb down, only his thumb like Jose said, and a spurt of steel shot out of the hole. It gleamed in the weak sun. Carefully, he sliced the ropes off Jose's wrists, watched him massage himself, then returned the knife. It was very, very sharp. "How come you never showed me that before?" he asked.

Jose pressed another button and the blade jumped back inside. "You're never around when I open my mail," he answered. "And at the dinner table I use regular silverware. What do you want, all my secrets at once or something?" Affectionately, he tousled McGill's hair. "Let's go home, huh kid?"

"Sure, Jose." Gravel squeaked and squirmed under their

feet. The wind was soft, now, like a friendly old lady patting your cheek on the street. When they got into the parking lot, McGill looked up. "Jose—where'd they go?"

"The bad guys?"

"Uh-huh. What happened to them?"

"I Flung them away, that's what happened." He unlocked the door and boosted McGill inside.

"Where'd you Fling 'em to?"

"Somewhere a long ways away."

"They going to be coming back to get me again?"

"I don't think so, McGill ol' buddy." Involuntarily, his eyes rolled up to pick out the sun. "Somehow, I just don't think so."

• Chapter VI •

"Explain fiasco with Feighan child," rasped the voice from the tank.

Hommroummy, watching the swirls of gas as warily as if he thought one might break through the glass to strangle him, did so. He explained the circumstances, his chain of reasoning, and his deductions about what had gone wrong. He did not minimize his errors or overstate his value: Gryll would react badly to a self-serving analysis. When he'd finished, he clasped his hands behind his back and waited. His muscles were tense, but his face was impassive.

"So," snorted the speakers. "Plan decent enough. Preparation inadequate. Execution execrable. Recap fate of threatened agents."

"The four most vulnerable have, ah, died. Unsuspiciously. A fortuitous thunderstorm enabled us to black out the Washington area. That earned us twelve hours, during which time we manufactured, for thirty-eight of them, financial histories detailed enough to prove their integrity. It wasn't easy, but I have a machine in Zurich." He cleared his throat. "We also investigated the investigators. Twelve were dirty, in one way or another. With our access to high places, we were able to have them suspended pending departmental inquiry. And *that* brought us the time to reprogram the appropriate computers."

After a moment's hesitation, the alien said, "Well done."

"Thank you, sir."

"Feighan boy. Now in chrysalis, which disguises desirable

characteristics. Do not approach until it achieves maturity. Understood?"

"Yes, sir," he said, backing away. In the corridor he looked at his hands. They'd come so close to death that they were shaking.

· Chapter VII ·

McGill Feighan was furious. Sent to his room without supper, like he was a little kid, instead of a fourteen-year-old who was almost 180 cm. tall. He paced up and down beside his bed, kicking savagely at the rust-colored hooked rug. Sent to his room!

All right, sure, maybe he'd said things he shouldn't have. Maybe. He wouldn't say he'd been wrong, but he'd concede he might have been—what was that word Ms. Thompson used? —intemperate. Right. But he'd been *angry*, and when you're angry, things pop out. Just like when you're afraid.

She'd been pretty nasty, too. Ol' bag. Screaming across the kitchen table, telling him he oughta be grateful for Jose instead of resentful, claiming he didn't know how lucky he was, that Jose was the only one who hadn't given up when he'd been paralyzed . . . crap. All mothers fed their kids that kind of garbage. None of it was true.

Grateful for Jose? He oughta thank the ol' wreck for tagging after him all the time? Crap. None of the other kids had a gray watchdog sitting in the back of the classroom. Every other kid could get privacy. None of the other kids hadda wear a ball and chain.

What had he done to deserve such treatment? It was cruel and unusual punishment, definitely, to saddle him with a watery-eyed old geezer who shadowed him everywhere, kept him from getting invited to parties, made him the butt of the school's jokes . . .

Oh, the kids thought it was hilarious. "Don't walk too fast, Gilly baby," they'd jeer, "you'll give your nursemaid a heart attack!" He'd told them Jose was a bodyguard, a guide, but who'd believe that a toothless old man could defend a lollipop against a baby? Gee—whillikers, it was rotten. He'd say, "Every Flinger has to have a change-ringer," and they'd say, "If you're a Flinger, how come you walk to school, huh?" And "Where's your tunic?" And "Are you really a Flinger or is your psychiatrist just humoring you?"

Jose was no help. Oh, he'd show them his tunic—which looked obscene on such a decrepit body, the neat tight patterns of energy glowing and whirling around a shrunken chest and withered arms and a hairy pot belly—and they'd mock him. "Who'dya steal it from?" And "You run a costume store?"

If only he'd *Fling* something for them—anything, a yo-yo, a car, a teacher—geez, McGill knew he'd be the most popular kid in school if he could get Jose to Fling the principal to Antarctica or somewhere . . .

But no, they all thought he was a little baby who couldn't get around on his own, some kind of mental retard like that kid in Metal Shop who made ice skate blades all day long and wouldn't do anything else.

Was it any wonder he'd asked Mom to let him go to school alone?

Maybe "ask" wasn't the right word. Demand. Well, he had a right. Yes. He had every right in the world to tell her he wouldn't go back to school if Jose had to come along.

She didn't care, though. *She* wasn't the one getting laughed at. No, she was just an overprotective mother; they'd read about her kind in Intro to Psych. The kids had recognized her from the description, too; they'd whispered and giggled and pointed at him for the whole week they were on that chapter.

The low rumble of adult voices rose through the floor. They were talking about him, he knew. His father bellowed like a bull with its horns stuck in a chain-link fence, puffing and snorting and pawing the ground. His mother's tone swooped in and out of the fence, now placating, now insisting, a hummingbird flying circles around that bull's horns. And rambling along, the farmer unhurried with a stalk of grass between his teeth, was Jose.

He paced some more, taking pleasure in slamming his heels against the patches of bare floor. That'd drive 'em nuts downstairs, he thought. Show 'em they can't just send me up here and exile me like Napoleon or whoever . . .

The door creaked open. Surprised that he hadn't heard footsteps, he spun, then realized, with a blush that didn't reach his face, that he couldn't have heard them over his own stompings.

Jose stepped into the room. He had an envelope in one hand and a belt in the other. His stubbly face was pale, and very tired.

"You!" said McGill incredulously. "You're supposed to guard my body, not whip it."

Jose managed a small smile that didn't lighten his eyes. "You should be grateful they sent up 'the old cripple,' and not your father. He's about ready to do a real job on you, kid. Was all your ma and I could do to talk him out of it. Shouldn't have called her a bitch, McGill."

"Yeah, well, other kids' mothers don't get so pissed about it."

Jose snorted. "Your name's McGill Feighan, not 'other kids.' And Patrick Sean Feighan doesn't take kindly to a son who curses his mother. Here." He gestured with the envelope, inviting McGill to take it.

"What's that?"

"Oh, it's one of those corny 'to-be-opened-after-my-death-or-disappearance' letters. I'm seventy-three, and though the actuarial tables give me a few years more . . ." He shrugged, and fluttered the letter onto McGill's desk. "Case I'm not around when you find your power, open it, read it. It tells you what to do, who to talk to about getting into the Academy." He sighed, then, and motioned with the belt. "Drop your trousers and turn around. Your old man doesn't hear me using this, he'll be up to apply it himself. Come on."

"No!" It was too humiliating. He was fourteen. Almost a man. A very important man, at that, because he'd be a Flinger soon. Flingers don't get whipped. Especially not by a shriveled old fart who couldn't take ten steps without pausing for breath. "No!"

"C'mon, kid, turn around and let's get it over with."

"No, dammit, I won't! And you can't make me, either."

Jose hesitated, as though balancing ideas in his head. A strange expression passed over his face. It contained resignation, but no recognition of defeat. "Come on, boy, don't make it harder on yourself than it has to be."

"I'm not a boy! And you can't do that to me!"

Jose shuffled forward, raising the belt in his arthritic right arm, moving it back behind his head so he could put whatever strength he had left into it. "Sorry," he said, as he snapped it forward and whipped it across McGill's left thigh.

"Ow!" He retreated. The mattress of his bed bumped him behind the knees. Falling backward, he saw the arm rise again, and lash forward. This one caught him across the shins. For all Jose's age, it hurt. And the arm was going up again. "Don't do that!"

"Got to."

"I'm warning you—"

"Sorry." The hand lunged forward for the third time.

Fury exploded in McGill, fury and shame and pain. It mixed with the reflex rebelliousness of the adolescent. It mingled with McGill's conviction that he was somebody special. It mated with the unbidden image of a tall, strong young man cowering before a cripple. Then it burst its bonds and took charge.

The room darkened, as though lightning had hit the power lines. Rage poured out of him like water from a fire hose. There was a hoisting sensation, and briefly, an eerie sparkle lit the darkness, but he knew it wasn't Jose's tunic, or the lights, or anything regular. When he brushed up against it, it was like walking near a friendly puppy. It would do anything he wanted it to do . . . but it had twisted away already, and the room lights were coming back on.

Pleasant fatigue weighed him down. He was much too tired to resist any longer. Rolling onto his stomach, ready to accept the inevitable—and Jose was right, better him than his father—he said, "Okay, go ahead." Anticipatorily, he flinched.

No whirr.

No crack.

No sting.

"Jose?" He propped himself up on his elbows and craned his neck. The room was deserted. Funny. He hadn't heard the door open or close—on the floor lay the belt. Had the old man given up, gone downstairs to enlist reinforcements? He listened, holding his breath so the sounds that wriggled through the floor would come in without interference. No. No voices. Maybe, then, he'd gone to his own room? Cautiously, he padded over the hooked rug, opened his door a crack, and glanced across the hallway. No. Jose's door was open and his room was dark. He wasn't there. Or in the john. Or...he didn't want to do it, but he had to. "Dad," he called out, "Dad, is Jose down there?"

"No, isn't he up with you?" floated back the reply.

"No, he, uh..." Scratching his head, he looked around. Footsteps sounded below; the staircase creaked under heavy athletic feet. On the off chance, he checked his parents' bedroom. Still no Jose. His father's bulk displaced the darkness behind him. He turned, warily. "I can't...can't find him."

Anger tautened Feighan's jaw muscles, but it was controlled, reined in. "What happened?" Behind him appeared Buongiorno, her face white and pinched with worry.

"Well, Jose, uh, he was— I mean, he had the belt, and was trying to use it, and...he, uh—" He had to stop, breathe carefully for a moment, and blink hard. "—he was getting in some good licks, too, and then...oh, yeah, that's when the lights went out, and when they came back—"

"The lights did what?" asked Feighan.

"They went out, didn't you—" His eyes went from face to face and found only bewilderment. "They *didn't* go out?"

"No," said Buongiorno. "We'd have noticed."

"Well, they went out up here," he insisted. "And when they came back on, Jose was gone, poof! The belt was on the floor, but he was..." He shrugged. "I don't know where he went."

Feighan and Buongiorno turned inward, and stared at each other for a long while. She was biting her lip; he was rubbing his right earlobe. Then, as if cued by an invisible prompter, they sighed in unison. She extended a hand. "I'm glad you listened to him, Pat."

For a moment, pride delayed his nod. "He was right. Poor bastard." As he drove his clenched right fist into his left palm, he pivoted to glare at McGill. "Where'd you Fling him?"

"I didn—" His stomach knotted, as though his father's fist had plunged into it. His spine turned to ice; his face, to a hot plate. For a long minute he couldn't breathe at all, and when his lungs finally got to working again, he broke immediately into tears. "I *did!*" he wailed. "I did. Jose, Jose, I'm sorry, oh my god, I—"

"Where'd you Fling him?" demanded Feighan, though more softly.

"I don't know!" he shouted. Burying his face in his hands, he stumbled into his room and collapsed on the bed. Tears, warm and salty, trickled through his fingers and moistened his pillow. "Jose," he moaned, "Jose."

He could sense his parents standing above him, indecisive, unsure of what tack to take. His father, he knew, was struggling with his flamboyant temper; McGill wished he wouldn't, wished he'd unleash it, wished he'd deliver the punishment that was so richly deserved. And his mother... before that bitter afternoon, he would have said she'd want to comfort him, but after the things he'd called her...

A weight sagged the edge of the bed. On his shoulders alighted hands as soft as mourning doves. The perfume of skin lotion swirled around him, evoking an entire complex of emotions, the strongest of which was grief. "Mom," he gasped, "Mom, I didn't mean I didn't know, I'm sorry, it j-j-just, I didn't want to, th-th-this thing inside blew up I didn't... oh, Mom!"

Her voice was soothing, hushing; her words were indistinguishable. He didn't care. It wasn't what she said, it was how she said it. Her fingers combed his hair and brushed his cheeks; they told him she forgave him, and wanted to help.

"McGill," said Feighan, "did Jose give you a letter?"

"Letter?" He lifted his head a centimeter and tried to think, but every visualization of Jose reinstigated the tears.

"He said he was going— here it is. It's addressed to you."

"Oh," he sniffed, "that. Yeah. He gave it to me just b-b-before—" The sobs came out in sporadic bursts that he could not control. He couldn't even *look* at his parents.

"May I open it?"

The old, smart-mouthed McGill tried to resurrect himself, tried to snap, "Asking permission? That's a first," but he choked that other, dumber half down and waved a hand behind his head. "Go ahead."

Paper tore and slid and unfolded. Feighan, clearing his throat, began to read:

October 3, 2097

"'MY DEAR McGILL,' it says,

'I have a feeling that tonight will be the night, that your justly earned whipping will trigger your Talent out of latency. I've been sensing its gradual strengthening; it's been swelling within its dormancy like a germinated seed inside its coat. It has to crack sooner or later, and physical punishment might well provoke it.

If you're reading this, it means I haven't returned from wherever you've Flung me. Don't worry about that. I'm old, and with your passage into maturity, I've lost whatever function I might have had anyway. Somehow it seems appropriate for me to die on a Fling . . . if I'd been able to return, I would eventually have chosen the Flingers' Death, and hurled myself into the sun.

My only regret is that you're a nice boy, and this will probably make you feel guilty as hell. It's likely to be futile, but I'll say it anyway: don't. Don't feel guilty. Guilt should be reserved for conscious, deliberate acts of malice—and if you're like every other Flinger who ever was, this . . . incident, caught you totally by surprise.

Just boiled up out of nowhere, didn't it?

That's the way it happens, kid. I've told you about Anita, my change-ringer, but I never did mention her departure. Same thing happened. One minute she was going to beat my butt, the next she was gone. She never came back, either. I had to read a letter sort of similar to this one to find out what had happened.

So. You're a full-fledged Flinger, now. But an untrained one. Without the training, you'll never probe the limits of your potential. Time to get it.

Go to the Flinger Building in New York City, tell them who you are—your name's on file, I gave it to them long ago—and tell them what you've done. Don't let guilt or shame shut your mouth. They won't care about me; I've done all I can for them. Besides, most of them got rid of their change-ringers in the same way I did mine . . . and you did yours.

That's about all I've got to say to you, kid. Everything else, I said before, when we were together.

Be a good Flinger. More important, be a good person.

> With love and affection
> JOSE SCHWEDEKER
> Flinger (ret.)'

And that's the letter," finished Feighan, folding it back into its sharp creases and returning it to its envelope. He let it lie on the palm of his hand for a few seconds, as if estimating its import, as if considering what to do with it—then, knowing he couldn't determine its influence through any physical means, knowing he'd have to wait to find its weight, he laid it on his son's desk. "Sit up, McGill."

Complying, he said, "Yes, Dad." His eyes were considerably drier, but his breath still came in uneven gasps. He couldn't lift his face. He studied the tops of his father's black shoes until a huge finger slipped under his chin and forced it up.

"Look at me."

Reluctantly, he obeyed. Sorrow gentled his father's features, sorrow and understanding and love. "What?" he asked.

"Jose's letter is over there." Without looking away, he gestured at the cluttered desktop. "Read it a few more times tonight, before you go to sleep. Understand that what you did was . . ." His massive shoulders rose and fell. "When a baby's born, he cries and shits and pisses and can't control any of them, even if they're obnoxious to the people who take care of him. They're reflexes, that's all. And in the Army, they used to have a rule that a man wasn't responsible for what he said or did in the first thirty seconds after somebody tried to wake him—because soldiers have reflexes that take over when their conscious minds aren't in complete control." He inhaled deeply, and took his time about exhaling. "What I'm trying to say, son, is like what Jose said—don't blame yourself for this, because nobody else is blaming you for it. It's a natural, normal thing, and it's okay." He smiled down at McGill, and ruffled his hair. "Nicole, give him a hand packing his things—and make sure our alarm is set for six. We've got a long drive tomorrow, if we're going to get into New York before dark."

▪ Chapter VIII ▪

The Chinese ideogram for peace filled the disp-screen, and Hommroummy meditated upon its paradox. It looked different than it meant, especially in grass writing. That plunging vertical stroke suggested a stylized dagger...

His pocket telephone rang; he fished it out and held it to his ear. "Yes?"

"McGill Feighan," stated the computer in all its blandness, "is fifty kilometers from home, on Interstate 80, headed east."

"Why?"

"A call from the Feighan household to the Flinger Academy in New York City last night indicated that he is to enroll in the Academy today."

"Thank you." He slipped the phone back into his pocket, and left his desk to pace. So Feighan had found his powers... something would have to be done, but what would be best? Gryll, who took such a personal interest in the affair, was elsewhere at the moment and wouldn't return until it chose. It couldn't even be reached... but Hommroummy thought he saw a solution. The idea was to enlist the boy into The Organization, to tug him toward the surface of the host culture so that he could become a cell of the interface. That meant knowing how to lure him... he had agents at the Academy; they could discover Feighan as well as anyone could learn another person, but that wouldn't be enough. If the boy were a pawn of the Far Being Retzglaran, as Gryll seemed to fear, and if the Far Being were out to cripple The Organization again, then that had to be clear well ahead of time . . . he summoned his captive telepath. Once they'd discerned Feighan's allegiances, they could lay their plans for absorbing him.

▪ Chapter IX ▪

On his first night at the Flinger Academy, snoring in an unfamiliar bed, unconsciously attuned to the foreignness of the room and the alienness of its odors, McGill Feighan nightmared.

Ambiguity distorted the opening sequence. McGill—older, bigger, and smarter—stood on an empty plain. The plain was brown. Like dry dirt. It flattened away as far as the eye could see. The horizon was smooth, God had sanded it to perfection, not a bump, not a hump, not a tree stuck up anywhere. In the orange sky moved the wind, birdless, beeless, even cloudless. He stood under it, and he waited.

He didn't know why, except he felt as though someone he respected had told him to. Irritation was growing, though: he'd been waiting for most of eternity. He supposed that he could leave, if he chose, since he was an adult, a free agent, and owed his time to no man, but...someone had said wait, and he did, shifting his weight from one foot to the other, altering the set of his hips and shoulders, occasionally digging his toe into the featureless brown ground.

Dust fountained in the west. First merely a smudge against the sky, it became a trail of smoke, then a billow. As it came closer, an entire stormfront of beige hung in the air, hurling its leading edge at him. It was surely what he'd been told to meet, but...why did it scrape nails of apprehension down his vertebrae?

Hours passed; he revised his estimate of the world's diameter. The horizon had to be further than it appeared, if that dust-kicker moved as fast as seemed likely. Scratching his jaw, he worried whether he should shave before it arrived, but decided not to. It had to be an eetie—this didn't look like Earth— and eeties were notorious for their unfamiliarity with Terran protocol. His fingers rasped on the skin under his jaw. There was no water for shaving, and the alien wouldn't appreciate the effort anyway. Probably not even notice that he was stubbly.

When it came closer, its shape clarified: it was a Jello submarine on wheels, and impossibly long. Two, three hundred meters. Rumbling toward him with no engine noise, no exhaust, no rattle-clack of moving parts . . . eerie, definitely eerie. His hand shook as he dried his forehead.

It braked to a halt in front of him. It towered a good fifteen meters above his head. The wind fled, leaving only sun and soil and the translucent ochre of the being's body. But it shivered, and broke in two; its aft end separated from its bow. One segment slithered to his right, the other to his left. He waited, and tried to will the weakness out of his knees.

"Good morning, McGill," boomed the bow end.

"G-g-good morning," he replied.

"Do you know who I am?"

"I haven't the faintest idea," he answered.

"I'm your father!" it shouted, while its companion exulted, "And I'm your mother!" The two leaped forward, squashing him between them, their gelatinous flesh flowing into all the nooks and crannies of his unyielding body, filling the spaces under his arms, between his legs, under his collarbone, squeezing, squashing, absorbing—

The bed threw him into a sitting position. Lights flashed furiously: the overheads, the desk lamp, even his tunic, which had been implanted that morning. The room computer extruded a tentacle that offered a glass of ice-cold water; its diagnostic section studied him with contactless probes. Once he'd calmed down, the machine dimmed the lights, hummed soft music, and lulled him back to sleep. This time it was dreamless.

But in the morning the Academy assigned him a roommate.

"Hiya, there, caddie," called a bright, amused voice. "Gimme a hand with this luggage here, willya?"

McGill rolled drowsily off his bed. In the doorway lounged a tall, very slender teenager; he was dressed in a three-piece suit of gray synthetics and his red tie was bright enough to blind. His hair was a tangle of tight brown curls that sideburned down to his jawline. Pale and dark-eyed, he had a two-bump nose and a smile of easy command. McGill had never seen him before. "Who are you?"

"Your new roommate, Marion Jefferson Greystein, the only other caddie in the Academy, brand-new like you but a few years older, yes, hmm," he said, advancing into the barren confines of the 3 m. by 4 m. room. "Good old cinderblock, painted dismal yellow and already peeling because the contractor was too cheap to moistureproof it. Uh-huh, just what I expected." He directed McGill to the insecure stack of boxes, crates, and suitcases that tottered in the hallway. "Just bring them in, my man, and stash them—" He held up a finger as if to announce the birth of an idea. His other hand fidgeted inside his coat pocket until it emerged with a large piece of purple chalk. "Ah-hah!" he bleated, "ah-hah!" Bending, he bisected the floor and the room with a wavery line. "Throw my gear anywhere on my side of that line, but do be careful with it because the foldout-holos are fragile and we would hate to chip off a lovely bare limb now, wouldn't we?"

McGill was too bemused to do more than nod blankly.

"Well, hop to it, caddie, got to get this stuff stowed before it's too late, that's right, bring it in, surely you can carry two bags at a time, you're a big boy, perhaps not in years but surely in size—" While he chattered away with apparent abandon, he concentrated on unpacking a small cardboard box. It yielded up a tangle of electronic gadgetry. Still talking so quickly that no normal person could have done anything more, he shielded his equipment from the computer-eye with his body and strolled to its blind side. His quick, sure hand thrust a jack into the appropriate hole. He glanced at his tie. Then he fell silent, leaned against the coarse wall, and heaved a massive sigh.

"Jesus," he said, in a rather different voice, "I'm glad I got *that* done."

McGill set down the suitcase he'd been carrying. *"What* done?"

Greystein looked askance at him, then nodded. "That's right, you don't know me. Well..." He seemed at a loss for words. "Put briefly, I suppose you'd have to say that I just castrated the computer."

"Huh?"

"I'm an electronics addict. Half the stuff in these boxes—"
He gestured vaguely at his laden bed. "—is solid-state com-
ponentry of one sort or another. You like my tie clip?"

McGill blinked at the apparent *non sequitur*, then shrugged,
and leaned over to examine the clip. It was a narrow strip of
silver inset with a many-faceted blue crystal. "Yeah," he said
at last, "but—"

"It's my detector," said Greystein. "Built it myself two
years ago; I was then, and remain today, a precocious young
man. The crystal changes colors as electromagnetic—and
other—fields impinge on it. The new color tells me what the
field is, and in one of those boxes—" Again he waved at the
clutter. "—is a nullifier for it."

"But why did you, um, do that to *this* computer?"

"Because it not only cares for all your wants, young— what
is your name, anyway?"

"Feighan," he answered, "McGill Feighan."

"People call you Mac?"

"Not my friends."

"I like that. McGill, then. Well, McGill, young daffodil,
this computer here monitors your behavior—"

"Oh, I knew that."

"—and it also modifies it."

"Say what?"

Beaming, Greystein bounced on his bed as if to test it for
softness. The tautly tucked blankets immediately wrinkled.
"This little device called a room-computer generates a field
which— McGill Feighan? *The* McGill Feighan?"

"Huh?"

"I'm an exologist in my spare time," explained Greystein,
"and I've got books and books of clippings about all the rare
eetie appearances, and are you the McGill Feighan who got
eaten by one at birth?"

"Uh-huh," said McGill warily. He wasn't sure what relationship the circumstances of his birth had to do with the room-
computer. "That's me."

"Damn, that's neat! I've been wanting to meet you— I'm
sorry, I was talking about this." He reached out a hand and
patted the aluminum flanks of the computer. "The field, yes—
it generates a field which acts directly upon the cells of the
brain, bypassing the conscious mind completely. The modu-
lated field can instill in you behavior patterns which the senior

Flingers would like to encourage—instant obedience to Flinger authority, for example, or for another, instant refusal to Fling for local authorities."

McGill slowly lowered himself to his own bed, and scratched his temple. The skin there was very smooth. "I don't understand . . ."

"Look, caddie, the Boss Flingers have a nice setup; they don't want it disrupted by subversive young Flingers who decide to go into business for themselves. They also don't want us doing something dumb for our national governments, like Flinging a large bomb into the capital of an inimical country . . . so they program us, with the field generated by this computer here, so that when we're fully accredited, we won't think of doing anything they don't want us to do." He paused for a moment to nibble thoughtfully on his thumb. "They do have a small point—they spend tremendous sums of money to find inhabited planets capable of staffing their own Flinger Booths—and if the Network is to keep expanding, they have to keep sending out those ships."

"Why ships?"

Greystein shrugged. "We're going to study the economics of the Flinger Network an hour a day for the next five years, so I won't try to give you a quick answer. What I will do is let you share the benefits of my marvelous jammer. It'll cut off not only the computer's monitoring ability—while encouraging it to keep reporting that it is monitoring us—but the field as well, although the computer and its supervisors will believe the field is still going strong. Now, about this alien . . ."

So many people identified him with the giant gastropod that he, adaptable as any adolescent, also began to define himself in terms of that experience. In a way it was inevitable; that it hadn't happened earlier was partly because his parents had shunned the notoriety, partly because his father was famous in his own right, and partly because the Talent had shaped McGill's identity up to then.

Perhaps his earliest memory was of Jose's arrival that cold, dark night when he was four. Jose, of course, who'd known dozens if not hundreds of aliens intimately, had found nothing too outré about McGill's ingestion. To him (and now McGill was beginning to think of Jose as having been brainwashed; he had probably been subject to the same behavior-modification field that Greystein had so wizardly eliminated), the foci of life were Flinging, and McGill's maturation into a Class A Flinger.

One views himself as those around him view him. And others view one in terms of one's oddities, one's peculiarities. They may publicly refer to one as "that nice little boy from next door," but in private, in the sanctity of their own minds, they pick upon whatever sets one apart from the general run of mankind: "Funny ears;" "runny nose;" "big mouth;" "black skin;" whatever . . . as one grows up, the mnemonic tags shift from purely phsyical characteristics to personal quirks, prejudices, functions: "meter-reader;" "drunk;" "eetie-lover;" etc.

Jose, his father, his mother, the neighbors, friends, relatives . . . almost all had thought of him as "the kid who was going to be a Flinger." So for the last ten years he'd been shaped by their viewpoints, as a desert rock is carved by the sandy wind, or as a granite outcropping is sculpted by the rain.

But in the Academy, where *everyone* was a Flinger except him and Greystein, who were going to become that . . . his Talent no longer set him apart, was no longer the easy tag by which he was filed in people's memories. Here, what was different about him was his birth.

So the Flingers, whose Talents did not immunize them to normal human practices and habits, immediately thought of him as one who'd been overexposed to alienness. "The kid who got swallowed," some would refer to him. On his first day he picked up a nickname: "Bellyful."

And people wanted to talk about it, even though he didn't remember it. But they'd ask questions, and speculate, and suggest, and the authorities vowed to examine him carefully, come physical exam time, and the staff psychologists determined to interrogate him about it, and the staff telepaths probed him on it, and . . .

McGill Feighan got caught up in it. Everyone needs something to set him apart. Although the textbooks keep saying we're unique, the mass-ness of the world rebuts them. Mass Media. Mass Advertising. Mass Production. Mass Indoctrination. Mass this, mass that . . . the common man, the average man, the man in the street . . . almost everybody who knows better is hell-bent on proving that he doesn't . . . generalizations abound, and in their abundance overwhelm uniqueness.

So when a naive teenager is offered uniqueness on a silver

platter, when he doesn't have to look for it or work for it, is
it unusual that he accepts it? Could one expect him to deny
that which envelops him in adulation and appreciation? So it
was an accident, so he'd had nothing to do with what made
him special—why should he not bask in it? How many beautiful
teenage girls coat their faces with mud to drive away the crowds
of drooling teenage boys?

He got very caught up in it.

Much to McGill's disappointment, the class schedule showed
that the first year was devoted almost entirely to book work—
and worse, most of the courses were identical to those he'd
have been taking at Fairview Park High School, if he hadn't
come to the Academy. The Federal educational bureaucracy
insisted that, to receive diplomas, Academy graduates had to
acquire the same type and number of credits as high school
students everywhere.

So he settled down to muttering over math and writing
papers that angered his English teacher (who, when she asked,
"Why did Cervantes write *Don Quixote*?" did not want to hear,
"Because he needed the money." But McGill didn't feel it was
his fault—he liked the books assigned, enjoyed reading them,
and sometimes even got a kick out of discussing them. It was
just that Ms. Grima was obsessed with dissecting them, stripping away the flesh to poke at the musculature of metaphor
and the skeleton of theme. How could anyone be happy reading
when he had to count the number of times "bluebird" was
used?) He did situps in gym and, in general, carried a normal
course-load for a fourteen-year-old. The only difference was
that he was alone in class. Greystein was two academic grades
ahead of him, and no other Flinger cadets lived in North
America.

Tacked onto the schoolday were the Flinger classes, three
his first semester: Introduction to the Economics of the Flinger
Network; the Theory of Flinging; and Extraterrestrial Life I,
which was an overview of the 693 member races of the Flinger
Network.

McGill found IntroEcon duller than anything connected with
teleportation should have been. Though pleased to learn why
the fare from New York City to anywhere was so low (the cost
of the expedition to Earth, plus 6.7% interest on the bonds,
was amortized over a 100-year period, and the way it worked

out, 70% of the 50 FNC [$750 U.S.] ticket price covered the amortization), he was appalled at the discovery that he was expected to be able to organize, launch, and captain a similar expedition, using only the resources of his native planet. But Greystein assured him that in time he would learn how many 1 mm. screws a starship needed, and at the worst would squeak though with a passing grade.

The Theory of Flinging, a catch-all course, presented physical and metaphysical analyses of the Talent and its proper use. While it was interesting to read that Knxalad of Mrxelpha deemed the Talent a mutation induced by solar flares, and that an equally learned scholar on an equally unpronounceable planet disagreed with old Knxalad, it had no practical application. The philosophical essays on its moral utilization were thought-provoking, but McGill and Greystein considered it hypocritical of the Academy to present differing points of view when it tried nightly to brainwash the student body into strict adherence to its dogma . . .

Eetie Life I, on the other hand, was absorbing, stimulating, and challenging. It was explained, on the first day of class, that when Feighan and Graystein were hired by the Flinger Network, they would have to be able to teleport animate and inanimate matter, massing up to 918 kilos a shot, to any of twelve different destinations. Ten of those, the ten planets studied first, were assigned to all Earth-based Flingers; these were the ten worlds with which Earth maintained regular transport. Only one was in Terra's neighborhood; seven were parsecs away. The ninth was Sector Headquarters, which supervised Flinger operations in that arm of the galaxy. The last was the Hub, the most cosmopolitan city in the universe, the Rome to which all Flinger roads led.

By tradition, the other two destinations were chosen by the cadets themselves. Any two, anywhere in the universe. The only requirements were that they belong to the Network, and that the cadet prove himself capable of safe teleport there.

"What are you going to pick?" asked Greystein, at the end of the first week. Sprawled across his unmade bed, he ate popcorn out of a ripped plastic bag while he leafed through a star catalog.

"I don't know," said McGill, looking up from the program he was writing for Computers I. "I've got three years, yes? Hey. You're the eetie expert, where did that giant slug come from?"

"Got me," said Greystein. "They used to think Thrmdiodl, but they found out, when they checked, that it had traveled on a forged passport. By that time, it was long gone. Nobody knows a thing about it."

"What about the, uh, whatchamacallit, the Far Being Retz-glaran? How about him—her? it?"

"To tell you the truth—"

"You don't know, huh?"

"No." Momentarily he looked crestfallen. But then he brightened. "Nobody else knows, either, not even the Flingers at the Hub. I was doing some research on it, though, and the Hub records have references to it going back seven hundred and eighty years. It keeps cropping up, usually as a being which sent a subordinate which was actually spotted, like in your case, though sometimes as an entity which is rumored to have visited a world which has sub-c commerce with a Flinger world . . . but nobody knows. The pattern that's emerged, according to the sources, is of a being of vast powers and a quirky sense of humor. Some books suggest that it's playing a large game. That's about all I know."

"Hmm." McGill frowned down at his homework, then shoved it aside with a weary hand. "Well, let me know if anybody finds out where it lives, because I want to make that one of my optional destinations."

Two weeks later, the principal's decision to move Greystein into McGill's room proved to have been wise. It was late at night, and both were asleep. McGill awoke at a tap on the shoulder. He sat up; his tunic rainbowed on the wall. Making a note to kid Greystein about his snoring, he looked for whoever had aroused him. The room was dark, but the shades hadn't been pulled down. Enough moon- and star-light slanted in to combine with his tunic and silhouette the doorframe, the desks, even the crumpled socks on the floor. But no one else was there.

"Dream," he slurred to himself, lying back and yawning. The pillow was warm under his cheek; he tugged the blankets up over his shoulders and—

It wasn't a tap this time, it was a grab. And it wasn't his shoulder, either, it was his head. Fingers. Big, strong, long fingers. Reaching into his skull, squeezing his brain like an orange.

He tried to get up. His body refused to respond. *Move*, he

ordered his legs, but they lay still. *Light switch*, he commanded his hands, but they were fallen branches from a dead tree. *Help!* he tried to shout, but his vocal cords slumbered on.

The fingers poked through his brain, peeling back lobes and bending over to examine them. Impatient they were, and determined.

"RMRMRMRMRM," he forced out of his throat, "RMRMRMRMRM."

The eyes of the fingers were inspecting him when he was five, when Jose had come to ring his changes, when Christmas had touched the spring night with lights and people and voices.

"RMRMRMRMRMRM!" The groan felt like he'd yanked a swallowed fishhook out of his throat.

The fingers, angry now, pulled his brain like taffy, stretching it unto transparency to isolate their prey.

"RMRMRMRMRM!!!" It hurt so bad he wanted to cry, but the paralysis wouldn't permit even that. He tried to think what he'd done as a baby, but couldn't remember. The fingers had stirred up so much stuff that drifting sediment smogged his mind's eye. "RMRMRMR!"

"What is it?" cracked Greystein's voice, fully awake, fully alert.

"RMRMRMRM."

The light snapped on. Curls flattened by sleep, Greystein leaned over him, peering anxiously into his face. "You okay? Say something, move something."

"MRMRMRMR." He sought to wiggle anything, a finger, his tongue, his eyes even, but nothing would respond.

The fingers continued to search. As his roommate sprang for the telephone, they found something: a sound, a name: Retzglaran. Voraciously, they dug for more. Memories flew like dirt from a mole's claws.

"Greystein here," bit off the teenager. "Feighan's under telepathic attack, get your staff— I don't care if he's asleep, this is an emergency! Yeah, I'll wait." Covering the mouthpiece, he swiveled his head to look at the immobilized McGill. "It's okay, man, everything's going to be okay, just hang in until the cavalry— Hello? Feighan. 12J. Dammit, you ought to know him, he's the kid who got swal— maybe 180 cm., 72 kg., uh, black hair, brown eyes, dark complexion, high forehead, Roman nose, square jaw— remember him now? Can you feel him? Good." Again he blocked the mouthpiece; again he turned to McGill. "Help's on its way; the staff Minder's sliding in now."

He could feel it, another hand approaching, grabbing the first, bending its fingers back, away from his brain, and he could move, he was free. Instinctively, as though the metaphorical hands were limited by geography, he rolled out of bed, landed on the floor, and scrambled on all fours to Greystein. "Keep them away," he begged, "please, keep 'em away, they're—"

"Hey, calm, easy, it's—"

"Please," he yelled, knowing he was hysterical but not caring. Emotions ran too high, like a tide that's breached the breakwaters and is curling inland. "Please, please, get 'em away, they're bad, please—"

Greystein grabbed him under the armpits and hauled him to his feet. After releasing him, he watched him for a half a second, as if afraid McGill would lose his balance, then— "Sorry, man," he muttered. His hand drew back. It cracked across McGill's left cheek, hard, stinging. It caught the other on its return.

Pain silenced McGill. His eyes filled with tears; he half-turned to hide them from Greystein. Sniffing, shocked, but nonetheless coaxing the emotions back into placid lagoons, he said, "Hey, uh—"

"It's okay, man." Greystein's hand comforted his shoulder. "It's okay."

A knock on the door spun them both around. "Come in," said Greystein.

It was the staff telepath, rumpled, sleepy-eyed, and swaddled in a terrycloth bathrobe badly frayed at the hems. "Are you okay?" he asked McGill.

"Yes, sir." He nodded.

"Uh-huh." He looked around the room, as if aware of a vague lack, but shrugged. "Are you in telepathic contact with friends or relatives or anybody?"

"No, sir."

"Good, 'cause I'm putting a trip-wire around your mind; anybody tries to get in, I'll hear 'em, and come help. Be cool. And I want to see you in my office tomorrow, all right?"

"Yes, sir."

"Fine." He tugged his bathrobe fully closed, gave the room another puzzled scan, and twisted the doorknob. "Good night, now."

The two boys talked about it for another hour before going to bed, but got nowhere. The next day, McGill reviewed the incident with the telepath and other faculty members, and they met the same frustrations. As his only memory was that the invader had been pleased by the mention of Retzglaran, they could decide little about the reason for the attack, or measures that would prevent a repetition. The staff Minder agreed to maintain his trip-wire for as long as he could; the principal instituted a computer search of all visiting aliens who might have had reason to violate McGill's privacy. As it turned out, the wire was never tripped and the search yielded nothing.

"All right," repeated the instructor, a tall, agile man whose tunic surrounded him like the aura in a Kirlian photograph, "let me summarize the procedure." He looked at their pads to ensure that both were diligently taking notes. He had a reputation as a stern taskmaster. If, when quizzed on this lecture, they didn't give him back his own words, they'd be in serious trouble. "Are you ready?"

McGill nodded. He was bored. Mr. Crafioni was a nice enough guy; his voice was clear and carrying; his thought processes were models of lucidity; but...the man repeated himself so often that you could scream! He stared blankly at the flat, shallow screen of his notepad. His stylus was in his hand—Crafioni would have noticed if it weren't—but he didn't expect he'd have to write anything. He had already ordered the summary printed out. It was the third time that afternoon that Crafioni had explained the process.

"First you visualize," said Crafioni, leaning forward against the podium to emphasize his point. "Visualize the destination down to the minutest detail, meanwhile studying the object to be teleported. Until the Fling has succeeded, hold *both* images in your head as clearly, and as completely, as possible. Once you have visualized them, you will *know* how to move the object from Point A to Point B. If you do not know, you are not a Flinger. Start the Fling, making certain to keep object and destination as sharp as possible in your mind. Still holding those images, and while you are Flinging, call in a third portion of your mind to adjust the angular momentum. This is the most difficult part. The best way is to bleed the original momentum into the dump—you will feel when it's all gone—and then to add enough to match up with the destination's. Very tricky. Very delicate. Only through experience and incredible concentration will you be able to do it over interstellar distances. Have you got all that?"

McGill nodded. It was crystal clear, at least in theory. What he was aching to do was practice.

And practice he did. The training area was a deserted hangar at the airport, one whose long axis ran east to west. It was easily 500 meters from one thirty-meter door to the other. Mr. Crafioni took him to the cobwebbed, dusty eastern end, and showed him Point One, a small, spring-mounted platform set into the floor. Point Two was at the opposite end of the hangar. Behind One, backlit by the sun that fought through the grimy windows, stood a head-high rack of metal shelves; flanking it were dollies piled with large wooden boxes. "Put an object on Point One," said Crafioni, "and Fling it to Point Two." He lifted a marble cube off a shelf and handed it to McGill. "I suggest you start with something this size."

He laid it on his palm, hefting its lightness, absorbing its cool. "Why so small?" he asked. "This won't be—"

"Try it," interrupted Crafioni. He shoved his large hands into his pockets and smiled briefly. His smiles came like nervous birds: they'd alight for a moment and delight with their beauty, but unexpected sounds would startle them away. "Go on."

McGill shrugged, and set the cube on the platform. Then, staring at it, he visualized Point Two—*felt* the line along which he should teleport the cube to get it there—knew that the east-west line of travel would obviate the necessity for momentum adjustment—and Flung. Simultaneously, the cube *thunked* as it landed on Point Two. He grinned. He snorted. He turned to Crafioni, spread his hands, and said, "Isn't that *neat?*"

The instructor pointed to a two-screen panel attached to the rack. Its left face said, "*Point Two: 83 cm.*" "No, McGill," he said slowly, "that isn't good. See?"

He looked, but didn't understand, and said so.

"'83 cm.' means the object dropped that far before it landed. Now, that's not very high—but a person could sprain his ankle, and a crate of delicate equipment could be damaged. You've *got* to visualize the lower surface of the object as resting on the upper surface of the destination—if you visualize them with space between, your transmission will arrive in the air, above the destination. Go down to Two— no," he said, as McGill began to close his eyes, "don't teleport. You're not good enough, not yet. That can wait. *Walk* down to Two, and send the cube back here. And tonight, remember to call your parents to tell them. It's something they'd like to hear."

A week passed before McGill could move the cube so precisely that it materialized where it should. It was a week of daily two-hour practices, with five minutes between each Fling because less rest would eventually damage his Talent. It was a week in which he learned to recognize the tension that besets even the best Flinger, the tension of making sure you do it right, absolutely right, the first time, because when you do it for real, you don't get a second chance.

Once he'd landed the cube without a sound, without a jar, without the slightest room for gravity to assert itself, Crafioni upped him to a five-kilo weight. And when that was mastered, to a ten. A twenty. A fifty. All the way up to the maximum 918 kilos, which anyone could Fling, but heavier than which no one had ever budged.

Under his instructor's tolerant eye, McGill tried: he laid the one-kilo cube atop the 918-kilo crate, stepped back, visualized, felt, knew, Flung— and nothing happened. Removing the cube, he teleported the crate with all the nonchalance of a man twenty years his senior. Crafioni patted him on the shoulder. "Don't feel bad, but think about it. Maybe you'll come up with the answer no one else has."

Almost his sole regret was that he and Greystein practiced at different times. "It'd be better," he said, as he watched his roommate disassemble Ms. Grima's computer/TV prior to repairing it, "if we could work out together, you know?"

"I doubt that, McGill, I really do." Squinting down a microscope at a suspect integrated circuit, he explained, "It would be fun, of course, except when Crafioni chews me out, which I'd really rather you didn't witness because I have an image to uphold, but— hah! Here's the problem." He tossed the IC into the wastebasket and added its model number to his "Parts Needed" list. Then he looked up, and his dark eyes were solemn. "Do you know why Crafioni is the only one who coaches us?"

"No." He scratched his temple. "I'd never wondered about it. Why?"

"Because it's hard to keep your Talent on a leash when somebody else is using his—very hard. Takes more self control than most Flingers have. Which is why we practice separately."

"Oh." He slumped down and leafed through his Asian History textbook. "Would have been nice, though . . ."

After eight months, Crafioni gave him the green light to teleport himself to Point Two. He stepped onto the platform (it sank beneath his weight like his heart sank into his stomach) and took five deep breaths to relax (that was the theory, but it didn't help. His body was knotted more tightly than kite string caught in a helicopter's rotors). He Flung with his eyes closed because he didn't need to see, he could feel just as well; he opened them sick with disappointment because he'd felt nothing. But when he turned . . . Point Two jounced under his feet, and Crafioni's wave was a blur of white at the far, dim end of the hangar.

Point Three was a hair over two kilometers from One, in a wooden shed alongside a runway. He was nervous about trying to teleport objects to a place he couldn't see, but clenched his teeth and— success! said the monitor. The buildup began again, from one kilo to the full 918. It took four months, this time, before he'd earned Crafioni's permission to Fling himself.

What Crafioni didn't know, of course (although he probably did, having been a cadet himself, once; it was likelier that he knew but wasn't letting on), was that McGill was Flinging himself to all three points every night—and back to his dorm twenty minutes later.

He'd wait till Greystein had started snoring, wait till the hallway was free of purposeful feet, wait till the traffic on the street was a somnolent whisper, and then, slipping on his shoes and throwing a bathrobe over his shoulders, he'd—

PING to Point One, where he'd read the glowing screen, chuckling if he'd landed perfectly, scowling if he'd added altitude in his visualization. Then, after a rest, *PING* to Two, peek through the giant metal doors into the starry (or, more often, cloudy) sky, scan the vicinity to see if the ground crews noticed a bathrobed cadet doing what he oughtn't, then *PING* to Three, where he'd shuffle around to keep warm, it was starting to get cold, and all that was left was the *PING* back to the soft, friendly bed, where he'd kick off his shoes and fall asleep.

Crafioni never mentioned it to McGill, and he never mentioned it to Crafioni, but an impartial, omniscient observer would have been intrigued to note that the dormitory out of which he teleported every night happened—just happened—to be on the same east-west line as Points One, Two, and Three . . .

Kids will be kids, and those who deal with them soon come to expect it.

In 2098, Crafioni started him on his next practice series. Going further afield, now, they left New York behind, Flinging to Pittsburgh, first, working from the cube to the crate, two hours a day, twenty-four Flings a session, odd days teleporting from New York and even days returning from the riverfront warehouse in Pittsburgh. Two weeks was all he needed, for on the fourteenth day Crafioni said, "You might as well Fling yourself back; I think you're capable."

McGill took it as the praise it was intended to be, but he already knew—since he'd continued his nighttime practices—that he was that capable.

After Pittsburgh came Lima, Ohio; a week saw that route learned, and on the last night he and Crafioni ate a restaurant dinner with his parents, who drove down from Cleveland for a private demonstration and celebration. Then Bloomington, Illinois, and Lamoni, Iowa; westward they reached, into Grand Island, Nebraska and Sterling, Colorado. His times were improving: four days to master Salt Lake City; three for Elko, Nevada; and only two to reach Eureka, California without a bump.

The secret he'd learned—the key that made it all possible—was that each destination felt different. It was compounded of many things, and some clung more tenaciously to his conscious memory than did others. New York was oil-spotted cement and echoing hangars; Pittsburgh, the smell of the river; Salt Lake, a pervasive, ubiquitous sense of righteousness; Eureka, the sea and the background thought of earthquakes.

Every place was different. He matured to where he could bend down, sniff*scratch*see a spot, and his memory would fasten onto it, seize it, imprint it on the cells of his brain so they could never forget it, even if he did. (Years later, when he was sick and wounded after a hand-to-hand battle on mountainous ice floes, he awoke, halfway across the galaxy, to the warm, earthy smells of Lamoni, the archetypal farm town.)

"Give you a Christmas present," said Crafioni. "Come on." He took McGill's hand and told him to sit on his Talent. By the time the boy had blinked, they were in Peking's Tien An Men Square. "Memorize it," said the instructor.

McGill sniffed the dusty air, absorbed the noise through the pores of his skin, and studied the smooth flat faces that swirled past. They didn't seem curious about the sudden appearance of two Westerners. Perhaps the square was a common reference point for Flingers; perhaps they were accustomed to foreigners; perhaps they were polite. "Got it," he announced.

"Good." And his fingers were cold on McGill's; darkness cloaked them for no measurable length of time. "Istanbul," he stated, when they appeared on the hillside overlooking the Bosphorus. "A little some different?"

"Much," he nodded. Here lay the sea, and uneven paving stones skewed by clumps of moss, and up ahead a cafe which he knew he'd come back to because it scented the air with coffee so strong that just breathing it woke him up. "I like it."

"Hold on." They emerged into darkness, high, dry, and Moorish. "Madrid."

City lights sprawled beneath them; McGill savored their unwinking brilliance. They stood before a whitewashed wall. He crumbled off a piece for its texture, and let the wind clean its powder from his fingers. He shook his head. "Quite a Christmas present, Mr. Crafioni. Thank you."

"My pleasure. Think you know the spots?"

"Yes, sir."

"Good." He was a silhouette against the stars. "Now take us home."

They materialized at Point One, and McGill again thanked him.

"You're getting good," said Crafioni. "Right after the New Year's, we'll start on north-south travel, and you can bash your brains out on adjusting angular momentum." He laughed, softly. "Hardest thing in the world, getting that damn momentum right. But I don't think you'll have too many problems with it. Good night." And he was gone.

A month later, a bundled-up McGill was at One, groaning as he lifted a fifty-kilo water balloon onto the platform. A van whooshed into the open hangar, and scattered dust as it stopped next to him. A young, flashily dressed woman hopped out. "Are you a Flinger?"

"Well, uh—" He hated to say no to a well-curved blonde, even if his tunic wasn't visible. "—sort of, I'm a cadet."

"Great!" Snatching a briefcase off the van's front seat, she set it on the cement floor and opened it. In seconds, a holographic display scattered the shadows. "Look, can you send me and my box here?"

It was not only a holograph, it was a full-sense: soft chitterings welled out of it, spiced by an alien tang; if he thrust his hand into it, he would make contact with the triangular blue tiles of the floor, or at least would think so. "Where is it?" he asked, instead.

"Malakina," she said. "I've just heard that they're going nuts over Terran pottery there, and I've got 850 kilos of handmade ashtrays and vases and all that, and if you could Fling me there—" She dipped into a pocket and pulled out a very thick roll of $100 bills. "$5000 U.S., and nobody knows about it but you and me."

"Hey, I can't—" he started, but she cut in:

"Please, I've got to get there right away." Her eyes were hazel, flecked with white and green. They were also imploring. "$6000."

"No, it's not the money. I'm a cadet, I don't know the place—"

"That's why I brought the holo; I know you have to sense it—"

"—or its momentum—"

"1645 kph, 13° to the north of ours."

"—but I'm a cadet!"

"So it's a bumpy ride, I don't care."

He threw up his hands. "Lady, come here, look into this TV monitor."

She approached the rack, and stood next to him while he flicked on the monitor. Its screen showed a dock that jutted into foamy waters. "What's that?"

"It's a practice pier in Ensenada, Mexico. There's a 155 kph difference in angular momentum between here and there. That's all. Now, you see that water balloon?" He gestured to the platform, brushing her arm as he motioned. She didn't draw away.

"Yes, I—"

"Now watch." He started to concentrate, then turned back to her. "Not me, not the balloon, the *monitor*."

"Oh." She fixed her eyes on its screen.

He stared—visualized—felt—knew—started to Fling—tried desperately to pull an extra 155 kilometers/hour out of the dump—and finished. With an instant pivot, he glared at the monitor. The balloon was just rolling off the end of the pier; the mechanisms mounted on it relayed to the monitor: "Velocity 52.3 kph."

"Damn!" he hissed.

"I don't...understand," said the woman, who did look puzzled. She was fluffing her blonde hair while he scratched the back of her head.

"What's to understand?" he muttered. "A lousy 155 difference and I can't hack it. And you want me to try an 850, with a change in direction, too. Lady, you know what you'd look like after I'd Flung you out there? You wouldn't look like anything," he groused on, not waiting for her reply, "you'd hit the wall at two, three hundred kph, you and your box, and they'd have to scrape you off, and then paint the wall to cover up what got jammed into the cracks. No. I'm not going to try it, holo or no holo."

She'd gone pale while he spoke, and her voice, when she found it, was shaky. "I...I didn't realize," she said faintly. "I thought...thought all of you were..."

"Good?" he asked bitterly. "Lady, I'm a third-year cadet. I won't even *start* to Fling off-world till next year. And I'll spend all of next year tossing water balloons around the galaxy, eight hours a day, nine days out of ten, and there is still a chance that I won't be good enough. Two out of five cadets have to spend an extra year on Interstellar Flinging because it is so damn hard!" He scowled at the screen, at the green balloon bobbing in the shallows beyond the pier.

"Water balloons?" she asked, as though she hadn't heard a word after that.

"Water balloons." The incomprehension on her fine-boned face frustrated him, yet pleased him, too. Holding special knowledge felt good. "I have to practice with real mass, but the kinetic energies involved are dangerous. When a half-filled balloon hits a wall, though, it spreads out, which dissipates a lot of energy. Then it bursts, and dissipates more. They still knock down a buncha walls—especially if you slip up and add instead of subtract momentum—but they're safer than anything else. Imagine a cube of lead traveling at 500 kph..." He pointed to the holograph. "You might as well pack up, I can't help you."

"Don't be too sure about that," she said thoughtfully. She cocked her head as she studied him, and moistened her lips. "You must know the other Flingers."

"Sure." Something in her expression made him nervous.

"They only work eight hours a day, right?" Still holding the roll of bills, she began to tap it into her open left hand.

"Yeah, that's right."

"Do you know one who'd work a few minutes overtime? At a bit better than time and a half?" She bounced the roll on her palm. "There'd be a commission in it for you, you know."

"Lady—" He sighed and half-sat on a shelf. "There are very strict rules about that kind of thing. The FNC doesn't allow it. I know you figure, 'What's an extra Fling?' but the thing is, it exhausts you. Ninety-six a day is pushing it as it is— there's a theory that if we cut back to eighty, we'd be good for another fifteen, twenty years."

"Well," she said, "if you save sixteen Flings a day, no wonder."

"No, that's not why. I'm not going to do the math for you; you can figure it out for yourself. Trust me, though—no Flinger's going to do extra work, at any price. The only reason they work as hard as they do is because the consortium is still trying to repay the FNC loan."

"Well, this will help, won't it?" she said, gesturing with the bills.

"Lady, you're asking me to do something that's illegal and I won't. I could get into a lot of trouble, and it's just not worth it."

Her smile became sultry; she edged a hip into his side. "Listen, if you'd rather get paid—"

PING

Shaking his head, he stepped out of his room and trotted down the hall to Crafioni's, where he knocked, waited for the "Come in!" and then entered. "Mr. Crafioni," he blurted out, "there's a lady at Point One trying to bribe me and we're supposed to report that stuff and—"

"Whoa!" He held up his large hands. "Give it to me slowly."

McGill did, point by point, even though he was impatient

to have the guards called so they could arrest her before she escaped. Hurriedly, he answered all of Crafioni's searching questions. In the end, the instructor nodded sagely and reached for his telephone.

"Crafioni here," he barked into it. "There's a woman in a van at Point One; arrest her on a charge of attempted bribery. Hurry." Turning back to McGill, he said, "You did the right thing. I'm glad you came to me."

McGill frowned. "You don't seem very glad. Even your voice seems . . . I don't know, disappointed . . . how come?"

Crafioni shrugged. "Well— first, you should have come to me right off, as soon as she made her offer. And second, I am upset. Not with you," he added hastily, "but with people who try to corrupt everything that is good and right and—" Angrily, he punched his right fist into his left palm, then stood, and paced his small room. "Damn!"

"What?" asked McGill.

"Ah—" He waved a deprecating hand. "I'm just in a bad mood. Any time this happens—oh, don't look so startled, all of us are offered bribes once in a while—but it bothers me. It's like . . . it's like a granite cliff, you know? The sea beats against it and it seems to laugh, but little by little it's being washed away . . . God, I hope that doesn't happen to us." He crossed to his window and looked toward the hangar. "The guards are coming out," he said. 'Alone. She must have gotten away."

· Chapter X ·

"I'm certain he does not belong to the Far Being Retzglaran," insisted Hommroummy. He held a Siamese cat in his arms and scratched it behind its right ear. It wouldn't purr, but its toleration of those deft fingers said much about its owner's empathy with felines. Its claws drew blood from lesser persons. "How could he? We've probed him thoroughly."

"Your ignorance shows. What FBR touches once, is always FBR's. Arouses wariness. FBR given to long-range plans against us. You scheme four, five years ahead. It plots four, five generations ahead. Might want Feighan at seventy. Might want Feighan's great-grandchild. Must block."

"How would you prefer I do that?"

The glassed-in gas roiled like an angry Medusa. "Best is to incorporate him. Always most pleasing to turn enemy's tools against it. Next best is to disrupt smooth flow of life. Whirlpool alters character of water downstream. Least satisfying last resort is to kill. Goodbye." The curtain leaped out from the wall and masked the tank.

Nodding, Hommroummy lowered the cat to the floor. Its tail swished; its claws honed themselves on the stone. He smiled absently at it, all the while wondering how best to bring McGill Feighan into The Organization.

A shame the usual enticements wouldn't work—in fact, they'd already failed. Wealth, power, and fame can't be offered to one who knows he'll achieve them soon, on his own, anyway...the boy would have to *need* The Organization. Hommroummy would have to find—or to create—that need. Then it would be done. Done right, the host organism would never know its loss.

· Chapter XI ·

McGill Feighan was sleeping, as only a sixteen-year-old can, when the gunmen kicked in his door. His lanky body reacted on its own, snapping him into a sitting position and throwing open its brown eyes. His mind, though, was fogged, diffused, enmeshed in dreamy lassitude. Even when the lead gunman flicked on the overheads, doused him with cold fluorescence, and snarled, "Gryll sent us," he couldn't accept what he was seeing.

His hand swept tousled black hair out of his eyes; his gaze wandered across the yellow cinderblock wall. His roommate's bed was neat, empty: Greystein had gone to Boston to attend an electronics fair. "Wha?"

The sparsely furnished dorm room stayed mute. The nearest intruder, a moonfaced black with a gold earring, raised his gun and took silent aim.

Events flowed in slow motion, as though his languorous dreams had infected the world. He watched the barrel drift upward, thinking, *A gun? Here? Don't they know this is the Flinger Building? Good scream'd bring Mr. Crafioni, two doors down, doesn't like guns. Catch somebody pointing one at a cadet, specially me his friend, prolly Fling the idiot into the sun.* Painfully, like a woman in labor, he forced an idea out of his sleepy, befuddled brain: *Oh. I coulda done that.* But no longer. The invaders had spaced themselves so widely that he'd have to teleport them one at a time. Even in his daze he knew they wouldn't wait minutes between Flings; they'd shoot him first, as Moonface seemed ready to do, what with his finger starting to tighten on the trigger, there, *funny*, he thought, *how that knuckle grays just a tad and say, why don't I get out of here before I get hurt?*

PING

(Inside one of Greystein's machines, a series of coordinates shifted.)

McGill sat trembling in a darkened, deserted airplane hangar. Its metal walls, contracting in the early June cool of a New York City night, dinged and scratched and scraped, but *sotto voce*, as though not wishing to disturb anyone. When he stood, the platform that marked Point One chilled his bare feet. Out of habit, he checked the monitor: 0.000009 cm. *Very good*, he decided. His thoughts, unready to cope with the fact that he'd just been attacked, refused to leave the mundane. *Geez, specially for middle-of-the-night, no warning, nothing.*

Scared and wondering what to do, he bounced on the balls of his feet. The monitor's numbers flickered. The lead gunman's words—"Gryll sent us"—echoed through him like a shriek in the night. Gryll: a being, a name, a rumor . . . a fish in murky water, Gryll had never been seen, even by those who ran The Organization under his—its?—direction. It made sense, though, that an interstellar crime syndicate would want a teleport. The Organization's smugglers would find one very useful.

The hangar was old; its walls were more like screens. Drafts cut through McGill's thin pajamas and he shivered. He would *not* let The Organization swallow him. All the money in the galaxy couldn't persuade him to work for rapacious, amoral sharks. Uh-uh. And as for force . . . who could restrain a teleport?

Stepping onto the concrete floor—and wincing as he bashed his toes against an aluminum box—he thought, *phone around here somewhere, call Mr. Crafioni, he'll help—*

The beam of a heavy-duty flashlight blinded him. He'd barely gotten his hand in front of his eyes when the anesthetic dart bit into his chest. His square jaw dropped. He tried to Fling himself out. Dizziness felled him.

(The coordinates changed again, repeatedly.)

He awoke on a dry, rough floor, face to a wall hewn out of living rock. For a moment he lay still, while his mind, trapped in the swirls of an anesthetic haze, pirouetted like an ice skater. Everything it perceived was chill, and slick. It couldn't hold reality because reality wore a skin of rime that slipped away from whatever would touch it.

"Unh," he moaned, shifting positions in search of a more comfortable one. His right cheek scraped across the gravelly floor. The unexpected pain brought him to full awareness. He pushed himself to his knees. Surprisingly—because, hungover, he hadn't pushed hard—he rose several centimeters into the air, hovered for a moment, then floated back to a gentle landing.

The Moon, he thought, though for the life of him he couldn't have analyzed that intuitive leap. There were, after all, other places with rock walls and low gravity. *Damn, the Moon! I can't teleport home from here; can't adjust momenti that different . . . hell, don't even know the angular momentum here . . .* fear shook him like a terrier does a a rat.

Behind him stirred a sound, a boot rasping on stone, and he twisted his head around to see it. Half a meter away was a plateglass wall, the green tint of which suggested unbreakability. Beyond that, in the other half of the cave, paced a Throngornian.

It looked like a lemur made mournful by excess height. Easily three meters tall, with long hairy arms that ended in six webbed fingers, it wore scarlet silk pants. Two violet sashes crossed in the middle of its broad chest. Its mahogany eyes were almost as huge as its pink-lined ears; protruding from its back were furled "wings" which, stretched out, would each measure four or five square meters.

For a moment McGill forgot his plight. Facts ingested at school—facts once viewed like sleeping bats, all dull and featureless and far away—came suddenly awake, to launch themselves at him and flurry around his head. The pants were a concession to Terran mores: Throngornians didn't bother with clothes; the "wings" were their winter capes. Furry on both sides, and with a meshwork of capillaries close to the inner surface—two major arteries and a voluntarily controlled second heart supplied them with blood—they were warmer than any wool, cotton, or hide could be. In summer, after the spring shedding, they were air conditioners: spread and poised capillary-side down, they vented the heat generated by the Throngornian's high metabolism.

Oh, he knew a lot about them—even that their planet was one of the few places in the galaxy where humankind could eat native food—the question was, would book-learning help him to enlist the Throngornian on his side?

"Good day to you, sir," he called in the alien's own language, wondering as he did so if his accent were correct. "Do you think you could tell me where, exactly, I am?"

The being fluttered its ears. "I'm a stranger here myself," it replied. "We're on the moon of your world. Beyond that—" Its ears twitched again. "You speak our language well, for an alien."

The proper response to a compliment was to touch the tips of the ears together, and then to spread them as far apart as possible. McGill didn't bother. "I shall tell my teachers of your praise," he said. His eyes were busy, probing the dimness until they found the regular outlines of what, he hoped, was a doorway. "If you'll excuse me—"

PING

But instead of standing before the door, hand reaching for the knob, he was barely past the plate glass, and almost stepping on the eetie's webbed toes. "Terribly sorry," he muttered, making a break for freedom.

A pair of huge hands clamped down on his shoulders from behind; he was lifted off his feet and carried back to the transparent wall. "You forgot to ask why I was here, little Stiff Ears." The Throngornian pressed his face into the glass, saying, "Cast yourself to the other side, now, and be quick about it! Your bones will break before this execrable wall will."

Though dangerous to Fling without the proper rest interval, it was a short hop, and—from the pain in his cheek—a necessary one.

PING

"Much better," said the alien, flaring its pyramidal nose into a cone, which indicated amusement. "Now stay there."

What happened? thought McGill in dismay, while aloud asking, "You alluded to my absent-mindedness, sir, and I am grateful for the reminder. Why are you here with me?" He rested his palms against the glass and stared into the barely readable face.

"I am an Anchor," said the Throngornian proudly. "I—and two of my fellows—are here to guard you."

An Anchor: an antiteleport, a being which nullified a teleport's Talent. Rare on Earth, for some reason, they were so abundant on Throngorn II that its Flinger Building was situated on a rocky, deserted island well removed from centers of population. Even so, distant Anchors often interfered with the Flingers, making teleportation impossible until they'd been found and convinced to stop broadcasting. The only thing that kept T-II from devolving into a complete nightmare was that one invariably teleported directly to the Anchor, who could then be identified.

In any event, it would keep him nicely penned. He couldn't Fling past it. If he teleported in front of it, it would catch him. If—

The door opened. A familiar two meters slipped through the rectangle of light. McGill's eyes widened disbelievingly. "Mr. Crafioni!"

"Yes," answered his instructor, "it's me."

Relief roared through him like a tornado. His knees almost buckled. Of all the saviors he could have asked for, the cool, detached, and superbly competent Crafioni was the one he would have wanted most. "Boy am I glad you're here—" He glanced at the Throngornian; it was ignoring their conversation. "—watch it, though, this guy's an Anchor and it's transmitting; you're not going to be able to get us home if . . . if . . . what's the matter?"

For Crafioni was shaking his perfectly barbered head. "I'm not here to take you home, McGill. I just looked in to see if you were all right."

Before McGill could say anything, a speaker hidden in the shadows of the ceiling crackled, "Salving your conscience, Crafioni?"

The instructor's blue eyes uptilted. "Yes, Mr. Hommroummy," he answered.

"What?" gasped McGill, who was beginning to catch on, but wishing he weren't. He looked up, too, and thought he caught the glint of a camera lens.

"That's right," said Crafioni calmly. "I'm the one who sold you out. How do you think they knew your Fling points? I also hired that woman to bribe you last January."

"Why?" he demanded. "How could you—"

"For the same reason," interrupted his teacher, "that you'll do whatever you're told, once they let you go."

"Leave," said the speakers.

Crafioni obeyed instantly. He didn't even pause in the doorway, just swung the heavy slab of smoothed stone shut.

McGill pressed his forehead against the glass. It was cool, firm, dead. "Why?" he asked softly, not expecting a reply.

He got one anyway. "We are interested in you, boy. You have had contact with a minion of the Far Being Retzglaran—"

"Oh, that was a long time ago," he broke in. Somehow, the voice seemed familiar—but it was buried in the same prehistory as the giant slug that had swallowed him at birth. "I don't know anything about that."

"You might not," conceded the spectral voice, "but the cells of your body certainly remember. Especially if they have been . . . altered, shall we say?"

"You know how many doctors made a career out of studying me?" There was fury in his voice, the burning, untempered rage of an angry youth, but it vanished when he visualized himself: hands on hips, in a Lunar cavern with a bug-eyed monkey, shouting at a shadow-shrouded ceiling. Incongruously, he smiled. "Look, let me leave, will you?"

"Oh, we shall, we shall. In four days. After your fourth injection of Breeze."

No, this is too much. He sagged as though he'd been struck. His palms slithered down the slippery glass until he found himself sitting on the rock floor. Breeze. The most addictive drug a human could consume. Four shots, one every twenty-four hours, would hook you for life. Then, if you didn't get it daily, withdrawal pains set in—and you couldn't wait them out. They got worse. And worse. Rumor had it that sanity lasted about a week. The body survived for two or three more, if the attendants could keep the addict from suicide.

Shivering, he hugged himself. It *was* The Organization that had him. Hommroummy . . . where had he heard that name? But the stuff about Retzglaran had to be a blind. What they really wanted was his Talent. Once addicted, he'd do anything to assure his supply . . . had Crafioni cooperated for the same reason? Who'd set *him* up? How many others were in on it?

"Sir," he called to the Throngornian, "please, allow me to escape. Your employers mean me evil."

The alien levered itself erect and crossed the cavern in two graceful arcs. "Show me your ritual scars," it commanded.

"Scars?" he echoed in bewilderment.

"You're not of my clan?"

"No, sir, I regret—"

"Then why ask my help?" Its ears drooped forward in honest puzzlement. "What are you to me?"

"A fellow being?" he ventured.

It made a rude noise, and tapped the glass with a clawed finger. "If you're not in the clan," it said slowly, "then you're prey. My prey if I want you, anybody else's if I don't. Learn that, and don't waste my time again." Turning, it retreated to the far wall.

While McGill was calculating the odds of besting the guard in a surprise attack—unlikely, given its height and weight advantages—the door opened again. An elderly Terran bearing two jet-syringes entered.

"Good morning," he said. "Roll your sleeve and thrust your arm through the aperture in the wall." When McGill didn't move he said, not unkindly, "Son, if I have to call for someone to get you out of there, I will. Now, the arm?"

He pushed up his pajama sleeve. "Is that—is that Breeze?"

"Yes indeed it is." He waved the syringes. "Would you like euphoric or noneuphoric?"

"I have a choice?" he asked sourly.

"Of course you have a choice. The euphoric will give you eight hours of vivid, but pleasurable, hallucinations. The other will seem to have no effect."

He was about to opt for the hallucinations, but a sudden idea made him ask, "How does that thing work?"

"This?" He held up the syringe questioningly. "Surely you've had your vaccinations—it works the same way. High-pressure air blows the drug right through your skin in, what, a hundredth of a second? No needle marks, no chance of infection—wonderful device. Now, your arm, son. And which will it be?"

He gritted his teeth and stuck his arm out the narrow hole in the wall. "The noneuphoric," he said, and watched the injector approach. His timing would have to be perfect. He'd have to concentrate on the Breeze without taking skin or metal. He'd have to eye the doctor's trigger finger so closely—

PING

The Throngornian didn't seem to notice.

In ninety-six hours, one has a lot of time to think, especially if one's captors fail to provide books, films, holo-vee, or any other form of distraction. McGill sat, and thought, and practiced Throngornian with his guards. Through their conversations, he tried to determine the layout of The Organization's Lunar base. He wondered how many years Crafioni had been their pawn. He told the ceiling speakers, over and over, that he had no knowledge whatsoever of the Far Being Retzglaran.

Each time, the speaker snorted, "We shall see about that later."

He understood the veiled threat: they were going to delay his fifth shot, make him squirm and twist and shriek out all he knew before they'd bring the injector to jet away his misery. Maybe they realized he knew nothing, and just wanted him to suffer so that the next time they had an errand for him, he'd remember the pain, the need, the pleading . . .

The thing was, he wouldn't be pleading. Nor would he be in pain, or even in need. He wouldn't be addicted. Each shot meant for him had wound up under the Throngornian's furry epidermis—on the fifth day, it would be the guard who screamed . . .

He knew that the switch wouldn't help him. The overhead surveillance would pick up the Anchor's plight within seconds after its need for Breeze became evident. A second Throngornian would enter, they'd carry out the first, and McGill would be back at Square One. All he'd gain would be four days.

And then?

Can't make me sit still for the injection, just no way, but I can't get free, either, so it's a stalemate. How long can I hold out? They stop feeding me . . . wait for me to fall asleep . . . he shivered, and hugged himself. He was more scared than ever before . . . *maybe 'cause this is the first time I know what's happening, what's at stake . . .*

Something landed on his head like a raindrop. He reached up to explore, but cautiously: he didn't know what kind of bugs eked out a living in the dry corridors of sub-Luna. His fingers grazed cool metal, coin-sized. He picked it up and brought it down to his eyes. It was a microtransceiver. A thread-thin voice was saying, "McGill—can you hear me?"

Cupping it in his hands, he raised them to his mouth. "Greystein?"

"Yes—where are you?"

"Dunno—a cave—prisoner of The Organization."

"There aren't supposed to be any caves there."

He rolled his eyes upward. "Well, I'm in one. Guarded by three Anchors. And Crafioni's in on it; he's one of them."

A minute passed on silent seconds before Greystein said, "Hang tough. I'll get back to you."

The fifth day arrived first.

Sure enough, the doctor was late. Very late. The guard began to look nervous. Then worried. Then definitely upset. But it couldn't leave the cavern to search out the doctor because then the spasming Terran might be able to shrug off his ordeal long enough to Fling himself into the corridor, or farther.

The Anchor trembled; McGill whimpered. He was certain that his act would be exposed at any moment, that Crafioni or the doctor or somebody would storm into the room and order him to stop faking it. But until that happened, he'd continue his fraud. Maybe whoever manned the overhead camera would focus his attention on him, instead of the Anchor, and if no one noticed the Throngornian's illness before it passed out . . . he doubled himself over and made horrid, retching sounds. For once his fear was useful: it kept him pale, and provided all the sweat he'd ever need.

When Crafioni entered, he shook his head with real sorrow. Not looking at the guard, he started talking before the door had closed. "They've got you, McGill, they've got you cold. Cooperate with them. They'll—"

The room exploded.

Sound and light burst together, sound like a bomb, light like a nova. Crafioni's scream was lost in the clamor; he fell to his knees with his hands over his eyes. The Throngornian crumpled like an airless balloon. McGill curled into a ball and prayed the pain would pass so he could take advantage of the chaos.

But two dozen booted feet hit the floor around Crafioni. Shouted commands echoed off the bare walls: "A Squad, secure this room. B Squad, the corridor, move it, move it!" The Mooncops had arrived in force.

McGill's vision was clouded; after-images of the stun bomb danced ghostlike on his retinas. Sitting up, he rubbed his eyes. Two huge, hazy figures were cuffing the Anchor; another two were hauling Crafioni to his feet. The far door had been opened and machine-gun-toting blurs twisted around its frame with their weapons ready. The Commander came over to McGill, features resolving into those of a bent-nosed woman in her mid-forties. She squatted before the aperture and balanced her rifle on her knees. "You all right?"

"Can't see, but otherwise . . . yeah. Timed it pretty close, didn't you? Where's Greystein?"

"At HQ, getting ready to— ah."

Another twelve officers materialized into the middle of the room. She directed them to their positions. "Cuff *everybody*," she repeated, "and don't let any of them get away." They sprinted out. Through the door rattled the distant sound of automatic weapons fire. The Commander said, "Damn!"

A thought struck McGill with the force of a falling boulder. "Hey! That guy—" He pointed directly at Crafioni. "—he's a Flinger, he can—"

Blackness washed over him like a breaking wave, and tried to suck him into the sea. Crafioni was fleeing, and taking McGill with him! For a millisecond terror paralyzed him. He was halfway to wherever, and angular momentum was bleeding away from him. *No!* he thought, *no!*

His Talent awoke; it slashed like a sword. Crafioni bellowed in anguish. The Talent restored the lost momentum and hurled McGill back to the cavern. He could feel the other dwindle into the darkness.

And then he was behind the plateglass wall, staring into the Commander's blink. "Am I, uh, having problems?" she asked. "Or did you—"

"Not me," he said, "him. I mean—" Because, of course, his former instructor was gone, utterly. "—the guy who was over there. Mr. Crafioni. He tried to . . ." Shaking his head, he trailed off.

A burly cop with a bloody bandage around his left arm came in. "We've found the exit, Commander. Leads to the surface. To a pad. A ship just took off."

"Notify—"

"We have, but they're gone."

"What do you mean, 'gone?' They—"

"Control says they're off the screens. They don't know why."

"Damn 'em for being so rich!" She slapped her knee and stood. "Any idea who was aboard?"

"No, but we caught some of their people, and they oughta talk."

"Right. You know what to do."

At about this time, McGill remembered the transceiver, and spoke into it. "Greystein?"

"Yeah, you okay?"

"Uh-huh." He looked around. "Guess I'll be getting out of here soon, but ah, I wanted to say . . . thanks, you know?"

"Hey," crackled the tiny speaker, "my pleasure."

And that's the problem, thought McGill. *Somebody else had to save my ass one more time . . . damn. Why can't I ever do it myself?*

▪ Chapter XII ▪

Milford Hommroummy was so certain that Gryll would have him eliminated that he lost his aplomb when the alien said, "Not your fault."

He stumbled across the cushiony rug of the passenger lounge, drawing an irritated scowl from the steward he'd bumped into. "That's— that's very kind of you, sir." He sank into an armchair and, through the disp-screen, watched the Moon shrink to a pebble. It had been too near a thing. And he still didn't know where Crafioni was, though he hoped the other would meet them at their backup base in the asteroid belt. They needed a good teleport. "How would you like us to pursue the Feighan matter?"

"Not to pursue; not yet. Let aftershocks dampen out. Loose ends could unravel us; trim off. Re-establish Lunar base. Restore profits. Then discuss."

"Yes, sir." Already he had plans for healing his branch of The Organization; it wouldn't be difficult, not at all. The anticulture hadn't lost more than a patch of skin—and probably little in the way of interface flesh. In a year or two, it would match and surpass its father...emboldened by his superior's forgiveness, he asked, "Why was it not my fault, sir?"

"In competition with Far Being Retzglaran. FBR noted for statistically improbable good fortune. Suspect FBR manufactures own luck centuries ahead of time. Unsurprised that short-lived creature unhorsed in joust. Major question is why our luck is not worse. Suspect Feighan on far periphery of FBR's blueprint for future. Wait for orders to resume operations on him."

"Yes, sir," he said, wondering where he himself fit onto Gryll's own blueprint, "yes, sir."

▪ Chapter XIII ▪

When he met Greystein in their room, the first thing McGill asked was, "How the hell did you know where to find me?"

"Your homing beacon," said his roommate in surprise. He gestured to the tangle of circuitry under his bed. "I'd modified a receiver two years ago, and wired it into the com—"

"*What* homing beacon?" His hands curled into fists, relaxed, and clenched again.

"The one in your— you didn't know about it?"

"No."

"I thought you, or your parents, or— how the devil did it get missed at your physical?"

They shared a look, then, nodding simultaneously, headed for the door. If one Flinger could be corrupt . . .

"This is truly going to shake things up," sighed Greystein, as they waited in the luxurious anteroom of the Director, North American Consortium, FNC.

And he was right.

In the ensuing tumult (kept entirely within FNC walls, due to the FNC's influence, which arose from its control of interstellar transportation, which allowed it to bludgeon reporters), one paramedic and one other Flinger, both at the New York Building, confessed to being Breeze addicts and Organization recruits. The Flinger had ensnared Crafioni—they'd been lovers, once, and she'd injected him while he slept. Serious consideration was given to having her discharged, or exiled, or worse, but the North American Consortium argued that it had already lost the revenue from one full-time Flinger, and couldn't afford a second such loss. The FNC agreed to provide her with noneuphoric Breeze, conditional upon her naming everyone whom she even suspected to be connected with The Organization.

Two days later, a sniper dropped her with a single shot, so the NAC lost its revenue anyway.

Upper echelons then decided that McGill should be quietly removed from Earth. His presence, it was reasoned, would only invite another attack. So, although it was early for him to be experimenting with interplanetary Flinging, they dispatched him to the Hirsnami, a solar system of eighty-two worlds. Some of their angular momenti matched not only Earth's, but those of its linkages as well.

Living and working under an assumed name, he spent half a year there, and mastered the art. "It's not quite the same," they warned him at the very beginning, "because when you do it for real, the distances are greater. Though that doesn't mean it's harder to teleport across them, it does mean that they'll take more out of you. Fling something to the Hub, and you'll feel like you ate a sleeping pill."

But he learned, he adjusted. And the first thing he learned was that while teleporting twenty-four times a day was no harder than, say, cramming for a final exam, doing it ninety-six times in eight hours was slow torture. He was in his space suit—Terra Base, a bleak and lifeless rock, had never developed an atmosphere—and after three hours he thought the smell alone would kill him. "Do you ever get used to it?" he asked his new instructor, Walking Mule.

"Yup. When your nose finally overloads. Even then, you shouldn't eat beans." Through the bubble helmet, the Indian's wink was almost invisible. "Getting tired?" He pronounced it "tarred."

McGill snorted. "It's all in my head, isn't it?" But he sat in the proffered chair and Flung from there. Halfway through the next set of twelve, he asked, "Could we knock off for an hour? Take a siesta?"

"Stand up."

He had to push himself to his feet, and that embarrassed him. He felt like a feeble old man. Long-distance teleportation drained more strength than donating blood. "Yeah?"

Walking Mule's tone was sympathetic but firm: "If you can

still stand, you can still Fling. Let's do it again."

At the end of six hours, his muscles were quivering. A hollow pain pulsed in the pit of his stomach, like nausea or cramps. He could barely grunt, "C'n we rest?"

Walking Mule shoved him, as if to knock him off the chair, but he wouldn't fall. "No," said the instructor. "Not yet. Listen. I know you're beat. But it'll never be this bad again. Almost, maybe—but never this bad. Keep on trying."

His vision started to blur somewhere around the eighty-fifth Fling. The suit had been drying his sweat, though it couldn't deodorize it completely, and his skin wore a crust of salt. He couldn't hold his head up. It kept falling to one side. "Please," he croaked, "stop?"

"Come on, McGill. Try. Harder. Do it."

And after ninety-six he asked, "'zat all?"

"Yup. Congratulations." Walking Mule thrust out his gloved hand.

McGill's helmet bounced off it as he passed out.

Walking Mule had to carry him to his room.

As promised, though, the first day was the worst, and soon he was teleporting both objects and himself to the ten Hirsnami planets that corresponded to Earth's link-planets. Within six months he did it so well that his superiors judged he was wasting his time; it was a propitious moment for him to move on.

Afterward, he never reminisced about those six months. Not that he avoided remembering them; just that there was little worth recalling. Most of the worlds had been as lifeless as Terra Base (he wasn't sure about the gas giants. He'd done no work with them because he'd never Fling to one; their gravity was too great for humanoid life). The food was awful. Had it not been for the long hours spent talking with Walking Mule, hours in which they rambled on about anything of any interest whatsoever, he never would have made it.

One worthwhile datum he learned from his teacher was that Earth's link-planets had been selected as such not because of propinquity to Terra, or even because of similar angular momenti (Throngörn II, for example, had almost the same momentum—but in precisely the opposite direction), but because the Hirsnami system contained their analogues. It was easier, and safer, to train cadets in a single uninhabited system than it was to let them attempt interstellar teleportation immediately after their third year at the Academy.

"You're some kinda powerful," remarked Walking Mule, as the monitor reported, seven minutes after the fact, that McGill had just landed the 918 with a separation of .00000001 cm. It was his forty-third consecutive success, and the instructor was impressed. "Damn if I can teach you a thing you can't do on your own. Hope I get to ring the changes on somebody just like you."

Through his fatigue he beamed. "Thanks. But how good am I *really?*"

The Indian frowned. "Put it to you this way: I'll let you take me home."

His eyebrows rose. "You trust me to Fling you between stars?"

"Yup." His nod was solemn. "Long as I don't have to smell you."

So after six months, they brought him home—or at least to New York City. FNC told no one he had returned except his parents. They were notified of his arrival by an inelegant artifice: without warning, Walking Mule Flung them to New York, where a brief, emotional reunion elated them all.

After swapping stories in McGill's Spartan dorm room for upwards of three hours, Patrick Sean Feighan hoisted his burliness off the edge of his son's bed and thumped him approvingly on the shoulder. "Let's go out on the town," he boomed. "Got things to celebrate!"

McGill spread his hands helplessly. "Geez, I'm sorry, Dad, but I can't—I have to stay in."

"Is it checking your bed they'll be?"

"No, no, nothing like that . . ." He stared at his knees. "See, The Organization tried to kidnap me before I went to the Hirsnami—"

"Again?" interjected Nicole, sloshing her iced tea onto her lap.

McGill was confused. "What do you mean, again?"

"Well, they did it when you were still in diapers. How old was he, Pat? Six months?" She dabbed at her blue slacks with a tissue.

"No, younger than that, he was. Two? Three?"

"Maybe." She frowned, berating herself for forgetting such a meaningful date. Then she chuckled and turned to her husband. "Remember the mess you made of my kitchen? Sugar

and flour all over the floor, and broken chairs, and that screen
door!" She shook her head. "Your father had to fight a real
Amazon—one of The Organization's best—we found out later
she had a black belt in everything you could think of. The
things she called him!"

"Don't forget the other time," said Feighan. "With Jose,
at the zoo?"

"I remember that," said McGill. "The thing that's driving
me nuts, though, is why? I figure it's because I'm a Flinger,
but—"

"You weren't when that woman came," put in his mother.
Her plump, smile-lined face tightened into pensiveness. "She
didn't know; she just followed her orders. But it must have
been that eetie. I can't see any other reason. Can you, Pat?"

"No." He studied the bare floor for twenty seconds. "So
they're still after you, are they? Is there anything you can do
about it, I wonder?"

"Been wondering the same thing myself," he answered. He
stuck out his long legs and crossed them at the ankles. "FNC
says I should just keep low, and stay alert. So—" He shrugged.
"—I am."

His father nodded. "I understand. Would you mind, then,
if your mother and I went out for dinner by ourselves? It's
been years since we were last in this glorious asylum of a city,
and I've a mind to re-see the sights."

"Oh, no, go ahead." He bounced to his feet. "I'll walk you
down."

Forty-five minutes later, Walking Mule peered around the
edge of the door. "Good, you're here." Abruptly, he *PING*
Flung them both to Throngorn II.

It was local autumn, and a bitter wind whipped off the gray
sea. The pinhead sun ambled towards the eastern horizon. As
the two sprinted for the protection of a low stone building,
McGill shouted, "Dammit, why'd you do that? My parents are
in town to see me—goddammit, you brought them *yourself*—
they'll be back from dinner in an hour or so and—"

Sorrow washed over Walking Mule's dark features. Puffing
and panting, he pointed to the lee of the building, as though
promising to explain all when they reached it. And once they
had, gravel crunching under their feet, he began, "McGill, I
don't know how to say this—"

He froze. Back against the coarse wall, hands grating up

and down its rough surface, he said, "My parents—"

"The Organization seized them five minutes after they left the Building. Then they—the kidnappers—telephoned for you. We routed the call through the computer; it provided a fascimile of your face and voice. The kidnappers said they'd trade your parents for you. 'You' said no deal. So they..." Turning, he inhaled deeply, as though gathering his strength. A scaled sea bird dipped out of the storm to investigate them, swooped by, and screeched its disappointment.

"Are they dead?" McGill heard himself ask.

Walking Mule nodded, and bowed his head. Silence hung between them like bad blood. When he raised his deep brown eyes, real pain marred them. "It was the computer's decision," he began, "but it was a good one. It hurts like hell when pragmatism collides with emotion. You have to understand. You're seventeen—they were in their forties. You have a Talent—they didn't. You also have a mystery about you—and they were transparent as glass. Put bluntly, you're worth more. I know that sounds cruel, but it's true. Look—" He reached for McGill's shoulder; he winced when it was jerked from his grasp. "I'm sorry. I extend condolences from myself and from all the other Flingers as well. Your parents will be avenged, we promise you that."

"And me?" snapped McGill. He could feel the anger in his voice and his pose, but he didn't try to dampen it. It masked too well his fear. And his grief. "What do I do? Warn everybody I know not to get close because they might wind up dead?"

"That's a distinct possibility," said Walking Mule, "but for the moment, we have other plans for you."

"Such as?" he bit off. He was cold, and with more than a physical chill. The Organization was too big, too avid. He was one person—one target. How could he— "What do I do, dig a hole and bury myself?"

"In essence," said Walking Mule. His gravity lightened at the surprise in McGill's face. "It seems obvious that they're after you because of your association with the Far Being Retzglaran—"

"Goddammit!" he shrieked. Bending over, he snatched up a fist-sized blue stone, and hurled it at the foaming breakers a hundred meters away. It would have fallen short, if a sea lizard hadn't picked it out of the air. "I don't remember a damn thing about that! It happened—it was all *over*—before I was four days old. Why is it haunting me like this?"

"McGill—" Again his tentative hand reached out; this time, contact was permitted. "—the gastropod came to Earth from Throngorn II. Our records show this. That's why I brought you here. We want you to backtrack it."

"What?" He couldn't believe what he was hearing. "Backtrack it? It left here seventeen *years* ago; how the hell—"

"You speak Throngornian," countered Walking Mule, ticking the points off on his short fingers, "you can't stay in any Flinger Buildings, you can't be seen in any of the galaxy's major cities, we can't investigate this without tipping them off—" He halted at the determination that outthrust Feighan's jaw. "McGill, somebody has to find out why the Far Being Retzglaran had that done to you—and The Organization is trying very hard. You're the only person we can spare. You have the best motivation. Will you do it?"

He looked out to sea for a very long time. Its crashing waves and swirling spume mirrored his feelings. He also was torn, and tossed by forces he couldn't resist.

My parents are dead. The words beat at him relentlessly, but shock muffled their impact. It was like they were written on a scrap of paper that a gale kept hurling at a window out of which he stared. He saw them—he understood them—but they did not hurt as much as he'd expected, as much as he wanted. He felt like a traitor.

I'm not, I'm a good son! He'd prove it—he'd tear out his hair, rend his clothes, wail louder than the storm . . . but he knew how futile and hypocritical that would be.

How could he honor them? How could he mark their loss? Only, he realized slowly, by fulfilling them. He was their son, their genetic grasp at immortality. They survived in the cells of his body, and in the span of his mind. He had his father's height and his mother's laugh; Feighan's fortitude and Buongiorno's hair. Only if he lived—and lived to his limits—could he guarantee that their years had not been in vain.

And he could not continue without shaking free of The Organization, without solving the mystery of the slug. He was two-thirds an orphan, now, and criminals hunted him because of that third parent. He had to know why.

"Yes," he said at last, "yes, I will."

Walking Mule's arm slid around his shoulder and hugged

him. It was a warm, solid arm, the kind that reassures by its very touch. "Before we go in," he said, "let's get our stories straight. First, your name—" Taking McGill's chin, he turned the boy's head to one side, then the other. "—well, you don't look very Indian, but you're dark enough. They're eeties anyway. How about Sun Spearer?"

Stiffening like a dentist's victim, he parried, "How about McGill Feighan?"

"It's too dangerous; The Organization—"

"It's my *name*, my parents, they—" He bit his lip and glanced away. It was a silly point to argue over, he knew. Indeed, one part of him wanted to accept the new name, and a new face, and a new past; it wanted to burrow into protective falsehood and stay hidden forever. But another part, less fearful and more angry, insisted on flaunting the name Feighan, on waving it like bait so his parents' killers would come for him, and in the coming, expose themselves. *Strange*, he thought. *Half my life I've been afraid, and I kept telling myself, when I grew up I wouldn't be scared any more, so now I'm grown up—most of the way, at least—and I find it's smart to be afraid*..."Sun Spearer'll be fine."

Walking Mule exhaled his relief. "The reason you're here: you're on vacation—from the Academy; we don't need to keep your Talent secret—but you're using your free time to track the giant gastropod."

McGill was cold, tired, and still dazed. Too much was happening. "Why?"

"Why do you need a cover story? Because—"

"No, no." He waved a hand. "Why am I tracking the slug? Why does Sun Spearer care about it?"

"It's a research project," sketched Walking Mule, "funded by the NAC, for the purpose of determining the gastropod's home planet. There's a couple hundred Terran scientists here, anthropologists and the like, so the Throngornians are used to the idea. Sound okay?"

He shrugged, and jammed his hands into his pockets. The wind blew his hair into his face, as it was doing to the strands that had escaped from Walking Mule's shiny braids. "Anything else I need to know?"

"No." He stamped his feet. "Let's get inside. I think the back door is around to the right."

They half-circled the building hunting for it, stumbling over rocks and fighting eighty-knot gusts. It wasn't until the heavy door sealed behind them that they realized just how cold and noisy it had been outside. Walking Mule shook himself; McGill let the dry heat seep into his bones. Then, since the ticket booth was unoccupied, they looked around.

A one-story building throughout, its ceilings were a good four meters from the stone floors. The bare walls were constructed of granitelike rock, cut into cubic meter blocks and laid without mortar. Studying where two of them came together, McGill could hardly see the line. "Got good bricklayers around here," he commented idly.

"Yup. It's a local art form, at least among the mammals, the Timili. In the lower right-hand corner—yup, over there, by the window—you'll find a plaque. You do read Throngornian?"

"I get by." He strolled to the window, which looked to be about five cm. thick. The wavy glass was starred, and cracked by wind-thrown rocks. He squatted. "It says, '1/82—Thamala.' What's that mean?"

"It means that there are eighty-two walls in this structure, and that is the best of them all. Thamala is the name of the being who erected it. A female, from all the 'a' sounds. Males have 'o.'"

"They do that for the best wall in every building?"

"They do that for *every* wall, in every building. Like I say, it's a local art form." He crossed the entrance hall and pushed open a wooden door laden with intricate bas-relief. It let into a long, wide corridor; from the far end pulsed light, and noise. "Come on, I'll bet they're back there."

"Sure. How do they judge the walls?" He ran his finger along a carved figure, trying to decide if it represented an animal or a vegetable.

"Smoothness, proportion, thickness, strength . . ." His boot heels thwacked on the corridor's stone. "One last thing: don't offend anybody. They're very touchy, both kinds."

McGill remembered, then, that Throngorn II had two intelligent races—one mammalian, one reptilian. The planet had such an eccentric orbit that summer was too hot for the former, and winter too cold for the latter, the Rhanghan. The Timili lived inland, among the rocky hills. The Rhanghan dwelt by the water. Though there was, apparently, considerable contact between the two, each had developed its own society and culture. "I'll be careful," he said. "I'm just glad I can pronounce their trade language... how many regional dialects do they have?"

"About ten thousand." At the end of the corridor, he checked that their tunics were visible, held his arms away from his body so that anyone could see he held no weapon, and very slowly stepped into the next room.

Half a dozen Throngornian Flingers lounged around two widely separated tables. Four were mammals, of the kind McGill had met sub-Luna. The other two, though, belonged to the race he'd seen only in pictures—so he gaped.

They were a mottled green, darker here, lighter there; the only other color sparkled from their tunics. Three of their 4.5 meters crouched horizontally, from the tips of their barbed tails to just forward of their front legs. Then their bodies curved upward, through a chitinous stomach plate, past a powerful, scaley torso, to the flat slab of bone that crowned their heads. Hundreds of teeth lurked in their long, triangular snouts. Nictitating membranes slid back and forth across their green eyes. Their thick arms terminated in six fingers. Stiff, knife-blade fins marched down their backbones, from their shoulders to their swishing tails. An automatic pistol belt girdled each's stomach plate. Each held a feathered spear in its left hand. Their eyes, cold and uncaring, swept across the two visitors.

"Greetings, all," said Walking Mule.

One of the Timili levered itself upright. "Greetings, Guildsbrother. You honor this ramshackle hut with your presence. How may we serve?"

Walking Mule relaxed, and let his arms drop to his sides. "This great mansion honors us by offering us its hospitality. I am the Flinger Walking Mule. This is the Cadet Flinger Sun Spearer, whose curiosity about the diverse peoples of the universe has brought us to your doorstep."

"I am Nojono, Director of this pitiable excuse for a Flinger Building. Come, sit. Dinner is being prepared." He made a sign and his companions hauled up two extra chairs.

"The young one sits with us, Nojono," commanded one of the saurians. Its voice was deep and gravelly; its tongue flickered in the air whenever it parted its jaws. "Send it over."

"They're mammals, Sahaang," bit off Nojono. His neck fur fluffed and bristled.

"My objections are not to *alien* mammals," she hissed. "Give it a chair."

McGill took the indicated chair and carried it over. It was heavy, and his muscles strained. The Rhanghan, he saw as he set it down, were lying on their underbellies, their stubby legs splayed. "I am honored, sir." In truth, he was so terrified that he could barely get the words out.

The magenta tongue probed the air around his face. "'Sir' is one of *their* words." Her tail pointed to the mammals' table. "Besides, I am female. Call me Sahaang, and nothing more."

"Yes, Sahaang." Bowing, he dropped into the chair, and immediately discovered it had been carved for a posterior not shaped like his. He wondered how Walking Mule disguised his discomfort.

"Are you a mature specimen?" asked Sahaang.

"An adult?" He blinked with surprise. "No,s— Sahaang. I'm about—" Hastily, he tried to figure in local years, which were roughly 225 Earth days long. "—a year and a half shy of legal maturity."

"Is that your progenitor?"

"No, my instructor. My father is—" Grief broke free, then, like a genie out of its bottle. Hot and demanding, it wouldn't wait for privacy. His eyes filled; his voice broke. Clenching his teeth, he tried to control himself.

The tongue snapped out and sampled the air. "I sense upheaval," she grated. "How did my question cause it?"

Walking Mule turned to answer, "His parents— died, recently. It was quite unexpected, and I believe he feels their loss keenly."

"You mammals," snorted Sahaang. "Emotion over dead parents. A waste."

"What would you know about love, cold blood?" jeered Nojono. "Parents are important to us; we care about them. When they pass over we mourn them, because the threads of our lives have been cut. You lizards—" he flattened his ears in the gesture of disgust.—"you don't care. You don't record their name feats, you don't distribute their possessions, you don't even lash their bodies to treetops like children should."

"Of course not," answered Sahaang. "How then could we eat them?"

And her tongue darted through the air as she stared at McGill.

· Chapter XIV ·

The curtains' rustle startled Hommroummy out of his brown study. He spun, and gaped at the gas-filled tank that the opening draperies had exposed. "Gryll!" he exclaimed. "I had no idea—"

"Information gap deliberate," it interrupted. "Worry not; not inspecting."

Hommroummy wanted to dry the sweat off his forehead, but that could be too revealing a gesture. One never knew what aliens would notice, and correctly interpret. So he contented himself with breathing deeply, and with ordering his stomach to untighten. "What can we do for you, sir?"

"McGill Feighan on Throngorn II."

"I'll attend to it at once, sir. What—"

"No. Handle Terran affairs, on Terra. Will direct matter personally."

"Oh." Again relief washed over him; again he refrained from displaying it. He was confused, though: if his superior were going to take care of it itself... "May I ask, sir, why you have told me of this?"

"Will need teleport. Am requisitioning Crafioni. Bad manners to weaken underling's staff without notification. Consider self notified."

"Yes, sir," he said, but the fabric of the closing curtains kept his words from their target. He exhaled, and bent over to scratch a drowsy Angora cat. Strange being, Gryll. Yet if it chose to take charge of the Feighan thing, Milford Hommroummy would not argue. He'd already suffered too much from it, and, frankly, did not want to go another round with the Far Being Retzglaran.

Let the cosmic gamesmen fight it out between themselves, he thought. Then he and the other lesser beings could pick up the pieces...

▪ Chapter XV ▪

At Walking Mule's request, Nojono and Sahaang arranged a briefing for McGill the next dawn—which, as it turned out, broke some twenty hours after sunset. By Earth chronology, a day on Throngorn II lasted 39 hours, 12 minutes, and 18 seconds. McGill guessed it would take getting used to. The two Terrans had awakened almost six hours before sunrise, and he calculated that he'd be ready for bed somewhere around Throngornian lunchtime.

The Fling Booths were empty because it was a slow season for commerce. As the Timili were just taking in their harvest, and the Rhanghan were preparing their dens for winter, neither race was shipping off-world. Thus all eighteen native Flingers could assemble in the communal dining hall, where Walking Mule had earlier set up a projection screen. Gray light softened the western windows, and the smell of breakfast drifted from the kitchen.

Nojono introduced them to the Timili, who, as if fearful of contagion, had clustered on the eastern side of the room. Sahaang did the same for her spear-carrying fellows. The names bubbled by like so many nonsense syllables, and McGill silently berated himself for not catching them. He hoped a smile would serve instead.

Just when Nojono was about to call the meeting to order, the Building's telepath strode in, a folded sheet of paper in her hand. Gold highlighted her gray fur, and her huge dark eyes swung from side to side until they fell on McGill. She edged through the crowd and handed him the note, leaving immediately after he had taken it.

Though written in cursive Throngornian, it was legible— and he began to shake as soon as he'd puzzled his way through its first half.

"Sun Spearer," it read,

"We are aware that your true name is McGill Feighan; we are aware of your purpose in visiting this world. You will not succeed without our help, which we hope to proffer in the near future.

Until then, I remain, sincerely,

Gryll"

Without a word—he was afraid that opening his mouth would free the terror that would coerce him into making a fool of himself—he passed the message to Walking Mule, who unfolded it, scanned it, and sat up very straight. Then he took his own pen and scrawled on the paper before returning it. His addition read:

"We can't talk about this in front of the others; using an alias is a breach of hospitality. Trust no one. Follow my lead."

Crumpling it into a wad which he thrust deep into his pocket, McGill nodded at his instructor. And swallowed hard.

"Ladies, gentlemen, and things," began Nojono, with a hostile glance at Sahaang and her associates, "Guildsnephew Sun Spearer is hunting the past of a being which crossed our portals some twenty-seven years ago. The alien is described as large, ochre, and malleable of form." He flashed a photograph on the four-meter-square screen. "Does anyone recall it?"

A slump-shouldered mammal in the front row stood wearily to speak. Its fur—pale, thin, and brittle—showed its advanced age. Obese and rheumy-eyed, it husked, "It was I who cast it, full twenty-seven years ago. I recall nothing more. Should the records of that time have survived down to the present, I will be able to state its destination."

"We know its destination, Venerable Sir," said Walking

Mule. "You cast it to Earth, Sol III. The Cadet's question concerns its origins and its prior travels—would you have such information in your records?"

It shook its head from side to side; its jowls sagged and flapped. "But Customs might," it added.

"I know," said a dun-colored Timili at the back. "It spent many days in the rugged hills of Kuturu, where my clan winters. I was a child then, which is perhaps why it seems less large on the wall than in my memory, but I remember well the sucking sounds it made while eating. It stayed eighteen days on a slope near our encampment, and caused us no ill. Neither did it cause us good. We spoke not to it; it spoke not to us. After eighteen days it left, gouging a deep trail in the drifted snow. That is all."

Even though he'd had little faith that his search might be successful, McGill was disappointed. He leaned over to mutter to Walking Mule, "I guess Throngorn's out; we'll have to find the planet it was on before this."

Sahaang's dry voice pre-empted the instructor's response. "Tell us, young warmblood, to whom you were referring when you said, 'We spoke not to it.' Did you refer to your entire clan?"

"Oh, no," said the female. Her ears fluttered in confusion. "We children spoke not to it, that is what I meant."

"Then," rasped the Rhanghan, "did any other member of your clan speak to it?"

"Why, yes—the Thread Splicer spent long hours conversing with it every day."

"What's a Thread Splicer?" whispered McGill.

"A medicine man—a shaman—that sort of thing."

Relentless, Sahaang continued, "Is this Thread Splicer of yours still alive?"

"Of course he still lives!" she replied. "He splices *truly*."

Amusement rippled through the crowded room, amusement signaled among the Timili by flared noses and among the Rhanghan by gently shaken spears. McGill surmised that T-II had seen some monumental quackery in its day.

When the laughter died down, Walking Mule asked, "Would it be possible for Sun Spearer to be told where in the hills of Kuturu your clan winters?"

"Of course," she said. "I myself will show him, on the map in the library. It is a good one, better than any I have ever seen. The FNC made a present of it to us when the first ship arrived."

"Would it also be possible," he went on, "for Sun Spearer to visit your winter camp?"

"Of course," she answered again. "Winter camp is very dull, and a visit from a stiff— excuse me, a Terran, would enliven it. My people would welcome him greatly."

"It looks like you're set," said Walking Mule behind his hand. More loudly, he asked, "How far are the hills of Kuturu?"

"In Terran measurement," she said, perhaps to show off, perhaps to spread balms on feelings wounded by her outslipped ethnic slur, "they are some three hundred kilometers."

"And how does one journey to them?"

"One walks."

Walks? thought McGill. *Three hundred klicks I have to walk?* For a moment he almost requested that she Fling him there—the territory was, after all, familiar to her—but then he realized that if she had been willing to do so, she would have made the offer herself. He tapped his instructor on the arm and asked, softly, "Is it taboo to teleport there?"

Walking Mule nodded. "Yup. In this culture, if you can't walk to winter camp, you don't belong there. The sick and the old . . ." He shrugged helplessly. "They're left behind."

"Isn't that a little—" He waggled his spread-fingered hand from side to side. "—ah, barbarous?"

"In the first place," said Walking Mule, "this is a low-tech world. Remember that. In the second place, ethnocentrism'll get you in trouble. *Real* trouble. Watch it; you can't afford it."

"Yes, sir." The meeting had ended, so he stood along with the rest. While the crowd broke into idle chatter, the Timili female made her way through it. Before she reached him, Walking Mule took his arm.

"Listen, McGill, I have to go back to New York—from here on in, you're on your own. If things get very dangerous, Fling yourself all the way home—but I wouldn't recommend it. I'm sure there are still informers."

"What about The Organization?" It was a straw that he clutched at, and he knew it, but the imminence of friendlessness on an alien world was like an invitation to walk unguided through a minefield. He'd rather avoid it, if he could. "What will I do?"

"Once you get out there—" He waved toward the coast. "—it's all wilderness. They'll never track you. Good luck." And he was gone.

Two hours later, McGill was on his way.

He looked from reality to its cartographic representation with growing disbelief. The Timili female, Bapasa by name, had photocopied the segment of the FNC map corresponding to the route through the hills of Kuturu. "This is the highway," she'd said, drawing a thick yellow line along it, "but it lasts only until the real hills raise their heads, a hundred kilometers inland. Then—" She'd been embarrassed for her world; as a Flinger, she had traveled to Earth and other high-tech planets, and had seen how underdeveloped T-II was. "—then, I must apologize, but it deteriorates. No Terran has ever gone there; your fellow scientists are in the other direction. The way might be difficult to follow. Just remember that large—" She'd tapped her head to show how big. "—round, white stones are laid in its middle every, um, forty-three meters."

Again he examined reality. The "highway" was a boulder-dotted goat track. The hill that wasn't "real" uplifted at a good 30° incline, and towered at least four hundred meters above him. The "highway" snaked up its front through two dozen switchbacks. And this was the easy part of his journey?

He shifted his knapsack so the straps would cut less deeply into his sore shoulders. Inside, winter clothing and a ten-day supply of food ("You'll find water everywhere," Bapasa had said) hung sullen and heavy. Despite the wind and the chill, he was sweating heavily. And his feet hurt.

Screw it, he thought, digging in his pocket for the binoculars Walking Mule had loaned him. *Fling right up top, save myself some pain*. He adjusted the focus on the field glasses and picked out a flat area. Yellowed, listless grass covered it. *Hope there're no rocks—*

PING

"You were told to walk, young warmblood," hissed a familiar voice.

"Sahaang!" he blurted in total surprise. He spun around to find her lying beyond a knoll, basking in the autumn sun. "I—I am pleased to encounter you again."

Her teeth were very white; she seemed to grin. "And discomfited to have your illicit behavior witnessed?"

He blushed. "That too."

"Come, sit beside me. We must talk." Her eyes rolled toward the sky; their membranes slid down protectively. "We have more time than I had planned, thanks to your precipitousness. Over here." Her swishing tail flattened seed-heavy grasstops.

When he dropped into a cross-legged position, thorns ripped through the seat of his pants and into tender flesh. He leaped to his feet. "OW!" he shouted, rubbing himself gingerly.

"I am sorry," rasped the reptile. "I didn't smell it." Her snout wagged from side to side. "Turn around and I will remove the barbs."

He did, and bent over. "What was it?"

"Both languages call it a Frindrin. Don't move. The Timili are very fond of it, because in summer it stands taller than you do, and its leaves are many enough to cast thick shade. The Timili spend much time beneath it. We do not. This is a deep one, I am sorry. When the heavy rains of autumn come, the stalk rots away, leaving a prickly pad to guard its roots through the winter. The thorns keep hungry animals from eating it. Stand still. People, of course, can dig it with tools—and we do, Rhanghan and Timili alike. Only one more. The roots are very delicious when baked for a day and a half. There. Better?"

"It's still, ah, sensitive." He scratched the ground with his toe. "No offense, Sahaang, but I think I'd be more comfortable standing."

"Of course you would," she said sympathetically, "but please stand on the other side of me. You are blocking my sun."

"Excuse me." He shuffled around her, wincing with each step. She smelled of leather and fish. "You came here to see me?"

"Yessss." She'd sunk her speartip into the soil and folded her hands on its butt; now she rested her chin on her hands and half-closed her eyes. "Sso warm...your name is McGill—" She had trouble with the alien sounds. "—F-f-feighan."

"Ah—" He cast about for something to say.

One eye moved, independently, to study him. Authority glittered in its depths. "Do not compound your difficulties with a lie."

"Yes," he admitted, "it is. How did you know?"

"I know all that transpires at the Building. The telepath

copied the note for me. Why did you thus abuse our hospitality?"

"It's a long story..." he said doubtfully. At her expressionless nod, he summarized, as briefly as he could, the incidents that had led to his flight to Throngorn. "So," he concluded, "I've got to find out why the Far Being Retzglaran did that to me—before The Organization does."

"I see," she said drowsily. "Very well. Let me warn you that someone at the Building—no, I will not mention a name; the matter is for Nojono and myself to settle—is in the pay of The Organization, and has told it of your coming and of your quest. Expect trouble, much of it. The Organization is very powerful, more so than any government or clan that exists here. It will defy us with impunity. Be warned."

The sunlight could not counter the chill that had settled in his stomach. "Wh-what do you advise?"

"Go to Kuturu, discover what you can. And trust no one."

That's the second time today I've heard that line, he thought nervously. *So melodramatic I want to laugh—when it's prolly so true I should cry. Wha'm I gonna do?*

He asked her that. She said, "Do not let Bapasa's clan learn that you have cast yourself part of the way to their winter quarters. This would outrage them. And I tell you sincerely, young warmblood, that the Timili know everything that happens in the hills. You would be best off if you walked the entire journey."

"You're probably right."

She straightened, and jerked her spear from the ground with an easy tug. "Before I go—" She twitched a yellow feather from the spearhead. "—a talisman, in our luckiest color. Keep it safe. Should one of my people cause you difficulty, show it this. It will help."

"Thank you," he said, not understanding why she'd given it to him, but grateful nonetheless for her concern. He bowed, and tucked it into his pack. "Are you returning to the Building?"

"Of course not," she snapped, with more asperity than his question had warranted. "I— forgive me, you are alien, you do not know all our ways. It is autumn; it is time for me to lock my den against winter's thieving fingers. I go to the chalk cliffs of Tentele that I might slumber with my mates." One nictitating membrane slid down in a slow wink. "Fortunately, we of the Rhanghan are not bound by silly superstition. Farewell."

And she was gone.

He heard the helicopter half an hour later, as he was inching along a precarious ridge. His reflexive frustration—*why couldn't I have just choppered up?*—was quickly replaced by worry. He couldn't have flown to Kuturu because aviation had yet to come to Throngorn II—so much of the Flingers' earnings were devoted to repayment of the FNC loan that almost none remained to import technology.

The Organization!

He scanned the surrounding terrain, searching for a place to hide. The granite ridge was half a meter wide, perhaps a kilometer long, and he stood at its middle. Its eroded flanks fell steeply into rock-jumbled gorges. Patches of moss grew on them, and withered leaves skipped across them, but there was no cover. His shadow sprawled a third of the way down the slope.

The rotor sounds strengthened, blew to him on chilly gusts. The helicopter was approaching and he was dangerously visible.

N'York? No! They'd think I was . . . here, then, but where?

The field glasses found him a large boulder in the western gulley; its overhang left little space but he had no choice. *Dammit, gotta risk it—*

PING

His knees pressed his ears tight against his head; damp rock cooled his neck. The pack was wedged into a cranny. His arms, at least, were free, but all he did with them was pull them deeper into the overhang's shade. The Frindrin wounds resented being sat on.

A brown, thousand-legged bug slid between his feet and flowed out into the sunlight. Its antennae fluttered like semaphore flags; its pincers gnashed with righteous fury.

"Sorry," he called softly. Then he shivered. *It could have been poisonous*, he thought, *coulda bit me, killed me . . .* in his pack was a guidebook to local wildlife; if he could have extracted it without showing himself, he would have. *So many things to learn . . .*

Along the gulley rolled echoes of the copter, gutter balls thrown by gigantic bowlers. THWACK-THWACK-THWACK! A diffuse shadow wove back and forth in front of his den. The chopper hovered right overhead.

Sweat drenched his shirt. His teeth chattered. He had to take a leak.

"POW!" barked a rifle; "TWIIIing," screamed its ricochet.

Were they shooting at him? Another target? Just venting steam?

"POW!" A dust cloud spurted twenty meters from his rock. The shadow covered it like a hawk on a chicken. Rotors roared in his ears.

They couldn't know where he was. He'd Flung himself under the boulder before the chopper had come into sight. They couldn't know. FNC doctors had removed the beacon once Greystein had told them about it. And he could not be seen from above, so they *couldn't* know.

"POW! TWIing, POWTWIIIiiinggg!"

A kicked-up pebble flew into his niche and nicked his skull. He wet his pants. And almost did worse. It smelled awful.

And then the rotor noises began to fade into the distance. They hadn't seen him. The shots hadn't been meant for him. Some Organization cowboy had gotten frustrated, or needed practice, or whatever, but hadn't been aiming to kill him. He told himself that over and over until, finally, it melted the icy paralysis that numbed him.

Twenty minutes after inaudibility had swallowed the chopper, he eased himself into the open, stretched out the cramps, and began to look for a stream or pond. He couldn't repack those pants until they were clean.

When he awoke, the sun hung an arm-length above the horizon; dusk wouldn't fall for hours, yet. He sniffed the strong wind. It smelled damp, decaying—from a million square klicks of autumn-struck forest, it had scooped up the scents of soggy leaves and rotting fruit. Somehow it smelled good. Natural.

He supposed he should, as a civilized citizen of a high-tech world, find the odor distasteful, too strongly suggestive of his own mortality for comfort—but he didn't. Rather, in those few post-sleep seconds, when ideas come effortlessly and complete, he thought of mounded leaves, crisp on top, compressed on bottom. Worms would tunnel up to nibble on them; spiders and gnats would nest in them; ants would break off pieces for afternoon snacks...they'd blanket the ground through the bitter Throngornian winter, blanket it so it wouldn't freeze too deeply, so the roots and the larvae and the moles would survive until the spring. And then, when the hand of ice had released the land, the rains would wash minerals out of the decomposing leaves, wash them down to the soil where the plants that drank them could burst forth in bud and blossom. Later, when the rains had passed, when summer scorched the forest and the air was drier than a furnace's, then the leaf piles would shield the moist ground, protecting it from drought...no, McGill didn't find the odors distasteful. Breathing deeply, he appreciated them.

The afternoon was quiet. Somewhere something chirped; somewhere else something more gravelly-voiced bellowed in anger. The dominant sound, though, was the wind: it rustled leaves, brushed branches, and whistled through bizarre rock formations. He listened closely for helicopters but heard none.

His pants had dried while he slept; he packed them and tied his shoelaces. It was time to return to the ridge. He weighed the morality of it for a moment, then with a disgusted *PING* Flung himself to the exact spot he'd left hours earlier. Settling his knapsack more evenly, he started walking.

It was all uphill, kilometer after kilometer, or so it seemed. He kept waiting to reach the top, kept anticipating the sheer pleasure of going with gravity for a change, instead of against it. It never came. What had looked, from a kilometer away, to be the crest would prove, when he'd surmounted it, to be a shoulder that had blocked the view of the true crest. So he'd slog up the next incline, only to find another rise behind it. And another. And another.

By nightfall, he'd covered thirty-five torturous kilometers. Not bad, though they'd blistered his feet. If he could maintain that pace...

A helicopter coughed in the south. The day's last light picked out the mouth of a cave. Cursing, he limped over it. "RRAAARRGGGRRAARRGG!" he screamed down its throat, and jumped back.

Claws clicked on stone. A large, furry animal raced out and disappeared into the deepening shadows. With a wan smile, he crept inside.

The tunnel was narrow, low-ceilinged; it bent sharply to the right, and then to the left. Thirty meters in, it ended in a large chamber. The whole place stank like an untended zoo.

He had a lighter, and wood littered the hillside. While a small fire would probably smoke the cave miserably and leave his eyeballs more bloodshot than a drunk's, it would also probably keep the resident from returning before it was welcome. And the double bends would retain the light. The chopper wouldn't see it.

With a sigh, he set to work.

Twenty hours is a long time to spend examining the gnawed bones in a predator's cave, even with a fire that demands constant replenishment. He heard the copter four times, and on each occasion slipped to the entranceway to wipe his eyes and see if it were coming toward him. Its running lights danced across the night sky, a black bowl filled both with star clusters new to him, and with two of T-II's three moons, but the helicopter came nowhere near his hideout.

He slept once, for how long he didn't know. A growl awakened him. The rank scent had strengthened. The fire had died to embers. A dark shadow blotted the tunnel. Controlling his fear—which he was sure the animal could sense, which he was sure would induce it to attack him—he slid his lighter out of his pocket and snapped it on.

The flame leaped high, leaped yellow. Two oval amber eyes caught it and held it unblinking. The whiskered face was feline, and fanged like a saber-tooth. As he lay, half-petrified, the powerful jaws opened.

"GGRRAAAHHHH!" yelled McGill. "GRAAAH!"

With a flick of its tail and a scrape of its claws, the dispossessed cave-dweller whisked into the open.

Sleepiness, displaced by anxiety, called it quits for the night. He ate something from his pack—a dried fruit sort of thing, sweet and very chewy—cursed himself for forgetting to bring water, and heard the helicopter when dawn began to brighten the mouth of the tunnel.

He'd had it with The Organization. It had chased him away from home, it had killed his parents, it had kidnapped him, and now it was trailing him through the forest like rangers do a rabid bear. No more.

Uncasing his binoculars, he crawled out of the cave. Rocks of all sizes littered its front yard. He picked out ten that were as heavy as he could hoist, and piled them at his feet.

The rising sun reflected off glass, threw slivers of chrome into his squinting eyes. He lifted the binoculars to study the machine.

One huge rotor whirled toward the front of the craft. Another, smaller, one beat the air by its tail. The cabin was a plexiglass bubble; five or six figures sat indistinct within it. Several clutched guns. "Bye-bye," he said.

PING

Ten large rocks, ranging in weight from thirty-five to fifty-three kilos, materialized directly above the helicopter's main rotor. They dropped, of course. One fell harmlessly past. One missed the blades but bounced off the cabin. The other eight made good contact with the metal.

The screech was horrendous.

Four jagged steel blades, ranging in length from three to fifteen meters, spun out over the forest. The engine roared, then died. Inside, arms waved. Voices shrieked. The entire machine plummeted behind a towering evergreen and exploded. Greasy smoke stained the clear sky.

"I can play dirty, too," said McGill, as he slipped his knapsack over his shoulders and started out.

· Chapter XVI ·

Hommroummy's pet computer riffled through the daily reports from the informants in Gryll's party on Throngorn II. He chuckled humorlessly as he read of the helicopter disaster; he could visualize the frustration of Crafioni, who would have to Fling another helicopter, 918 kilos at a time, all the way there. He almost wished he could see it. Almost.

While his supervisor was gone, he had work to do. Dangerous, difficult work. The Terran branch of The Organization was riddled with people who served two masters—himself and Gryll. He had to eliminate them; they couldn't be trusted to place his interests first. Yet they couldn't simply disappear. That would be too suspicious. They had to fall victim to age, to accidents, to illness . . . and all of it natural.

As he summoned his experts, he wondered why his superior didn't apply the same technique to McGill Feighan. It wasn't smart for an anticulture to attempt to absorb anything that didn't seek absorption on its own. Resistance brought attention, and anticultures, like fungi, grew better in the dark.

The Earth spun in his disp-screen like a beach ball on a turntable. It was that, oddly enough, that had convinced him to diminish Gryll's influence in The Organization. Ultimate responsibility for Terra should belong to a Terran, not an alien. He was no xenophobe—indeed, he approved of The Organization's multispecies nature—but before he surrendered control of his planet to an eetie, he wanted to be given control of its world.

The computer whistled and he went to review its findings. He hoped it was calling to tell him that Feighan had just killed Gryll . . .

▪ **Chapter XVII** ▪

The winter camp of Bapasa's clan clung to the mountainside like a fly to a wall. McGill, seated on an uprooted tree made soft by rain and rot, examined it through his glasses for a long time. To the valley it presented a puzzling sight.

Thirty-two smooth, inverted cones jutted towards the cloud-thick sky; gray smoked curled out of most. Five to ten meters below each, a square of garishly painted hide stretched across the mountain's face. The predominant color was yellow, but reds and blues and cruel greens abounded. No order arrayed the hides: a line drawn between any two would have to bend to touch a third. Linking them, though, were light-colored threads, *footpaths*, he figured. The whole looked like a web spun by a drunken spider with a taste for quilting.

He was in better shape than he'd been after the first day, but not by much. His feet ached abominably; he hadn't known blisters could pop up so easily and in so many places. Where they had broken, red smeared his socks. The knapsack was lighter—was almost empty—and no longer pulled at his shoulders as if to topple him over backward. On the other hand, his legs were exhausted; his body was stiff from sleeping on bare ground. And a thousand rocks had torn the hands that had hauled him up the mountains.

I could Fling myself there so nicely—somehow it seemed wrong to have to climb the last four thousand meters. The air was thin this high, thin and very cold. Breathing hurt without satisfying. He knew from bitter experience that his lagging body would need five or six hours to force its way up that winding, rock-strewn excuse for a path. *Path, shit, it's more like a string of toeholds.*

But he had to walk it. Not counting concealment-Flings that had moved him no closer to the camp, he hadn't teleported once since meeting Sahaang. He couldn't risk ostracism at this, the penultimate moment. Bark squished as he pushed himself erect. Clenching his teeth, hyperventilating, he started up the cliff.

The camp stood twenty or thirty meters above the treeline. The scrub growing in the shallow patches of soil was stunted, gnarled, and sad. There wasn't much of it, either: most of the mountainside was a tilted slab of stone. Great-winged birds circled in the sky, and on a distant slope teetered a Throngornian sheep or goat.

Grunting, he clawed his way up. The effort cost him dearly: his blood dried on dozens of rocks, his heart hammered madly, sweat dribbled over his eyebrows and blinded him . . . he had to stop every fifteen or twenty minutes to gulp air and fight off swirling dizziness.

"Hello, Sun Spearer," chortled a high, light voice.

He straightened—almost falling back downslope in the process—and found his bedraggled image reflected in the huge, soft eyes of a Timili child. He—she?—perched on a rock in the sun, wingcape unopened. "Good day to you," he said. "I see you know my name."

"I know more than that," said the child. "Oh! I'm sorry. I am Rothono, and I've been waiting here for you for two days."

"Two days?" He had to laugh, even though his chest ached, even though the sound tapered into a wheezing cough. "I think perhaps you overestimated the strength of my legs."

"Oh, no," giggled Rothono. "The Thread-Splicer thought you might cast yourself—I was placed here to stop you."

"Stop?" Dully, while his lungs recovered, he eyed the boy. "How could you— oh, I get it." He should have expected to meet another antiteleport. "You're an—" He had to use the Terran word because he didn't remember the Throngornian. "—Anchor."

"Ang-kor?" echoed the child. "No, Rothono. And I am the tornado that stops the cast. Were you to use your Power, you would cast yourself directly to me."

Suspicion confirmed, he nodded, and slid his thumbs under

the straps of his pack. "If I promise to walk, may I visit your camp?"

"Sure!" Bouncing off the boulder, he caught the footpath with the tips of his twelve splayed toes. His balance was superb—he didn't even sway. "I'll lead you," he said, loping ahead.

"Ah, Rothono—" When the boy turned, he asked, "More slowly? Please?"

"I am sorry." He was nearly as tall as McGill, and much of his height was in his legs. His eagerness was in his youth. "I forget that you are a footless people."

"If I have to go much farther," admitted McGill, "you'll be right. They'll fall off. But why do you think that?"

"We had a book last winter," explained Rothono, "and it told us all about Sol III, how you have things that move on the ground, and things that fly in the air like a bird only so much bigger that a thousand people can sit inside them at one time, and boats a hundred times larger than the boats of the Rhanghan, and—"

"Why does that—" Inhale, exhale, inhale. "—mean we're footless?"

Rothono gave him a logician's look of exasperation. "If you were footed," he said patiently, "then you wouldn't need all those machine-things, would you?"

"They get us places— a lot faster— than feet can."

Rothono thought about that for a moment. "Why do you want to go faster?"

He almost replied, but stopped himself. A truthful answer would be composed of rationales that would themselves make no sense to the boy. If he couldn't see why speed was important—at least to an individual, if not to society as a whole—then explaining would waste breath that was sorely needed. Instead, McGill asked a question of his own: "Why do you winter up here— in the mountains— where it's so much—colder?"

"It doesn't get cold up here," Rothono protested. "Except in a blizzard, maybe . . . but when the sun shines, it's warm as coals."

"Isn't that true down in your valley?"

"Well, yes, but . . ." His ears waggled to express his confusion. "I don't know why we come here. We always have. I never asked before . . . maybe it's the snow?" At McGill's quizzical grunt, he chattered on: "In the valley the snow is seven people deep—I saw it last year, when I was in hunt school—it covers the rooftops and the orchards and goes halfway up Frindrin Hill. Maybe that's why."

"Seven persons deep?"

"Oom-oo." He did a dance step of impatience as he waited for McGill to lose his dizziness. "No wonder you need things to make you go faster; you walk very slowly, even for an adult."

"Uh-huh." Seven persons deep...twenty meters of snow...maybe they were trying to avoid the spring floods, as well as winter-long entombment in houses that would shrink remorselessly as the days wore on without exhumation...he thought of twenty meters of snow melting, and shook his head. That explained winter camp, all right. He'd like to see their houses, though, the valley ones. Must be solid stone— of course, they would be, if wall-building were a local art form. And what a test of wall strength, those spring floods... "I didn't see any people around," he gasped as they started onward again. "Where is everybody?"

"Most of the adults went back to the valley." Rothono had left the path and was now hopping from boulder to boulder on a parallel course. "They wanted to bring more food and stuff."

"Do you carry— all your food— up here?"

"Oh, no." He sniffed, made the flared-ear sign for silence, and overturned a small rock. His hands blurred as they darted into the moist depression; when they reappeared, they contained a squirming, rat-sized mammal. It had smooth brown fur and tiny eyes that blinked frightenedly. "This is a Tyty; there are lots of them around here. They make a great stew." He bent over and released it; it headed for the nearest stone's shade and promptly burrowed beneath it. "Don't tell my mother I let one go. She'd be angry."

"It was cute," agreed McGill. "So you hunt a lot, huh?"

"Oom-oo. The snow drives the animals out of the valleys, the ones that don't hibernate. We estivate, did you know that? I read you didn't do either."

"I did know. And we don't." Bending backward, he estimated that at least three thousand meters remained to be climbed. He groaned. "Too hot for you in summer?"

"Even at night. And daytime's too bright. In fact," he added, "we start going to bed at dawn in the middle of fifth month—

we estivate from mid-sixth to mid-first—and we don't sleep at night until mid-third month. It really hurts our eyes."

"Well, what do you— do up here— when you're not hunting?" The path broke, literally: a one-meter section had washed out. Rothono hopped lightly across it. McGill peered down, which was a mistake, and had to fight off vertigo before he could emulate the boy. Then he leaped, landed, and sprawled on his face. As he accepted Rothono's hand, he was grateful that the Timili hadn't laughed. "So how do you pass the time?" he repeated.

The boy looked glum. "Now we have to go to school," he said, "all winter long. And it's not fair. When Grandfather was my age, the whole clan sat around and told stories and smoked Dinimi, which was a lot more fun. But now—" He stopped. His ears perked up and swiveled to hear the mountainside above them. A low rumble from the sky loudened into inrushing thunder. "A slide!" he shouted. "Quick, quick—" His ears fluttered like wind-tossed petals. He didn't know where to go.

McGill's binoculars practically jumped into his hand. He jammed them to his eyes sockets and spun the focus knob. A stony gray wave swelled in their field. Spitting rocks and dirt and broken bushes, the avalanche raced toward them. For a moment, a tumbling body appeared, then vanished into the tumult. "If we run—"

"No. Too wide, too quick." He crawled between a boulder and the ground. "In here."

"Too small. And—" Tall as a Timili, the boulder balanced precariously. One good slam against the uphill side would tip it forward, to flatten whatever lay beneath it. "Come here."

"You come." The avalanche's roar already blurred his words.

"Dammit—" Unable to hear himself, he knew Rothono couldn't either. The slide advanced with a freight train's speed. It clattered a mere hundred meters away. He dove forward and seized the boy's ankle. "Let me cast!" he shouted.

PING

They lay in the dust at the place where they'd met. He looked uphill. Yes, he had figured it correctly. Assuming nothing diverted it, the avalanche would sweep harmlessly past them. When calm returned, he could Fling them back. "Does this happen often?"

Dazed, Rothono sat up and touched his temples lightly. "Ungmmm," he moaned. "Ungmmm."

"You okay?"

"Ungmmm..." Hesitantly, he took McGill's hand and pulled himself to his feet. Dust darkened his fur. It rose in a dry cloud when he slapped at it. "You cast us."

"I had to. Otherwise—" He pointed to the rearguard rocks still rolling down. "But I Flung us backwards, not up to the camp."

"Oo," said the boy, shaking his head as if to clear it, "oo that is good. I was afraid..." Trailing off, he turned, and folded his arms across his chest while he studied the avalanche's last trickle. His wingcape shivered, unfurled, and wrapped around him. For a moment it hung limp and wrinkled, but as his second heart awoke to pump blood, it stiffened and thickened. Rothono seemed to need its fleecy warmth.

"Why don't you lie down a minute?"

"No, I— you're right. I am in shock." Stretching out on the path, he accepted McGill's pack as a pillow. "How did that happen?"

"You're the one who lives here, you tell me." Having taken food out of the knapsack before surrendering it, he shook several pieces of dried fruit into his hand. "Want some?"

"Thank you." He popped one into his mouth, but didn't chew—rather, he let his saliva moisten it until it bulged inside his furry cheek.

McGill did the same, somewhat ruefully. Meals would have been more pleasant the last few days if someone had taught him to do that. "Do you have many slides here?" he asked politely.

"Almost none," said the boy. "That's why—" His ears rotated in tiny circles. "Of course. Hafala did it."

"Hafala?"

"Yes." He nodded, saying, "It was she I heard die." He waved vaguely toward the mounds of loose rock.

McGill realized her body was what he had seen. "Who is she? Why did—"

"Hafala? She is the mother of Kodono, who left our village several years ago. You are acquainted with him, I believe?"

"Kodono? That name doesn't—"

"It was on your account that he was imprisoned." Brief hostility gleamed in his eyes. His lips lifted a centimeter to show the tips of wet white fangs. "Hafala was told that you had asked for his death."

"Wait." He'd just had a horrible thought. "Kodono— did

he travel to Earth, I mean, Sol III?"

"Yes. And he has not come back."

Kodono must have been one of the Anchors holding him on the Moon, he realized. What rotten luck. "How did Hafala hear of this?"

"When we learned you were coming, we were told of what you'd done."

Was the whole thing a complicated trap? Had Bapasa lied about the gastropod, just to lure him to the mountains where her indignant clan could kill him? "Do all of you bear me enmity?"

Rothono seemed astonished. "Why should we?"

"Well, Kodono . . ."

"No, not at all. Hafala hated you—desperately—but when the Thread-Splicer sees what she has done . . ." He began to get to his feet. "She did wrong, and we will not honor her body."

"But the rest of your clan—"

"No. It bears you no hatred. Be easy about that." He looked at the sky, at the deepening purple in the west. In the east, the setting sun drew bars of red and gold above the horizon. A tide of shadows was rising up the northwest face of the hill. "We'd gotten a fourth of the way."

"Would it be wrong of me to Fling us back to where we were?"

Briefly, Rothono contemplated ethics. "No," he said at last, "no, I don't think it would be. It would be only right, in fact. You may cast."

"Thank you." He took the boy's hand. It was thin, strong, and furry.

PING

"Such a strange feeling," said Rothono, when they stepped apart on the pebble-littered path. "It feels like you're a hide stretched across the sky. Thank you."

"You're welcome."

They set off. For the next while, a broad and gentle trail invited them to ascend it quickly. Within an hour, they had less than five hundred meters to go.

"Tell me," asked McGill, "have you heard stories of a giant slug—a large ochre being that visited here a long time ago?" He held his breath while he waited for the answer. If it were "no," then perhaps he had been decoyed here to die.

But the boy said, "Yes, a little... I do not remember them well, though, because the teacher makes us study. She will not abide our listening to the old people."

The track steepened; McGill again began to puff. "Maybe— Thread-Splicer— can tell me— more."

"You?" asked Rothono in surprise.

"Yes, me— why?"

"Because—" His ears drooped forward. "—adults don't converse with outsiders. Only with clan members."

"But— but—" He gestured over his shoulder. "—they talked to me at the Flinger Building, why—"

"This is clan land," explained the boy. "On clan land, only children see strangers."

"See?"

"See." He studied McGill's face while he searched for words that could carry an idea across an abyss of alienness. "When an adult sees an outsider on clan land," he elucidated, "then he is saying that the other has come to do wrong. So they do not see each other. Thus no one has to kill."

"So that's why *you* were sent to meet me," McGill said glumly.

"Yes."

"And when I get up to the camp, I can talk only to children?"

"Yes. Oh, the cubs will love it. You're the first stiff— excuse me, Terran, we've ever met. Teacher said she will allow us to question you in class, if you will."

"But—" He tried to remember what had been said at the Flinger Building. Only a week had passed, but memory's mists already clouded the conversation. "When that alien came here, your Thread-Splicer talked to it, talked to it a lot."

"Naturally." He balanced on one leg while he picked a sharp-edged pebble out of a callus on his right sole. "It wasn't a warmblood. But you are. Now do you see?"

"Uh—huh." His legs, weak and trembling, felt ready to quit; he leaned against a smooth-faced outcropping. "See, I have to find out about it, that's why I came."

"We know."

"Well, look..." He wiped sweat off his forehead while he thought, then dug into his pack for more dried fruit. "Have one. What I was wondering was, you can talk to me, right?"

"Yes."

"And you can talk to your Thread-Splicer, right?"

"No."

"Ah, shit," he said in English. "Sorry," he apologized, returning to Throngornian, "a native phrase of exasperation. Can you talk to someone who can talk to Thread-Splicer?"

"My father."

"All right, then!" Stuffing his handkerchief back in his pocket, he forced his feet to move. Though the camp offered its comfort less than two hundred meters up the mountain, those two hundred meters rose at a 60° slant. "How about, I ask you a question that you ask of your father that he asks—no?" For the boy was shaking his head. "Can't do that?"

"No. I am sorry, but children may not inquire after knowledge that has not been proffered to them. The clan's learning is often given freely, but that which hasn't been, belongs only to the adults. Do you see?"

"Not really..." He was equally frustrated by the way Rothono could scamper up a slope that slowed him to a crawl. "So how do I learn what I need to know?"

"Didn't they tell you?"

"Tell me what?"

"You're going to become an adult—me, too—we start tomorrow morning."

He rested his forehead against cool, dry rock. "Start *what* tomorrow morning?"

"The journey."

"*What* journey?" he demanded.

"To Tentele, to the chalk cliffs where the Rhanghan live—we have to steal their spears."

If the camp hadn't been just over the next rise, McGill never would have made it.

He awoke in the middle of the night—at least ten hours after he'd gone to sleep—and looked around. Rothono's brothers and sisters, all twenty-three of them, slept in random patterns on the cave's seamless flagstones. The only light came from the embers in the chamber's fireplace. It was a remarkable piece of work: a pyramid with man-sized openings in each face, like the base of a miniature Eiffel Tower, it stood in the middle of the room, and threw heat almost to the walls. Smoke curled out of the mountain through smooth-hewn ducts of slate; fresh air drafted through the room's doorless archway.

He'd found another reason why the Timili wintered in the hills: not only were the caves high above the floodline, and less snow-buried through the winter, but they were also warmer. Though chilly and damp, the mountain's innards never fell below 5° or 6°: thus the Timili saved firewood while staying tolerably comfortable. Burrows in the valley would have achieved the same thermal effect, but would have been vulnerable to the rampaging waters of spring.

Pulling on his coat, and sealing it tightly, he stood, and stepped carefully across the scattered sleepers. Some twitched in their dreams; others uttered soft groans and snorts and chortles. It sounded—and smelled, he realized—like the inside of a guinea pig cage. Their fur might insulate them, but it didn't emit the nicest of odors.

The guard outside the children's chamber "didn't see" him, but moved his spear away from the archway. McGill nodded his thanks and strolled down the exit corridor, appreciating the effort generations of winter-bored Timili had put into improving it. The stone floor was more level than poured concrete; bas-relief crowded the walls, pillars, and ceilings. Here crouched a Rhanghan, there a Tyty, and this— he blushed and hurried on.

At the hide flap that served as a front door, he knelt, unlaced the lower left-hand corner like Rothono had showed him, and slipped through. Outside he fastened it up again. Though he'd re-enter before too long, the Timili insisted that the flap be tied down at all times. They said it kept wandering spirits out.

Through the sky swung but one moon. He couldn't recall if it was Mufu, Rufu, or Lufu, since all were approximately the same size . . . it looked huge to him, who was used only to Luna, but he knew that it seemed half again as large merely because of its proximity. The largest massed about 3.2% of Luna.

It was almost overhead, which meant the next would float over the horizon in a little more than three hours. And thirteen hours after that the third would appear, and in another thirteen hours . . .

Squatting in the lee of a boulder, he wondered what he should do. Somewhere out there, somewhere that he maybe couldn't see, Sol III orbited Sol and Luna orbited Sol III and he wanted so badly to go home that it took all his self-control to restrain the tears. He was scared, scared worse than he'd ever been before. And he couldn't bring himself to believe that it was wrong to be afraid.

In the morning, he and Rothono would commence the 280-

kilometer trek to Tentele. Timili custom insisted that they travel unsupplied—that if they wanted to eat on the journey, they kill their own food, or at least gather it from the autumn forests. They'd be armed with a knife and a short spear apiece—and nothing more. With those poor weapons, they were supposed to break into the den of a Rhanghan—a den which, Rothono had said, was so thoroughly closed that the reptiles themselves took a week to exit it, come spring—and, once inside, to snatch the feather-fringed life-totem from the hand of the cave-dweller. *Of all the* . . . Rothono said they resisted, furiously; it wouldn't be like an Earthside scavenger hunt. The Rhanghan treasured their spears, and would not surrender them before death.

Great, he thought. He'd have to invade, kill a saurian twice his size and ten times as quick . . . and then walk back to Kuturu. Two hundred eighty kilometers through gathering chill. Fight to the death. Then another, colder, two hundred eighty kilometers . . . all so his questions could be answered.

Why don't I just go home? It wouldn't be hard: a few moments of concentration, a timeless instant of transition, and then he'd be there. New York City. Or Peking. Or Fairview Park . . . no, no, he'd never go back there, nothing waited for him there. His parents were dead, Jose was dead . . . friends and neighbors lived there; they'd welcome him back, honestly and sincerely and as warmly as they could manage, but . . .

But what does a friend understand of things he's never done, places he's never seen, people he's never met? He can listen. He can question. He can note the facts, absorb the atmosphere, empathize with the emotions—but then? The difference has opened a distance. The former friends sit, legs dangling into emptiness, on opposite sides of the canyon, shouting back and forth at each other. It's bridgeable—sort of—but the span must be spun of sameness, of proximity, and of shared experiences. These things take time.

If McGill went home, he wouldn't have the time. He'd be a Flinger, or he'd be a fugitive. Perhaps both at once. If the former, the FNC would order him to live in New York. If the latter, he wouldn't dare live anywhere for any length of time, lest The Organization find him.

And that was another reason for not returning: had he the right to endanger his friends and neighbors? *No* . . .

So what was left for him? He stood and brushed gravel off

his pants. The night wind, crisp and clean, brought to him the sounds of a sleeping forest. Overhead sparkled the stars, but they didn't care.

He might as well go to Tentele—it was his only chance to establish a life of his own, a life free of jeopardy.

He just wished he could feel optimistic.

· Chapter XVIII ·

Crafioni looked so haggard that Hommroummy felt a flicker of sympathy. "Please," he murmured, "do be seated. It appears as though Gryll has been working you overtime."

"You might say that," answered the teleport as he sat, "if you had a taste for understatement."

"When are you due back?"

Crafioni winced. "Its words were 'As soon as possible.' Which means a minute before I arrived." Even the sparkle of his tunic seemed dulled by fatigue.

"Then I shall be blunt: I believe that in this Feighan matter, our interests are, if not identical, at least parallel."

The Flinger's eyes narrowed. "How so?"

"Gryll wants him captured." He stroked the fleecy belly of the Persian on his lap. "I do not. Nor, I believe, do you."

"I follow orders," said Crafioni emotionlessly.

"But you have a fondness for the boy," pressed Hommroummy. "While I hardly know him, I must admit that I have less fondness for the one that would enslave him . . . shall we assist each other?"

"How?"

"The details can be left till later." He rose, and motioned his visitor to do likewise. "You really should return now. I shall be in touch."

Crafioni nodded, closed his eyes, and disappeared.

Alone, Hommroummy smiled.

· Chapter XIX ·

As if to emphasize the bleakness of McGill's mood, the morning achieved perfection. Not a cloud marred the brushed blue silk of the sky. Visibility was infinite: from the cave of Rothono's family, he could see, even without the field glasses, mountaintops rippling away in all directions, rumbling into hazy serrations on the horizon. The wind blew softly, with enough of an edge to have character, but hinting at sufficient warmth for him to unseal his coat. Far below, treetops rubbed together, old friends sharing a private joke. Sunlight lay on him like a lover.

He stood. He saw. He was not cheered. An iron knife hung from his belt and bumped his thigh each time he moved. The steel-tipped spear was too heavy for easy toting, too short to use as a walking stick, and surely too flimsy to kill a Rhanghan. His fingers squeezed the raw wood of its haft, and one impaled itself upon a splinter. Cursing, he teased it out with his teeth.

Shoulders sagging, legs still sore, he waited for Rothono to emerge. The path dropped below his feet, but his heart had fallen further yet. He did not want to go. Firefish swam in his belly; his body's coalition of aching muscles was about to disintegrate; mist blurred all his brain but the single thought: *I am leaving here to die.*

He kicked a rock over the edge and watched it tumble, plummet, rebound into an emptiness that consumed it before it hit bottom. For one long moment he contemplated following it, as his instincts commanded. It would be easy. A step, a full stride with a push at the end, like a platform diver's, and then— weightlessness. Wind squinting his eyes, whipping his hair. The kaleidoscopic view as perspectives shifted with his spiraling glide. The rush, the uprush, the swelling and looming and exploding of the ground that would reach up to meet him...then no more McGill Feighan. No more wondering. No more hiding. Just...whatever happened next.

He stepped away, and turned his back on the brink. Slowly, he let out his breath. It wasn't that he'd decided to live—he was much too depressed to decide anything—it was, really, that he hadn't had the energy to die...

A red-pelted cub was building pebble castles in the sunlight; he recognized her as one of Rothono's sisters. "Is your brother ready to leave yet?" he asked.

"If he were ready, he would be here," she answered gravely. She tapped a prism-shaped rock into a chink just too big for it.

"What's holding him up?" The delay grated on his nerves. "I thought he wanted to leave at dawn."

"Would you hand me that stone by your foot, please? Yes, the blue one." Hand outstretched, she waited for it. "Thank you. It is precisely the size I needed." Placed in a corner of her castle, it metamorphosed into a turret. "Rothono is not here because he is offering himself to the future, and as you know, it is an experience which one wishes to prolong. He will come when he has offered all he can."

"You talk pretty fancy for a little girl." When he stood above her, his shadow blotted out the castle's courtyard. At her impatient gesture, he moved obligingly to one side, but continued the conversation because he didn't want to be alone with his gloom. "How old are you?"

"Seven." After balancing on the turret a tiny warrior made of sticks, she leaned back to examine her handiwork. "And I apologize if my manner of speech disturbs you."

"No, it doesn't, it just surprises me. You use, ah, very large words for your age."

"As Teacher says, 'What you don't learn young, you won't learn well.' And I wish to become a storyteller when I grow up." She cocked her head to study him. "You won't object if I use you in one of my stories, will you?"

"No, not at all." His heart wasn't in it, but protocol demanded that he bow. "It is a compliment."

"I would not say that, precisely." Her dark, deep gaze challenged him. "It is simply that you are the only alien I have ever met, and these days, one must make one's aliens plausible, if one is to use them. That is why I have been watching you. I hope that I did not make you nervous."

"No." *I didn't even know you were watching me*, he thought. "Did you learn anything?"

"Only that you Terrans can not seem to stand still—you shift your weight and you scuff the ground with your toes and you pivot your head first to one side, then to the other—do you not frighten away the animals when you hunt?"

"I've never hunted," he said apologetically. "On Sol III we, ah, we don't need to."

"Oh." While her ears drooped forward, she pondered that. "May I borrow your spear for a moment?"

"Sure." He handed it to her.

She stood to accept it, then suspended it horizontally a meter above her castle. She closed her eyes; her fingers opened. The length of wood *thunk*ed onto the castle. Its walls quivered. One watchtower tore free and crashed into the moat. "O-o-ohhh," she mourned.

"Why did you do that? And why are you sad?"

"I'll *never* be a wall-builder." She pouted. "See how it dislodged the turret? And look, the foundations cracked . . ." She picked the spear up, but before returning it, she used its butt to knock down her construction. "Rothono's coming—I can hear him."

"Thank you for the conversation," said McGill politely.

"I thank you, alien sir. You were patient with this child."

His smile was genuine. "It wasn't hard—and you speak beautifully."

"I'm the best of the class—" She scowled at the rubble. "—at least for that."

The hide flap snapped in the wind as Rothono crawled out. He sealed it, hoisted his own spear, and turned. Fatigue tugged at his eyelids; his fur was ruffled in some places and flattened in others. At the air's touch, his jealous wingcape embraced him. "Good morning, Sun Spearer." He yawned. "Sorry I kept you waiting." He reached down to scratch his sister between the ears. "Good-bye, Gamana—if you write this story while we journey, be sure it ends happily."

"Good-bye, Rothono." Her hand rose to smooth his neck pelt. "Who was she?" she whispered.

"Masana—watch over her."

"I will. Good-bye." She folded her hands behind her back and stepped away. Her eyes brightened, shimmered, threatened to spill over—but she turned and attacked the cave door's lacing.

"Let's go, Sun Spearer." He set off down the path at an easy lope, then brought himself up short after fifty meters. "Too fast for you?" he called back.

"A little," admitted McGill, hurrying to catch up. At Rothono's side, he asked, "Your sister said you were 'offering yourself to the future'—what does that mean?"

The Timili flashed him a sleepy grin. "It means that I spent a very pleasant night with Masana, is what it means."

"Masana?" He looked at his companion in surprise. "I thought— I mean, I didn't realize that you— is she your wife?"

"My wife?" His nose flared as he laughed. "No—I won't marry until after I return. Watch your step here."

He inched along the trail, knowing that a slip could drop him a hundred, even two hundred meters—but also aware that the descent would be much easier than the climb. In five minutes, they'd already covered what had taken an hour the day before. As long as he didn't look down . . . "But you and Masana, ah—" *Dammit, why don't they ever teach sex words in language classes?* "I don't understand your, ah, relationship—" He chuckled ruefully. "—and I don't speak your language well enough to know how to ask the right questions."

"I see," nodded Rothono. A blue, still-winged bird soared past the hikers. "Masana is older than I, twice my age, at least thirty. Her husband died last summer—his own fault, really; no matter how thirsty he was, and he must have been parched to wake up, he should have waited till night to leave the house—but she had only dropped three litters." His eyes swept across McGill's face and found incomprehension. "Most Timili women," he explained, "have at least five. My own mother has had eight. And is working on a ninth."

"Wait a minute." He was calculating Masana's age: *thirty in base 12 equals thirty-six in base 10, times point six to give Earth years equals twenty-one, twenty-two . . . why am I doing this? What does it matter how old she is in Earth years? She's old enough to be a three-time mother and a widow.* "How many children in a litter?"

"Two to six. But you see, Masana felt bad about having had only three—so when she asked if I would offer myself to the future through her, I said yes." He blinked, and licked his lips. "Father told me that experienced women are better; I don't know if he's right, but I have no complaints."

The ground leveled out, taking McGill aback. They'd already reached the valley floor, which they would follow to the northeast. There it poured down the side of another hill. "I'm pretty confused," he said. "Does 'offering oneself to the future' mean fathering children?"

"Oom..." He unsheathed his knife, and stopped to cut a reedlike plant at its base. "Would you like some?"

"What is it?"

"A Stiblis—here, chew on this slice. It's sweet, and it eases the boredom of walking."

"Sure, thanks." He popped the section into his mouth and caught it between his molars. Under the sugar-taste lay a tartness; he let its juices drip down his throat. "You were saying?"

"I was only with her half of one night," said Rothono modestly. "I hope I have sired cubs—but even she won't know for another month. She said the time was ripe, though." He shrugged. "I merely offered myself to the future—the future might yet reject me."

The trail curled around a lightning-blasted tree and began to slope; here the footpath was broader, permitting them to walk side by side. Every forty-three meters a white rock raised its head. "Does everyone do this before he makes his journey?"

"Yes," said Rothono, "but few are lucky enough to lie with an older woman. Most must be content with the maybe-women."

"The what?"

"The maybe-women." He eyed his companion curiously. "Don't your people have maybe-women?"

"I don't know," confessed McGill. "What is a maybe-woman?"

"Oh, language again. This way." The path had forked, and he headed to the right of the triangle of brambles. "A maybe-woman is a female who has entered puberty but not yet proved her fertility. You don't have that?"

McGill tried to explain that while, centuries ago, that concept had shaped some Terran cultures, things had changed. On contemporary Sol III, females tended to prove their sexuality first, and worry about fertility later, if at all. "In fact," he finished, "lots of our women are too busy doing other things— working, studying, whatever—ever to have children. And those who do, don't have many. Take me: I have no brothers or sisters."

"They all died?" asked the startled Timili.

"Oh, no—they were never born. My mother only wanted one." *That's not really fair*, he admitted to himself. *No telling how many she'd have had if that slug* . . . "Only children are very common."

"But the b-b-book," said Rothono, "it said Sol III was a very crowded place, that people built their houses one on top of another—how can this be?"

They splashed across the ford of a narrow but deceptively deep stream. The water was clear and ice-cold. Great-whiskered fish lazed in its depths. "We live a long time," said McGill. "Ninety or a hundred of our years—that works out, ah, to a hundred fifty of your years? No, wait." He divided by three point six and multiplied by five. "A hundred twenty-five, hundred forty."

"That many?" gasped the boy. "That's older than anybody— how old are you?"

"Seventeen, that's ah . . . twenty-two, or three, of your years?"

"And you're only starting to become an adult?" He was plainly flabbergasted. "Why do you wait so long?"

"Uh . . ." He sifted through the facts for a hasty answer. "We grow more slowly! Sure. Here, stand close to me—do you see that you are nearly as tall as I am? Even though I'm twice as old?"

"Oom-oo," said the Timili. "It begins to make sense. That's why you're footless."

"Pardon?" He blinked; the bushes visible over Rothono's left shoulder were shivering. But there was no wind.

"You grow almost as slowly as the trees do—and the trees don't move at all." He winked. "You're lucky you don't grow slower, or you'd have roots, too."

An ivory lance poked through a gap in the shrubbery and slowly jabbed at the empty path. While McGill watched, more and more of it projected, until at least a half meter of white menace jutted out of the bushes. "Rothono," he whispered, "what the—"

Sniffing the air, the boy whirled. His spear rose into position as though it had a mind of its own; his left hand dropped to the hilt of his knife. "Kyjyly!"

Branches snapped and leaves rustled. The rest of the animal crashed into view. The two backed away as another half-meter of horn threatened them. The head was round, huge—a good two meters in diameter—and mounted on a green neck thicker than McGill's torso. Its eyes gleamed red; its square and plentiful teeth gnashed ferociously. Its scaled, low-slung body looked like a hippo's—only meaner.

"Wh-wh-what do we do?" asked McGill.

In response, the boy flared his ears—and became a gray-furred statue.

It was the sign to keep quiet and motionless. He tried. The kyjyly, five meters away, froze as well. The three stared at each other menacingly.

The wind blew McGill the odor of herbivore: rank sweat, moldy leather, rotting grass . . . patches of rust discolored the smooth, sleek horn, and many minutes passed before he realized that blood had dried there. Dead leaves cartwheeled down the path, oblivious to the drama of the tense tableau; the animal's small eyes flickered to them but kept returning to the voyagers. Insects clouded its flanks, raising a steady, faint buzz. Some rode the breeze to investigate McGill.

One landed on his nose. Crossing his eyes almost brought it into focus. Its wings were short, transparent; emerald veins made them exquisite lace. The touch of its many legs irritated his skin. It crawled to the tip of his nose, down the bar of flesh between his nostrils— then in.

He sneezed!

Alarmed, the kyjyly charged. He hurled himself to one side. The beast's massive shoulder brushed his feet as it roared past like a green land-rocket. Bushes broke beneath him; crushed leaves scented him with chlorophyll. He sneezed again, and again, and again, until finally he expelled the bug. It buzzed after its host, whose rumbling hooves receded in the distance.

"Sun Spearer?" quavered a high, faint voice.

"Just a minute, Rothono." He twisted and turned and tore himself free of the undergrowth. Thorns had ripped his coat in a dozen places, punctured his pants and prickled his skin, but he was grateful. The pain could have been worse. When he regained the path, he looked around for the young Timili— who was nowhere to be seen. "Rothono?"

"Here—above you."

At least four meters up a gnarled tree lay Rothono, arms and legs twined around a cleft-barked branch. His whole body trembled. His eyes were clenched shut.

"How did you get up there?"

"I— I'm not sure. I guess I jumped."

"Well, jump down. The kyjyly's gone."

"I'm afraid."

McGill lowered his head and pinched the bridge of his nose. After a long, patience-gathering moment, he raised his glance and said, "Crawl out here, to right above me—" He waited while the boy obeyed. "—good, good. Now. Let go with your legs, just hold on with your arms— uh-huh, uh-huh— now, swing your legs over the side—"

"AaaAH!" shrieked Rothono as, balance upset, he slipped off to hang only by his locked arms.

McGill reached up and caught an ankle with each hand. "See, you're not that high up, just let yourself down real slowly—" Shinbones slid through his fingers, then knees. "—okay, I got you by the thighs, you're gonna let go of the branch—"

"Oo-oom!" disagreed Rothono violently.

"To hell with this, man," he said in English. Tightening his grip on his companion's thighs, he jerked him and broke his hold. He did manage to keep him from falling too quickly.

When they'd picked themselves off the path, the boy glared accusingly at McGill. "You *pulled* me down."

"Told you to let go." He stepped back into the underbrush to hunt for his spear. "Wouldn'ta had to if you'd listened to me."

"You scraped my palms." He displayed them for inspection. Roughened, they bled slightly. Bits of bark clung to their fur.

"I'm sorry," he said sincerely. "I think I hear a stream up ahead. Let's go wash them off."

At the creek, Rothono came out of his sulks to complain, "If only we'd had real spears!"

"Why?" He winced as he splashed cold water on his thorn-torn arms.

"The casters will give us twenty good knives for a kyjyly horn—and twenty good knives is more wealth than the entire clan possesses. Why, with twenty good knives..." His eyes unfocused as his daydream unfolded. "... we could buy enough food to last us for a whole year, and then we could spend the spring damming the head of our valley to hold the snow-melt, and that would store enough water to last all summer long so our crops wouldn't die of thirst, and . . ." He sighed. "If only we'd had real spears!"

"Next time," said McGill. "Next time."

Four days later, they reached the chalk cliffs of Tentele. A grass-matted headland stood two hundred meters above the crashing sea. A low, wooden building with slatted sides snared Rothono's gaze.

"Why do you keep looking at that?"

"I, oom—"

"Do you expect a Rhanghan to come out?"

"No, but— I must look." He broke away and ran to press his face against the louvered wall.

McGill followed more leisurely. "What do you see?"

"Nothing." Relief was strong in his voice.

He frowned. "What did you expect to see?"

"Oom . . . the Rhanghan are very clever. This is . . . one of their food houses, a place where they store food through the winter."

"Oh?" He tried to peek through the two-centimeter gap between the slats, but his Terran eyes could coax no shapes from the interior darkness. He couldn't smell anything but dust and old wood. Still, the idea of food triggered a reflex, and he touched his stomach. "Is there anything in there now? I'm hungry."

Rothono shuddered, uttered a noise of distress, and spun away to vomit. His wingcape spread lest it be soiled, and gave him privacy. Kneeling, shoulders shaking, he heaved up the Tyty they'd had for breakfast.

"Hey, what's the matter?" Tentatively he touched his companion, who quivered his hand away. "Are you sick?"

Rothono stopped retching. "No," he groaned, "but you must be."

"I feel fine—what's wrong?"

"You—" The boy rose, and pivoted. His spear snapped up to nip at McGill's belly. "You would eat from a Rhanghan food house?"

He had no idea what he'd said wrong. It was a perennial problem: Flingers dealt with so many alien races that they couldn't possibly remember—or even learn—all the flashpoints of each. With 693 worlds in the Network, it was impossible to recall every taboo. All he could do was what he'd been trained to do: bowing, he said, "From the depths of my heart I apologize. I have, unwittingly, given you offense. I did not intend to. Being an alien to this world, I am ignorant of many of its customs. Pray forgive me my offense, and enlighten me so that I will not repeat it."

The blade wavered, then dropped. Abashed, Rothono fluttered his ears and his wingcape. "No, forgive me, Sun Spearer, I— in so many ways you know us that when you stumble, it seems deliberate. I am certain you meant no insult." He also bowed.

"But what—"

"The food house..." With the speartip he pried a milk-white pebble out of the hard ground. "In it do the Rhanghan freeze their meat. They are clever; they have arranged wheels and belts and tubes so that they need not come to the surface. In their cavern is a lever. When they pull it, a . . . a wheel turns and a clasp opens and the . . . the meat slides down to them."

"I am sorry," said McGill gently, "but I still do not understand."

"Do you know nothing?" blazed the boy, stiffening, and again half-poising his lance. He caught himself; his nod was sad. "No. I apologize. You do *not* know, that is why you ask. The meat . . . is Timili." His anger sparked anew. "They capture us when we come for their life-totems, and they butcher us, and they hang us in their food houses till we freeze rock hard, and all winter long they slither through their caverns GNAW-ING ON OUR BONES!" He threw the spear into the ground. The blade disappeared. The butt vibrated. "Now," he asked quietly, drained by his outburst, "now do you understand?"

"Yes." McGill nodded. "Yes, I do . . ." And he, too, began to kick at pebbles.

Rhanghan ate Timili. None of the books had ever said that. No one had ever told him. They ate Timili. His stomach knotted. *Cannibalism.*

No, demurred his last shred of objectivity, *not cannibalism. They're not eating their own, they're—*

Cannibalism, he insisted. *Remember Sahaang said they eat their parents?*

Objectivity vanished.

They ate the Timili. He studied Rothono out of the corner of his eye, seeing him in a new light. It was one thing for a boy to cross mountain range after mountain range knowing he could die, but it was another, a completely different thing, for him to set out aware he might be eaten.

He trembled. He had just realized that the Rhanghan might do the same to him. And he didn't think he had Rothono's courage. He knew he didn't.

The boy pulled his weapon from the ground, and brushed dirt off its barbed tip. Holding it to the light, he scowled at a nick. "Are you ready to enter?" he asked.

"Enter?"

"The cavern." He gestured at their feet. "We should start now, because night will fall soon, and we have a cliff to descend."

"Oh, my God," he groaned in English. "Can we wait till morning?"

"Winter comes on flying legs," said the boy. "I would prefer to be with the clan when it arrives."

"All right." The Timili's calm bravery was . . . not an inspiration, but . . . a pride-prod. In the face of it, he could not be a coward. It would be too humiliating. He steeled himself. Forcing his shivers to abate, he walked to the edge of the cliff. "How—"

"There is a path." He moved lightly along the brink. "Come, follow me."

Down they went, and the footing was surprisingly easy. The path—here a shelf of rock, there steps hacked out of the stone—had been designed by and for long-tailed quadrupeds with broad bodies. McGill had trouble only when he glanced over the side. Then he froze, as the surf broke on the jagged rocks below, and spread his arms against the cliff face.

"Is your world flat," mocked Rothono, "that heights terrify you?"

"No, it's—" *it's not I think I'm going to fall, it's that I might throw myself over with every look down I think I want I ache to fly like a bird when I'd drop like a stone* "—it's okay." And he averted his eyes, gluing them to the inner edge of the path. All was fine.

Half an hour later, they stood on a basalt ledge slippery with sea spray. Before them, a round hide, whitened by salt accumulations, covered the mouth of the Rhanghan's lair.

"There are many such seals," explained Rothono in a low tone, "six, eight, twenty—depending on the age and wealth of the three within."

"The three?" he croaked. He'd only been expecting one.

"Three. Mother, father, and child-raiser. The nurse is harmless; it carries no spear. The other two are vicious." His ears swiveled to probe the cliff, then relaxed. "Within, it is very tight, very narrow—their heat shields are in position now. It is like a maze; find your way to its center. Let the warmth—and the stink—be your guide."

"Wait—aren't you c-c-coming?"

"Of course not." He seemed astonished. "It is you who seeks the life-totem here, not me."

"But I thought you—"

"Oh, I seek one, too—but I will seek second." He padded away from McGill, then glided along the ledge to the path. "I will wait above for you, Sun Spearer. And—" pausing, he cocked his head, and added, "—and if you find yourself captured, or in danger of death, cast yourself up to me. It's illegal—but I won't tell." With that, he swarmed up the rocky footpath to disappear into the sky.

McGill drew his knife—watched his hand shake like a hummingbird's wing—and stepped toward the cavern mouth.

▪ **Chapter XX** ▪

The problem with an anticulture, Milford Hommroummy mused, was that it was composed of particles whose centrifugal vectors had driven them from the primary society—and the vectors never became centripetal. Thus few parasites could grow large enough to compete with the host for dominance. On the rare occasions that such an event had appeared to happen, it actually hadn't. In reality, the leaders of the one had ousted the leaders of the other, and inherited the primary culture largely intact. Of course it hadn't always stayed intact, but with the defensive skin gone, the cells of the body were helpless . . .

He controlled his facial muscles as Crafioni materialized. "I believe," he said coldly, "that we had agreed that I should get in touch with you?"

"There's trouble," said the Flinger, dropping uninvited into a chair.

"Oh?" He tapped a dicta-pen across his left thumbnail; its speaker burped static on each impact. "Elucidate."

"Our agent in the camp where Feighan's staying died in a landslide. We have a long-range surveillance post; the men saw him go into the camp. But we haven't seen him since. Gryll wants to attack, and—"

Hommroummy punched a button on his computer and read off: "'Feighan is in caves at Tentele (see outprinted map); expected to return to Kuturu if he survives.' Is that sufficient?"

Crafioni gaped. "*If* he survives?"

"Yes, *if*. He might not." He shrugged his disinterest. "If there's nothing else—?"

· **Chapter XXI** ·

After two hours of sawing, he broke through the final seal. Woodsmoke and sweat assailed his nostrils, along with grease, long-ago broiled meat (his stomach panged), sea salt, mildew, rot, and shit. It hit his gut like a fist, and almost hammered him back outside. While he braced himself on the wooden frames which had stretched the eighteen hides, he seriously considered flight.

But that would blunt the point of it all. Rothono's Thread-Splicer wouldn't talk to him until he became an adult of the clan. He couldn't do that without a Rhanghan spear (a part of his mind suggested that he simply buy one—surely some saurian, somewhere, would be willing to sell? Again, no—they gave up their life-totems only on death). He had to take it from the cave's inhabitant.

His eyes, straining into dimness, touched what might have been a speck of light. He stepped forward, and immediately bumped his knee against the edge of a wooden platform. His hands traced its outline. It was a small passageway. Maybe a meter wide by one-and-a-half high. Once inside, he had a choice: to walk stooped over, or to crawl. He got down on all fours. It lowered his center of gravity, which would help if he had to brace the spear against the charge of an angry reptile.

At least it was warm, much warmer than the sea-ledge. Sweat already trickled down his back, moistened his armpits, and stuck his shirt to his skin. Not all of it came from the heat.

His palms flattened on a wood floor. It was beautifully

sanded, and either waxed or varnished. The Rhanghan would hardly want splinters in their tails, and the tails themselves would further smooth whatever they swept across. He wondered how large the cavern was, how broad and deep its flooring, how high above the surf-moist rock that stood. A clever idea, though, the deck.

He probed the blackness with his spear. *Thunk* straight ahead—to the top, bottom, and right as well—silence to the left. The tunnel bent. He followed it.

Two meters on hands and knees brought him to another turn, this to the right. Stench solidified in his nose. Heat throttled him. He wriggled out of his coat, then *PING* Flung it to where Rothono waited. The Timili would understand that nothing had happened, and that McGill was progressing safely toward his goal.

Twenty meters later the passageway angled into another right-hand turn. The texture of the darkness altered at the corner, lightening indefinably. He hoped it meant he was almost there. Nearly gagging on the fetid odors that rose and hung and swirled, he moved on.

Another twenty meters and another right-hand turn. The entrance hall must have run along the perimeter of a hollow square—his only question was, how many circuits would he have to make before he debouched into the central living area?

Twilight filled the passage before him. He guessed that his prey lurked around the next corner; the hunch paralyzed him. Fear raged like a blizzard, demanding that he turn back. He didn't stand a chance against an adult Rhanghan in its own lair. The tail alone could kill him. The spear, so much longer than his, would pin him to a wall, would shred his vitals and drink deep of his blood. He was an ass, an idiot. He should Fling to safety immediately!

Voices mumbled in his memory. Immobile, he listened. His father was talking, a long time ago, while he had been leafing through the family scrap books. He'd discovered a cutting from the Cleveland *Plain Dealer*, a sports editorial headlined, "Browns Don't Stand A Chance." On the facing leaf had been a column by the same man, one written six months later, after the Browns had destroyed the Yokahama Bears in the Super Bowl. He'd read them both and asked, "How'd you win when you looked so bad at the start of the season?"

"Sure and we just kept hitting," Patrick Sean Feighan had

replied, cracking his knuckles reminiscently. "We'd get knocked down, so we'd stand up like heroes and hit some more. We never lost faith. We never gave up. We just kept hitting until there was not a body left to hit."

And Jose was trying to attract his attention, too, with an excerpt from a chat they'd had after the zoo incident. "A Flinger can take anybody," he'd said, "anybody at all—if he's cold enough. He's got a guaranteed edge even when he doesn't want to put the guy in the sun. Ping he's there, pong he's here, and as long as he doesn't mind killing the other guy, he's home free, 'cause in hand-to-hand, kid, a tenth of a second is all you need."

Even Crafioni had some advice for him: sitting on his desk in the small classroom with McGill and Greystein, swinging his legs freely, he said, "Figure that in a tight fight you'll get two Flings, at most. This is because, first, a tight fight doesn't last very long. Second, one Fling ought to be all you need. Third, even the short hop will drain you, and if you try three in a row, the third will leave you wobbling like a zombie. Save it. Wait till your opponent is off-balance and clearly vulnerable from a given angle, or until he's getting ready to finish you off. In the last case, the best time is just after he starts to deliver the death stroke."

Great. He had voices in his head, telling him how to win. The only problem was, they all sounded like halftime strategy talks in the locker room. *But this isn't a game,* he thought, *this's for real!* So what if he didn't discover the Far Being Retzglaran's intentions? So what if Rothono thought he was a coward. So what if The Organization . . .

The notion chilled him more than did the idea of fighting a Rhanghan. He had to know what the gastropod had done to him, and he had to know it first. If they got it, they would use it . . . somehow . . . to manipulate him. He would be theirs, never to avenge his parents' murder . . . *No!*

He'd fight, then. Even though convulsions racked his stomach. Even though he couldn't breathe for fright. Even though his rabbit's heart shivered his entire body every time it beat. He would fight. *And prolly die,* he thought, *but I got no choice.*

Yet he couldn't storm the reptile's quarters in that state. He had to psych himself up, first. Fear wasn't reliable enough; fear would tense him at the wrong moments. He needed more. He needed hate.

They eat Timili. He visualized it: his friend, Rothono, being captured, being slain, no slaughtered, like a steer, the mallet and the knife and the hook through the guts to hoist him to the rafters, and the skinning bleeding disemboweling trimming quartering butchering cooking . . . his breath came faster, now, faster and hotter as his fists clenched and unclenched.

Then he thought of its happening to him—and he was ready.

Twenty meters to the final turn. He took them slowly, softly, stealthily—giving his fury a chance to build, to dance white fire before his eyes, to stoke his heart and boil his adrenalin. The vision glowed of Rothono's head on a platter. The need pulsed to smear his spear with Rhanghan gore.

He flew around the bend like a banshee out of hell. Knife in his right hand, spear in his left, he screamed and leaped for the center of the room. Time slowed because hypo'd perception wrestled it to a halt. He saw the woven-reed walls, the massed racks of scrolls, the glass-globed lamps—he noted the carpet's intricate patterns of interlocked gold rings—he glimpsed the piled blankets and the stacked musical instruments—but most of all, most clearly and sharply, he saw a haunch of meat turning on a spit in the fireplace.

"AAAAAARRRRRGGGGHHH!" he bellowed.

Three saurians slithered out of their blankets. A stringed instrument twanged onto the floor. Papyrus crackled as a scroll unrolled in the air. "VVAWW!" bleated the one that dove for a corner. "VROO!" growled the other two. They whipped their spears into position instantly.

Haft met haft with a wooden crack; McGill's palms stung. His forearms quivered. He thrust, parried, dodged—

A great green tail swept through his legs and tossed him face forward into the scroll rack. Dusty cylinders smacked his head. The tiers of shelving tottered, and threatened to overturn. He scrambled a meter or two on all fours. A spearhead dug into the paneling to shower chipped raffia on his legs. He bounced upright and whirled.

The larger Rhanghan came in on the right, fast, weapon outthrust. Its mate blocked McGill's escape route. He almost teleported, but couldn't spot a location that would guarantee a quick kill. Instead, he reached out and tumbled the scrollcase into the path of the charging lizard. It crashed down, pinning the feathered life-totem. He leaped onto it. The reptile cried its anger as his weight tore the weapon from its hand. He jabbed with his spear; the saurian recoiled.

What luck! All he had to do was hop down, grab the lance handle, and Fling—

The mate's tail slapped his back and pounded him to the floor. An exultant shout rang out. Eight heavy feet thundered toward him. The platform shook.

Stunned, he lay motionless for half a second. He clung to the weapons as though rigor mortis had set in. Feebly, he twitched them. The feet hesitated—

That was all he needed. He pushed himself up and stumbled to the wall. Leaning against it, he fought dizziness, caught his breath, and sought to regather his strength.

The Rhanghan would give him no peace. The spearless one ripped the leg off a table, and waved it like a club. The other leveled its life-totem. Their tongues lashed the air. Hot emeralds glittered in their eye-sockets. One at ten o'clock, one at two, they advanced.

This time, he saw the tail flash death. He blocked it with his knife. Impact jolted him to the right; cool blood spurted up his wrist. The wounded saurian shrieked in pain. It hurled its life-totem.

For a second he thought he'd been punched in the biceps. Then he looked at his left arm. The lance had ripped halfway through; its barbed tip gleamed wet, gleamed red. "Oh, Jesus!" He gasped, dropped his own spear.

Pain burst like a skyrocket. His vision blurred. He swayed, and the stained speartip touched the wall. "AAAH!" Knees giving way, he started to collapse. Two satisfied grunts sounded soft and distant. Consciousness flickered like a breeze-blown candle. *Just a second longer—*

PING

The sky was dark. It had started to rain. He knelt on the headland, in the cold mud, calling, "Rothono!"

No one answered. No one came.

Tears mingled with rain. The wind thrummed the spear, torturing his torn muscles; chill air salted his wound. He cried out.

No one answered. No one came.

Blood ran down his arm to trickle onto the saturated soil. It puddled at his knees, and dripped across the drenched coat that lay before him. "Oh God Rothono where are you?"

No one answered. No one came.

Weeping, he knew what had to be done. He grasped the

spear—and shrieked with anguish. But he had to do it. Gritting his teeth so hard that his jaw cramped and cracked enamel flaked onto his tongue, he pulled the long haft entirely through his arm.

Blackness lapped at him like the surf. Patient rain began to cleanse the life-totem. Its fringe of feathers soaked up mud and blood.

Wobbling, knowing he had all too little time, he ripped the sleeve off his shirt. Lifting the arm was hell. He looped the cloth around the wound—caught the cuff between his teeth—and fumbled the other end into a crude knot. He pulled it as tight as he could.

Through a cloud, he found the soaked coat, and threw it over his shoulders. Then he fell forward. Unconsciousness swallowed him before his cheek splatted into the ooze.

Awakening a little before dawn, he lay in cold sickness for an eternity. Dried mud sealed one eye. He chipped it away with a fingernail, and each movement wasted him. Then he blinked.

The sky had cleared—to the west, pink backdropped the mountain tops—but the temperature had plummeted. His breath fogged white. Shivering, groaning every time he had to shift his arm, he forced himself erect.

And promptly collapsed.

He screamed. Pain clawed his throat ragged. A whirlpool of vertigo swirled him around. The sky spun like it does when you lie supine on a live carousel. He would have vomited if his stomach hadn't been empty.

After a while, the world slowed down. The agony in his arm quieted to a blunt, demanding ache. He tried again.

This time he got to his knees, first, and waited till the nausea passed. Then he hauled himself to his feet, clutching the Rhanghan lance for support. He leaned on it, eyes clamped. His inner ear gradually adjusted.

He looked around.

To the east, a die-hard flock of birds, each screeching its unhappiness with the weather, fluttered over a white-capped sea. They dipped and snatched at unwary fish. In the west, where the foothills began their slow march into rising dignity, naked trees slumbered like abandoned scarecrows. North and south stretched the headland, bleak and empty except for isolated food houses.

Rothono was nowhere to be seen.

He didn't know what to think. He wasn't even sure he was thinking. It seemed unreal enough to be a nightmare. His sight was misty, like a picture shot through a vaselined lens. He had no peripheral vision. He— he tottered. His arm swung and pain moistened his eyes. He knew he was awake, then.

But where in hell was Rothono?

He didn't want to believe that he'd been deserted. The Timili hadn't seemed the betraying type; he'd appeared too warm and open and friendly. Moreover, he hadn't had a reason.

But where was he?

Mapless and unguided, McGill could not walk to the winter camp. The route to Kuturu was too long, too complicated—it twisted through mountain passes and meandered through valleys and once, because of a river, actually doubled back on itself. He would not—he could not—find the way himself.

He could Fling, of course. Very easily. Two seconds of concentration, even in that godawful physical state, and ping, he'd be there. But what good would that do? Custom said one had to do it on foot. If he didn't, the clan wouldn't accept him as an adult. And should that happen . . . his arm throbbed mournfully. It would be stupid to walk 580 kilometers, risk death a couple times, maybe lose an arm, then wind up disqualified for cheating. No. He couldn't teleport back.

He had to find Rothono. But how? The Timili was a consummate woodsman. He could be motionless behind a tree trunk, silent in a leaf pile . . .

Why was he assuming Rothono would hide?

Thinking through the static of pain was like hearing a quarterback's signals from Row Z, but he tried. He balanced himself on the life-totem, closed his weary eyes, and tried to reason it out.

He could see no cause for Rothono to have run away. None. Therefore, he must have been . . . what? Hungry? Sick? Wounded? What, though, could have wounded hi— *oh Jesus*, he thought, *oh my god the Rhanghan musta captured him*.

The sun cleared the mountain tops and sprawled his shadow across the brown, wet grass. He scanned it for footprints, for signs of struggle, but the rain had washed away everything, even the blood he'd spilled the night before. The only mark was the squishy hollow where he'd lain unconscious.

Dammit, I'm in no shape to—

Inspiration rode over the hills like the cavalry, scattering

desperation before it. He knew exactly how to locate Rothono—or, failing that, at least to have his arm treated.

The Timili was an Anchor, a natural antiteleport, and unless
he made a conscious effort to stop broadcasting—which he
wouldn't in an emotional state—he'd jam McGill from anywhere within a few klicks.

Gathering up his knife and spear, sheathing the one and
wrapping his knuckles around the other, he thought of the
Flinger Building in New York City. He concentrated—visualized—felt—knew—and—

PING

His nose, quicker than his eyes, recognized the stench of
a Rhanghan cavern. Yet surprise was on his side. The off-
guard reptiles would need a few seconds to recover. He had
to move quickly. He had to—

"Well, good morning, young warmblood," hissed a familiar
voice. "Isn't this a treat?"

"Sahaang!" Startled, he tripped, and fell across a furry bundle: a tied Timili: Rothono.

He passed out.

When he came to, the Rhanghan Flinger lay beneath a blue
and gold blanket eight meters away, almost on the other side
of the room. Another lizard sat in the far corner, breathing
wistful, minor-key music out of a flutelike instrument. He tried
to sit up.

"Ah, M— Sun Spearer, you're awake." She rewound her
scroll and crossed to his pallet. Bending over, she fiddled with
the hides of his bed. "How are you?"

The meat on her breath turned his stomach. "Rothono," he
mumbled, "Rothono, is he—"

"Alive, well, and very angry. He's in the cage." Her snout
dipped to point through the floor. "And you?"

"Ah—" With her help, he achieved a sitting position. Sweat
from the effort streaked his forehead. "Not in the best of shape,
I'm sorry to say." His muscles spasmed. A new wave of pain
ran hot and cold; its alternating pulses curled his toes. He
suppressed a moan.

"Poor thing, you." Solicitously, she eased him down and
tucked the blankets around his neck. Their fleece was clean,
but itchy. "Lie still; you'll start it bleeding again."

Too weak to resist, he obeyed. Her touch was surprisingly

gentle. When she spooned broth into his mouth, he drank it—and refused to suspect the source of its stock. The thick rug was warm, and softer than the bare ground. He looked elsewhere when she unwrapped the stained bandages to examine his injury. After a few days, the varied stinks numbed his nostrils and he stopped reacting to them. The flute played dirges without end.

"Well," announced Sahaang, on the fourth or fifth or maybe fifteenth day, "your fever has broken. The infections seem to have subsided. Your Terran medicines are most impressive."

Blinking her looming body into focus, he sensed that her concern was genuine. It puzzled him—why did she care? "Terran?" he repeated blankly.

"Of course, you do not remember," she clucked. She lowered a spoonful of broth to his lips, then pulled it away. Three droplets fell to the blankets. "No, you should feed yourself, now."

"Is that—"

"It is not Timili, if that is what upsets you." Her teeth flashed; it might have been a grin. "We reserve our delicacies for those who would most appreciate them."

"How can you eat Timili?" His voice was weaker than his feelings. "They're intelligent beings, they're *people*, and—"

"Hush. The doctor said you mustn't twist and turn like that."

"What doctor?" The soup was warm and spicy; slices of red and blue vegetables bobbed in the mollusk-shell bowl.

"I cast myself to Sol III and returned with one of your own physicians." Her eyes glittered hypnotically. "I would not have an alien die in my winter quarters."

"Oh." He pondered the difficulties that the search must have entailed for one who spoke no Terran tongues. "Thank you."

"It was my duty." She inclined her head in a bow. "And as for eating the Timili, I fail to see how you have the right to criticize our customs."

"Customs!" He choked, and sprayed broth on her scales. She did not react, except to shake it off. "It's murder! It's savagery! It's—"

"—necessary," she stated firmly. "You know so little about us, and yet you feel knowledgeable enough to accuse us of wrongdoing. But ask yourself: were we Rhanghan criminals, would the Timili coexist with us?"

"Huh?"

"Yet you—" Tail coiling with suppressed anger, she pounded across the room to a scrollcase, where she lifted from a hook the spear McGill had taken. "You!" She shook it so its feathers flapped. "You break into a peaceful being's home, destroy her furniture, assault her husband with a knife, and steal his life-totem— then you call us criminals?"

The music stuttered into silence; the other saurian slipped out of the room.

"But—"

"Are we not intelligent beings?"

"Well, ah— yes, of course, yes, but—"

"But you felt need of this trophy." Her sarcasm flowed thick and bitter. "Those backward hill-people refused conversation with you because you had not been initiated into their clan— and so you felt need of this. How dare you?"

"But—"

"Oh, yes, I know." Folding her arms, she scowled down at him. "You are warmblooded, they are warmblooded, but we are not. Therefore, they are correct in whatever they do. Is this not so?"

"Sahaang, I—" He let his head fall back to the carpet. She was right. He never would have behaved like that on Earth— or in Kuturu. Feebly, he raised the only point that justified him in his own mind. "But you eat Timili."

"You are a fool, McGill F-f-f-eighan!" With a tremor she caught hold of herself; she mastered her temper. "But you are also an alien. An ignorant stranger. A prejudiced, ignorant Terran. Perhaps it is not worth my while, but allow me to explain: the Timili breed and breed and breed. Were there food for them, they would stand shoulder-to-shoulder on every square meter of land within three hundred of our years. But there is not food for them,. This is a poor, harsh world, and there is not food enough for everyone. Were it not for us, they would starve."

"That doesn't follow," he protested. "You're saying you feed them?"

"Of course not!" she spat. "We thin their ranks. Nonagressively. Every fall the young males invade us to seize our spears. Our life-totems. They sweep over us as the seas the sandy shores. Do we not have a right to defend our lives, our property?"

"Well, ah . . ." Her logic, thus far, was irrefutable. "Yes. You do."

"What would you have us do with their corpses?"

"Treat them with decency!" he said hotly.

"We do not mutilate them. We skin them, yes. But with respect. And we butcher them, but not because we enjoy the process. It is necessary. We must eat. The world outside is too cold for us, even bundled in layer upon layer of hide. Before our cave, the water becomes a plain of ice reaching far into the sea. Snow buries the headlands and the foothills. Would you have us lie in our dens and starve?"

"Well, ah . . . Sahaang, I—"

"We are doomed, McGill F—eighan! Every year we slay ninety-nine out of a hundred. The strongest, the smartest, the quickest Timili youths—they kill us. And return to their clans to breed another generation, a generation a little bit stronger, smarter, and quicker than the one before it. Once—" She turned, searched the racks, and fingered out a dusty, shell-capped scroll. "This is a volume of our most ancient legends. They were spoken from nurse to child for a thousand, even ten thousand generations. When they mention the Timili, they call them rock apes. They say that they do not speak. That they use no tools. That they are nothing but animals. And these legends are true."

"No, they use—"

"*Now* they do!" Her eyes were afire. "After a thousand, ten thousand generations of culling, now they speak, and think, and endanger the survival of my species." Reverently, she eased the scroll back onto its hooks. Her tone, when she spoke, was softer, resigned. "But what do you know? You feel a kinship with the warmbloods, and none for us. Enough. Just ask yourself, if what we do is a crime, why do the adult Timili continue to send their children to our caverns?" And she left the room.

When the flautist crept back in, it piped of helpless sorrow.

Sahaang returned an hour later, nudging before her a bound Rothono. She was still angry. "You see?" she said. "Your friend is alive and well." She pushed him toward McGill; he stumbled, but saved himself.

"Rothono!" He searched the youth's face and body for signs of ill-treatment; none were apparent. "Are you all right?"

"In all but my pride I am unharmed." His wingcape was furled. The cords constricted it. "But you—Sahaang tells me you are wounded?" His huge eyes lit on McGill's bandaged arm. "Oom—she tells me truly. What happened?"

"Ah . . . I was outnumbered." When he shrugged, the arm ached, but no more than that. The Terran medicines and Sahaang's nursing had gone a long way to healing him. "I got the spear, though."

The youth's face fell. "And I haven't."

"Here," grated Sahaang. She offered a life-totem butt first. "Take it. We have no need of it."

The two were astounded. "But—"

"You need a spear. This is a spear. Take it." She shook it impatiently. "M— Sun Spearer will be ready to travel tomorrow."

"I will?"

"Perhaps not," she said easily, callously. "But winter is almost upon us. As your warmblooded friend can tell you, to travel from the sea to Kuturu in winter is not advised." She thrust the spear at McGill, who accepted it. "Unbind your friend." She started to leave.

"Sahaang—" he called.

"Yes?" She answered without looking back.

"The life-totem—is it yours?"

"Of course not," she snapped.

"Then whose—"

She leaned against the doorframe. Her skin color dulled; her arms hung loose. In a softer, sadder voice, she said, "My husband's. He needs it no longer." She left.

Shaking his head, McGill untied Rothono. "Can you use it?" he asked.

"Certainly." He rubbed his furry wrists, and flexed his fingers. In the dimness of the cavern, his pupils had dilated till the irises had nearly vanished. "It is the obtaining that marks one's passage into adulthood—not the method of obtaining. It will serve well." He flipped through the feathers. "Six yellow and two red. Sixty-two years old. A ripe old age for a Rhanghan."

McGill refigured the calculations in his head. Forty-four Earth years. Or seventy-four hungry Throngornian winters.

The Timili caught a scent, and inhaled until he'd found its source. "I see you haven't finished your broth. Are you planning to?"

"Would you like it?"

"Thank you." He spooned some into his mouth and sighed with pleasure. "Rhanghan soup—excellent."

"Is that a specialty of the Rhanghan?"

"It's not called that because of the cook's species," explained Rothono. Sipping from the bowl itself, he smiled. "The name comes from the main ingredient." He took another mouthful, which he swirled on his palette like a winetaster. "A bit gamy. I'd say an adult male."

And the flute cried of summers lost to time.

▪ Chapter XXII ▪

When Crafioni appeared, his hands squeezed his temples as though to hold his skull together. "Is this headache your idea?" he snapped, groping for a chair.

"Certainly not," lied Hommroummy. "The telepath must have slipped."

"Accidentally on purpose, I'm sure—look, Gryll gets nervous when I'm gone for more than a couple minutes—he thinks I'm in the john, so..." Eyes closed, he kneaded the nape of his neck.

"It's my considered opinion that our superior is making a grave mistake," said Hommroummy. "Attempting to subvert a tool of the Far Being Retzglaran can only redound to our disadvantage. We could never trust him. Far better, I feel, to leave him in peace, and pursue our own, more immediate, interests."

"I'm glad to hear you say that," grunted the Flinger, opening one eye a crack. "But what do you want me to do?"

He slid a disc of metal across the desk. "Take this. By the edges," he warned, before Crafioni could lay his thumb on it. "It is an explosive device triggered by pressure on the faces. Gryll's tank is pressurized, as you know, and should that coin be teleported into it, it will detonate."

Crafioni looked at it with respect. "You want me to be your hitman?"

"Only," stressed Hommroummy, "if Feighan's capture is otherwise inevitable."

"Sure." He stood. "If there's nothing else—?"

"Please." He swept his arm toward the sky—and smiled once the Flinger had gone. With Gryll eliminated, his men in the expedition would insure Feighan's death...

· Chapter XXIII ·

They gathered at dawn. Under the carpet, the platform trembled as surf pounded on the cliff-face, and drummed against the heat-shields. Flames leaped and crackled in the fireplace; chill drafts curled along the floor. McGill and Rothono were ready to leave.

"When you have learned what the Thread-Splicer has to tell you," said Sahaang, "come visit me. No—" She answered the question in his eyes. "—I have no information about the object of your quest. Rather, I am greedy for conversation, for insights into alien minds. If you have time—"

"Thank you," he said sincerely, adjusting his sling. "I will come, if I can." He looked around her living quarters; they were imprinted on his memory. Too much had happened there for them to be forgotten. "I'd like to get to know you better."

"I am complimented." She stooped to open a drawer in the base of the fireplace. "This is for you."

It was a cream-colored egg the size of his fist. Its shell was soft, leathery. "What—"

"One of my children," she told him, taking it out of his hand to wrap it in a square of fleecy hide. "Carry it next to your skin, and it will hatch in six months. Be certain that the infant sees you before it sees anyone else. Then it will regard you as its parent, and die before it allows harm to come to you." She returned it, and shuffled back. "Now go. Fling yourself to the headland, for I will not lose my heat to give you exit."

Rothono nodded, so McGill said, "Sahaang, I—" Tucking the egg inside his shirt, next to his stomach, he continued, "—I have no words to thank you. I will return. We have a lot to talk about." He zipped his coat, and—

PING

The wind, gusting at sixty knots, practically bowled them over. The breath it tore out of their mouths fogged briefly and then whirled away. Dark clouds scudded across the sky.

"We must move quickly." Rothono had to raise his voice to be heard. "It will snow soon, and it is not good to be trapped in the storm."

"I believe it." He wished his beard were thick enough to protect his cheeks; already they felt numb. "You want me to, ah, cast us?"

"No!" Disapproval washed over his face, but quickly receded. "We must walk. I thank you, though." Wingcape enveloping him, he found his bearings and strode toward the foothills.

McGill had to scurry to catch up. "You never told me—what happened to you? How did you get caught?"

"My own stupidity." The youth scowled. "I thought that there might be Timili alive beneath the food-house, so I broke into it and clambered down the shaft. There was a cage, which sealed upon me like a cave-in, but there were no Timili."

"None?"

He paused. "None who could be rescued," he said at last.

"Oh." Even immobilized, his arm throbbed. The pain would continue until he slept indoors, and did not need to slog up cold, cheerless hillsides. But what did a little hurt matter? He was on his way to Kuturu with the symbol of adulthood, and could soon question the Thread-Splicer at length. That awareness kindled joy, and the joy was almost enough to warm him.

Rothono, too, felt better. The thought of what awaited them had done wonders for his mood. He ascended the first slope like a bird, or a wind-wafted leaf. When he had to wait for McGill to catch up, or to catch his breath, he hummed strange music to himself, and did small dances of happiness.

"What is that song you keep singing?" asked McGill, about noon of the first day. They had stopped to eat a pair of tyty Rothono had captured, and he was drowsy. With luck, he'd be able to talk the youth into lingering a few hours, so he could sleep a while. The endless days were enervating him. "Some kind of folk tune?"

"It's the Groom's Wedding Song," replied Rothono. Quiet satisfaction smoothed his facial fur. "Now that I am a man—or now that the clan will recognize me as a man, once we return—I must think of marriage. There are many beautiful women in winter camp, and . . ."

"Is that how you choose a wife? By her beauty?"

"No, not at all—but it does make the experience more pleasant, yes? And it enhances one's pride to have a woman who bulges other men's eyes . . ." He laughed, softly. "Of course, I have heard that it also makes one more nervous about her fidelity, but one can't have every wish granted."

"I've been wanting to ask you—"

The youth stood, and kicked dirt over the fire's embers. "Ask me on the path; we really must go."

"I was hoping we could sleep."

He glanced at the cloud-heavy sky. "It will snow very soon, and when it begins we can camp. Daylight is short now, though, and we must use it while it lasts. Come."

Reluctantly, he levered himself to his feet. The arm felt heavy and misused. He adjusted his sling, checked that the egg was safe, and said, "All right." The spears in his right hand clattered together; he swung them over his shoulder. "What I wanted to ask was, are there a lot of unmarried Timili women?"

Rothono looked back. "No. Very few. Why?"

"Well." Sensing that he might be edging onto touchy subject matter, he tried to be diplomatic. "So many young Timili males go to the Rhanghan, and so few come back . . . it seems that that would, uh, create an imbalance? That there would be a lot more women than men?"

"Oo." He extended a hand to help McGill up a particularly steep section. When he spoke, his tone was somber. "This would be so, but . . . our women often die giving birth. Especially the youngest, the new-women. In our clan last summer, out of—" He tallied them in his head. "—forty-three maybe-women, thirty-two became new-women, and eighteen of those did not awaken from estivation. Their children died with them."

McGill was horrified. "That's awful—why do so many die?"

He shrugged. "I am not a midwife, Sun Spearer. I have heard it said that the maybe-women with narrow hips have the least luck. Something to do with the cub's head."

McGill nodded. It did make sense . . . it also fit in with what

Sahaang had said about the rapid evolution of the Timili. Could intelligence be even roughly correlated with brain size, then the largest-brained men would have survived to breed more than once. And since the females were mating as soon as they were pregnable, they probably hadn't completed their physical growth. "Maybe if the narrow-hipped ones waited until they'd grown a little larger, they wouldn't die," he suggested.

Rothono fluttered his ears. "But that would mean that they would have to endure childhood longer," he argued. "Why should they want that, when they could become adults so easily?"

"But at such a risk," McGill pointed out.

"Life is a risk. Eventually it kills us all."

"But they're children, they shouldn't have to—"

"You reason strangely, my friend."

"How so?"

"Oom—" He hesitated at a fork in the path, and then chose the way to the right. The wind hissed threats of full winter, and the bare branches in the forest shivered. "Children should not, I agree, be compelled to take risks. But who is to decide what a child is? We Timili allow the cub to choose for himself. When he feels old and strong enough, a boy says, 'I would be a man,' and leaves to test himself. If he returns with a spear—" He waggled the one in his right hand. "—then he has proven himself. If he returns without one, he is still a child. If he does not return—" He shrugged. "He knew beforehand that that was possible. No one orders him to go, though. It is his choice. He alone determines when he is ready to become an adult."

"Yes, but—" The logic had to be flawed. After all, Earth was a civilized, high-tech world, and it didn't force its children through that sort of rite of passage. Not anymore. Therefore...*But this isn't Earth*, he reminded himself, *and the question isn't, "Do we do it like that?" It's "Does it work for them?" And it must, if they keep using it...I think.* "I don't know," he said aloud. "It just seems..."

"Different?"

"Very."

"We are."

And that was irrefutable.

The snow began two hours later, as a light sprinkle of white on a gray background. Rothono immediately pitched camp at the base of an eighty-meter conifer. With their knives they lopped off evergreen branches two and even three meters long; they arrayed the branches around the fat trunk in teepee-fashion.

"What about a fire?" asked McGill, when they had crept into the darkness of their shelter and thatched it up.

"There would be no exit for the smoke, and it would kill us both."

"Well, what about leaving an opening?" Flakes had melted in his beard; he handkerchiefed it dry.

"The snow would come in." Through the gloom he touched McGill's good elbow. "You are tired, friend, and I'm sure your arm must grieve you. Sleep, now, and worry not."

"It's a bit cold, isn't it?"

"And it will be for a while yet. Look outside." He spread two needle-heavy branches apart so McGill could peer through them. "Notice how heavy the snow falls?"

He couldn't see more than five meters. The blizzard was thicker than any he'd ever experienced, and he'd grown up in Cleveland, the east side of which, at least, lay in one of the country's snowiest zones. But this— "There must be twenty, thirty centimeters down already."

"And more is waiting in the clouds. Within the hour it should blanket this hut completely—and that will keep us warm. So sleep. Worry not."

It was good advice. He took it.

In the morning, the snow was so deep that they could leave their hut only by shinnying up the tree trunk, and shouldering through a thick layer of powder. At least two meters smothered the ground, and as McGill clung to a resinous branch, his heart sank. How could they ever get back to Kuturu? "How?" he asked his companion.

The youth was already bending four branches into loops, tying their ends, and weaving vines across the openings. "Here," he said, handing one to McGill, "do what I am doing."

He watched for a while, realized they were making snowshoes, and did his best to be useful. It wasn't easy; the skill itself was arcane, and only one of his hands worked. Yet within the hour, each of them had a pair. "Is that good enough?" he asked, showing Rothono the one he'd finished.

"It should suffice. Here's the other. Test them."

Lashing them to his feet, he dropped from the branch onto the drifted snow. He did not sink in. Walking was difficult, but— "Yeah," he said, "yeah, they do the job. That's not bad."

"I am glad you approve, friend. Let us be off."

They were, immediately. Their pace was slow, but the exertion kept McGill warmer than he would have liked. In the beginning, he fretted: too many kilometers separated them from Kuturu, too many kilometers and too many treacherous slopes. Snow masked everything: firewood and hibernating tyty and possible shelter . . . the trip was bound to take eight or ten days, especially since it was all uphill, and he didn't know how they were going to survive it. He said as much.

"You are an alien on this planet, yes?"

"Yes," he puffed.

"You are a Far-Caster, yes?"

"Uh-huh." The sun conquered its shyness and strutted out from behind the clouds; its dazzle made him wince, and wrung a pained moan from Rothono.

"And yet you walked, first from the Cast-House to our camp, then from Kuturu to Tentele, yes?"

Scooping a hand into the soft surface, he fashioned a snowball. It packed beautifully. He lobbed it at a tree trunk—and missed. "Yes, I did."

"In Tentele," continued the Timili, "you entered a Rhanghan cavern, fought two adult Rhanghan, and stole a life-totem, yes?"

"Yes, but—"

"You were wounded. Wounded, you bandaged yourself, located me, got a Rhanghan to nurse you—"

"But she's my colleague, my friend."

"—saved my life, were given an egg, and caused her to give me her late husband's spear. You, an alien on this planet, do all that—and a little snow worries you?" His laugh ran up the slope before them. "At times I wonder what sort of people Sol III produces, that they question their capabilities so much."

McGill subsided. Rothono had exaggerated his accomplishments, but he did have a point. A warm glow spread through him. Yes. Maybe he did doubt himself too much. He wouldn't call what lay beneath his feet "a little snow," but they were traversing it without too much difficulty. His arm hurt—pain nagged him like an enemy—but he'd borne it this long, and it could only lessen. Yes. Rothono was right.

You're not a kid any more, he told himself. *You're an adult. Maybe you can't vote yet—or maybe you can* (he couldn't remember how much time had passed back home)—*but you've got a classy, high-paying, responsible job waiting for you, once you clean this mess up, and the Timili are about to welcome you into their clan, and . . . by damn. You have grown up.*

The white-coated landscape sparkled like his spirits. He pressed on, felling very good indeed.

They trudged into camp nine days later, hungry from the poor hunting, exhausted from the ice-slicked mountains, and much in need of baths—which the Timili shunned. Briefly, McGill thought of pinging to New York for a long hot shower and a shave, but he was too tired. Besides, the cave wouldn't smell any better for his washing—and he'd notice everybody else's stink more acutely.

The Thread-Splicer, a towering male with blond fur and chocolate eyes, met them at the entrance, wordlessly to study their gauntness and to stare into their wind-chapped faces. He seemed pleased that they held his gaze with easy confidence. Then he relieved them of the Rhanghan lances, and disappeared down a side-tunnel, leaving McGill puzzled. "Is he going to keep those?"

"No, he will return them once he has inspected them."

"I thought now that we were adults, he'd talk to us."

"Impatient, are you not?"

"Well . . ." He shrugged, and felt only a small twinge from his arm. "I have come a long way to talk to him."

"There will be a party very soon," said Rothono, "a party in our honor. Then will the Thread-Splicer formally anoint us as adult males. Once he has done that, he and the other adults will be permitted to speak to us again. Let's eat."

"Sounds good." He followed him through the twisting maze of vaulted chambers. They were chilly, damp, and drafty—a far cry from Sahaang's snug, hot den—but freedom from snowshoes, and from lung-searingly bitter air, came as such a relief that he didn't mind the drawbacks.

In the kitchen, a smooth-walled grotto with a fireplace, and with stout shelves buried under dried fruits, roots, and vegetables, Rothono lifted a bubbling pot off the grate. "Tyty stew," he said. "We grow tired of it towards spring, but today I could swallow the whole vat. What else?" He poked the coals with a sharp stick. "Baked frindrin!" Teasing out what looked to be a brick, and setting it on the flat-topped, scoop-sided boulder that served as a preparation table, he smashed it with a stone ax. The baked mud cracked, and flaked away. A delicious aroma watered McGill's mouth; it reminded him of stir-fried bamboo shoots.

"You know," he said, helping himself to a bowl of stew, "my first day here I sat on a frindrin—never been so surprised in my life. God, this is good."

"Then stop talking and start eating," commanded Rothono, gesturing with his spoon. "Like this." And he proceeded to set an example.

By the time they'd finished, the Thread-Splicer had returned. Silently he jerked his honey-furred head. Rothono rose, washing down a last mouthful of frindrin with ice-cold water. "Come on," he said.

"Sure." He scrambled to his feet, warm all the way through for the first time in days, but sleepy from the food. "Where to?"

"Our anointment ceremony. It's about to start."

The cave the Thread-Splicer led them to was packed with men of the clan, from Rothono's cavern and the other thirty-one as well. Torches flared and sputtered in wall-holders, endowing the frieze of fighting Timili with false life. There was no fireplace, but at the far end a brazier glowed cherry-red. Side by side they walked toward it. "What's happening?" whispered McGill.

"Just do as I do," he hissed. "And hold speech till it's over."

Positioning them on either side of the brazier, the Thread-Splicer stood behind them. Looking out over the hushed ranks, he presented the life-totems they'd brought home. "I have investigated these," he sang, "I have read their runes and felt of their feathers. They are genuine. In truth have these maybe-men ventured into lairs of Rhanghan and emerged bearing trophies. Unless there be a man among you who can testify that these are counterfeit, let these two maybe-men become full men!"

McGill held his breath. He hadn't know that anyone could blackball him at his late hour. Could The Organization have slipped someone in to ruin his chance? Could—

The crowd kept its dark silence. The Thread-Splicer raised

his arms high above his head. His wingcape unfurled, and mandalad behind him. "Let them join the clan!"

Two of the oldest Timili shuffled to the brazier. Bent, they were balding in patches, and weakening vision had dulled their eyes. One took a metal rod from the coals and offered it to Rothono.

Bemused, McGill watched him accept it. Half a meter long, its heated end was a tangle of loops and whorls of white steel, like a— *Oh Jesus God it's a brand!*

Rothono bowed, spread his own wingcape, and—with a huge inhalation—stabbed the iron at his chest like a samurai committing seppuku. Fur singed. His entire body stiffened. His jaws bulged but contained his pain. A moment passed, and he removed the metal, returning it to the old man. He bowed again, and fainted. The crowd roared its approbation.

It was McGill's turn. Holding up a finger to the bearer, he unbuttoned his shirt. Gasps of awe met the brilliance bursting from his tunic. The hide-wrapped egg he slipped into his pants pocket. Then he took the hot iron— *God I gotta be outta my mind!*—and with a silent prayer for strength shoved it against his breastbone.

It was worse than being speared. Pain flooded through his system. His eyes popped, and spun in their sockets. His jaws shuddered to part so that the scream in his throat could find the air. The muscles of his arms quivered with the desire to rip the torment away. But he held his pose for six heartbeats.

Keeping the whimper out of his exhalation, he handed the cooling brand back to the ancient Timili. Teeth gritted, he bowed to the men. They screamed and shouted and surged forward like the ocean. He was one of them, they yelled, he was a man! Gurgling gourds were pressed into his hands, and questions hit him from a dozen directions.

A deep, sure voice in his ear said, "They have wanted to talk to you for a very long time—and this is their first chance."

He looked; it was the Thread-Splicer. "And I want to talk to you."

"Tomorrow," he promised. "Tonight we celebrate."

▪ **Chapter XXIV** ▪

He was lacquering the sharp claws of his favorite Manx cat when his telepath staggered in, exhausted by the distances across which she'd had to transmit. He quirked his eyebrows. "Well?"

"The boy has returned," she said, in the toneless voice of one grasping at the cotton candy of a dream. "They are ready to start the operation."

"When?"

"Tomorrow, their time."

"Are my people prepared?" He screwed the cap back onto the bottle and rubbed the cat's stomach. It filled his lap like a warm, furry sack of flour, moving only to lift its head and rasp its sandpaper tongue across his thumb.

"They say they are."

"They would, naturally, say that. Did they *feel* prepared to kill him?"

"Yes, sir...although my empathy is only 60% reliable at that length."

"Crafioni—has he suspected?" He sat the cat down and nudged it away from his chair, where it had tried to scrape the polish off its claws.

"No, sir. He still believes the idea is to let the boy escape."

"Excellent. You may go." As the door closed behind her slim back, he reminded himself that once the takeover was complete, she would have to be sacrificed. She would know too much about how he had achieved ascendancy to be allowed to live . . . a shame, really, but unavoidable.

And the men on Throngorn II . . . he could deal with them on their return. It was imperative that the upper echelons not suspect he'd thwarted Gryll's plans . . .

• Chapter XXV •

The hand that stirred him from his sleep did not belong to the Thread-Splicer. It was the guard's. "Arise, Sun Spearer! There is trouble. You are summoned."

As he sat up, McGill catalogued his pains. Though his left arm was almost back to normal—at an experimental touch, it grumbled but did not scream—his chest was so sore that mere breathing hurt. The branding had left it swollen and inflamed; every time the fabric of his shirt slipped across it, he wanted to yelp.

And his head. Oh, his head. He couldn't even keep it upright; he had to let it fall into the cradle of his hands. The Timili did more than bake the frindrin: they also fermented it into an amber beverage so potent that after his first, celebratory swallow the night before, he'd choked, and fluttered his eyes, and wondered why steam wasn't wisping from the gourd's neck. The second sip had gone down more smoothly, perhaps because the first had burned out every nerve in his throat. Tipsiness had entered, then, as a lightness in his head and a not unpleasant thickness of his tongue. A gulp had drained the gourd, and it had been refilled before he'd caught his breath. From there . . . the evening disappeared into darkness, a darkness interrupted by half-remembered songs and smiles and backslaps . . . the Timili had taken him into the clan, had accepted him as one of them, and had gotten him rip-roaringly drunk. What a night. He wondered how many hangovers would wobble through the caves of Kuturu that day.

"Are you awake?" insisted the black-pelted guard.

"I think I'm dying," he croaked.

Despite his urgency, the burly Timili chuckled. "It's only a crack-skull," he promised, "the second step into manhood. You'll recover, impossible as it may seem now. But hurry, rise—you are summoned."

"Oh." He rolled onto his hands and knees. His mouth tasted like a sewer pipe. Head hanging, he groaned, and willed himself to his feet. "Is it the Thread-Splicer?"

"No, it's a strange stiff-ears who demands to speak to you. Here." He grasped McGill's right biceps and half-led, half-dragged him out of the sleeping chamber. Rothono and the other unmarried males of the family slumbered in the far corner, snuffling and snorting as essence of frindrin distorted their dreams. "We told him you were resting, but he threatened us with great harm if we did not do his bidding. Can he?"

"Harm us?" For half a second he marveled at the ease with which he'd said "us." He felt that he belonged with the Timili, as though his passage through their rite had truly bonded him to the clan. "It depends on what he brought with him, I guess. If he's got Terran weapons . . ." And at that thought, he realized his visitor represented The Organization. Neither Walking Mule nor any Terran Flinger would have threatened the Timili. No other Terran could have found him . . . except The Organization. "I'd say," he went on, as they turned right, into the high-ceilinged exit tunnel, "that he has weapons, somewhere, and that if he uses them, we could all be in trouble."

The guard grunted as if his suspicions had been confirmed. "What should I do?"

The hangover blew smoke in his eyes, roared in his ears, beat on his head with a baseball bat. Coherent thought was almost unattainable. Stopping, leaning against an embossed forest scene damp with seepage, he tried to read the future. "Is there another way out of here?"

The question amused the guard. "At least a dozen."

"Good. Ah—wake everybody up, tell 'em to be ready for anything, from ah, a normal day to an evacuation. I have a hunch about who those people are, and if I'm right, it could be serious." He patted the guard on the shoulder. The bone and muscle under his fingers reassured him. "I'll see what he wants."

Light darted through the flap as he unlaced it, light and cold air and a powdering of snow. He zipped his coat, and stooped to slip out.

"Good morning, McGill," drawled a familiar voice.

He blinked through the dawn sun. A tall, slender figure stood outlined against the snowpack. He shook his head; his eyes began to adjust. A face came into focus. A well-known face, with bright blue eyes and a tired smile. "Crafioni!"

"None other." He extended one of his oversized hands. "Nice to see you again."

McGill scowled at the hand, which hung between them for a moment before retreating to a pocket. The pocket bulged. He could guess what else was in it. "What do you want?"

"You," said the ex-instructor calmly. "Come quietly and we won't hurt the eeties."

The word jarred on his ears. Eeties. Common enough Earth slang, not derogatory, it was one he'd used frequently through his childhood. Somehow, though, it had become too facile, too cheap, to describe the reality of alien intelligence. Stalling for time, he asked, "Why?"

"Who knows why?" Crafioni shrugged. The brisk wind sculpted the snow around his booted feet. "We have our orders, that's all."

"Gryll again?"

"Who else? Are you coming?"

"Uh-uh." That word had escaped easily, too. He felt obscurely proud of himself for not having stuttered or shivered. "Tell Gryll he can stuff it."

Crafioni's smile was sad. "That's hardly the kind of thing one says to one's employer, McGill. I'll give you a chance to change your mind. An hour to think it over."

Funny, he thought. *Couple months ago I prolly woulda been half-nuts with panic by now, but I'm not. I'm just standing here cool and collected and not scared. Jeez, it feels good. 'less it's the liquor* . . . "And then?"

"And then, McGill, we'll come in and snatch you. Anybody gets in our way, he dies. Simple enough?" He half-turned, as if to go, but stopped and glanced back. "Oh—you're probably thinking that you can Fling yourself out of here. You can't. There's an Anchor down below, and if you teleport, you'll wind up on her lap. Surrender."

"Not a chance."

"Your choice. Another thing. We've got a chopper, and I thought I'd save you a hernia. The rock trick won't work. Not with our Anchor. You've got an hour." With that, he *PING* disappeared, twitching McGill's Talent as he went.

He stayed looking outward for a while longer, wondering at half a dozen things. Surely that had been a gun of some sort in Crafioni's pocket, probably a transquilizer/anesthetic dart gun. Why hadn't he used it? One quick pfft! and McGill would have been unconscious, easy prey. Why?

The warnings about the Anchor, what had brought them on? Without them, he might have tried to Fling to safety, but teleported into a trap. He scratched his temple. It was like Crafioni didn't want him captured—which made no sense.

And then he'd given him an hour to change his mind. More nonsense. If he had the troops, the helicopter, and the Anchor, he could have launched the attack immediately. It—

A noise to his rear spun him around. The Thread-Splicer stood before the hide with a brace of strong-armed guards, all just beginning to lower long and lethal spears. "We heard the anger in your words," he said, "but as you spoke in your own tongue we could not understand the cause. May we help?"

That's why Crafioni hadn't drawn his gun—he'd been gazing uphill into the measuring eyes and ready lances of the guards. "I fear," he said, speaking formally because he wasn't sure how to address the shaman, "that I have brought ill-fortune to the clan. That man wished my obeisance. He threatens the clan if I do not go." A thought burned through the haze of his hangover. "Sir. His henchmen might even now be creeping into the cave, through the other passageways. The guards should—"

The Thread-Splicer held up a golden hand. "The other entrances are closed and guarded well. Worry not."

"But these men have very powerful weapons," he protested. "Guns, lasers—they could cut through a hide this quickly." He snapped his fingers. "And they can kill from a great distance."

"Come inside." Once McGill had entered, he relaced the flap and stepped away from the entrance. At his gesture, the nearest guard reached into a shadowed alcove and depressed a lever.

A bass scraping shuddered the tunnel. Slowly, a huge slab of stone slid out of the ceiling and settled in place behind the hide, sealing the cave completely. It was at least a meter thick.

"Now," said the shaman confidently, "can your enemies cut through this?"

McGill nodded. "If they brought the right weapons—" He

thought of plastique, of bazookas, of aerial rockets. "—they can blow it apart." Then, reasoning more carefully, he added, "Of course, that would probably bring the roof down and clog the tunnel up even more...but we might not be able to get out, if that happens."

"It happens more frequently than our pride cares to admit," rebutted the Thread-Splicer, "and we have grown skilled at clearing away debris. Worry not."

"All right." Actually, he wasn't worried. Again he suspected a relationship between last night's liquor and this morning's calm, but he didn't care. It was good not to quake like a rabbit. Danger bristled, certainly. He could even die if things went wrong. But...somehow, gambling with death excited more than scared him. The stakes made the game worthwhile. "We have about an hour."

"We shall have to discuss strategy." Whirling, he stalked to a conference chamber. Moisture trickled down the ornate walls and splatted in the run-off channels that bordered the flagstone floors. Racked torches hissed and sparked. Their footsteps echoed up and down the corridors. "Here," said the shaman, entering a well-ventilated room with an abstract mosaic on the ceiling, "be seated. Tell us what you know of their war ways."

"Very little," he confessed. Someone handed him a cup of soup and he drank it down, relishing its heat and its spice. "Thank you. They'll try to capture me alive—they want to use me, you see. Despite their threats to kill all the Timili, I don't think they'll be that indiscriminate. The kind of people they are, they're happiest when noticed least. A slaughter would bring them more public attention than they want. So if they break in, it's my guess they'll kill only those who attack them."

After pondering that information, the medicine man turned to one of the guards. "Put the pregnant women, the children, and the maybe-adults in the warhole. Seal it tightly. Douse the torches in the corridor leading to it. Remind them to stay inside until we come for them." He paused, then qualified, "Or until all sound has ceased. Go."

The man bowed, and backpedaled out of the room. His bare feet slapped the stone as he ran to obey.

"What else, Sun Spearer?"

His head was clearing, now, and he could almost think. "Ah...they'll probably use tear gas, at least for openers—"

At the blank looks around him, he explained, "—it's a special kind of smoke. If you breathe it, you cough, and get sick, and go nearly blind. It's not lethal, and the effects do wear off after a few hours, but . . . in the meantime, it's very difficult to deal with. A wet cloth wrapped around your mouth and nose might help, some, but I'm not sure how much."

Several Timili frowned. One asked, "Is there more?" Anxiety warped his voice.

"I'm afraid so. One of them can cast, and might. Is Rothono your only tornado?" When they nodded, he said, "Damn. Ah . . . just in case . . . he should be, let's see, near me so he can stop if I want him to, and . . . against a wall, or in a corner, with his spear, so that if Crafioni—he's the caster, the stiff-ears who talked with me—if Crafioni casts himself up here, he'll come straight to Rothono, so . . ." Dismally, he trailed off. He felt little fear for himself, but it worried him to think that his best Timili friend might have to go up against Crafioni. Might die at Crafioni's hand. He'd never forgive himself. "I don't know, maybe I should surrender."

More than a few men snorted at that. The Thread-Splicer's warm, furry hand descended on McGill's. "You are one of us, Sun Spearer," he said, softly but very firmly. "No one takes you without your permission. No one. The clan dies first."

"I—" He swallowed to clear his throat. "—thank you. You are good."

"We are family," corrected the shaman. "What other tactics might they use?"

"Ah—" Staring into the flames of a torch, he thought. "Oh. Some of them might walk up the hill, but others are going to fly—they have a helicopter, a flying machine, and will probably drop men on the peak, to come down on us."

"We can deal with the walkers—" He grinned. "—as I understand Hafala almost dealt with you." He pointed to the long-armed, black-furred guard who'd awakened McGill that morning. "See to it, Lolono."

"Sir!" he said, before he slipped away.

"Can you deal with the flying machine?" he asked McGill.

"I don't know." His hand raised in a wave as a bleary-eyed Rothono stumbled into the chamber. "If it comes between me and their tornado, yes, I can deal with it. But if it doesn't . . . you know how tornadoes work." He tapped his head at his forgetfulness. "Also, I have to see it."

"We have vantage points. You will see it. Can you think of anything else?"

"Ah . . . just that the men attacking us are very well-trained, and very well-armed, but, ah . . . they're doing this for money. I don't think any of them is really willing to die . . . I could be wrong, I don't know . . . but I think that if they're in a position where they have to choose between surrendering and dying, they'll surrender. I think. Oh, yeah, they probably don't speak Throngornian—except the one who talked with me, he does."

"Then let us position ourselves," said the Thread-Splicer, rising from his chair and prowling to the corridor like a hungry lion. "Come, Sun Spearer. And you, Rothono."

After collecting McGill's binoculars, they walked toward the center of the mountain. The rooms they passed were empty of people but scattered with possessions, as though the occupants had dropped whatever they were doing and hurried off. In the kitchen, a stewpot boiled over, and the coals below it were sputtering with indignation. The classroom torches had been extinguished, but light from the corridor slanted through the entrance to illuminate a book, forgotten on the floor, its pages ruffled by the drafts. In the distance burst a babble of childish chatter. A guard's gruff, "Hush if you'd live," silenced it.

"Up here," said the shaman. Darkness perforated the corridor wall; he reached into it, found a toehold, and ascended the narrow shaft. His bare, splayed feet were the last to disappear.

"Go ahead," said Rothono. Instinctively understanding his friend's hesitation, he added, "I'll be your eyes; just do what I say."

"Thank you." He groped into the alcove and raised his arms. It was pitch black. Clammy but fresh air blew down the shaft. Coarse stone scraped his wrists. Rothono's head wedged into his right hip.

"A little higher," said the Timili, "and to your left."

His fingers, fumbling in that direction, came upon a stout wooden board fastened to the shaft wall. It was about ten centimeters deep and twenty wide. Grabbing it, and searching with his toe for the niche, he pulled himself up. "Is there a place for my other foot?"

A hand seized his left ankle and guided it into position. "Go higher, you'll find another board."

"I'm not tall enough. Is there a third toehold?"

"No." A moment of silence hung in frustration. "Wait. Put your right foot—" It was lifted and moved away from the wall. "—on my head. Careful, those ears are sensitive. That's better. Now reach."

He found the next rung. "Thanks."

"My pleasure," upfloated the voice.

They progressed like that for three or four minutes, until suddenly the shaft opened onto another corridor. Binoculars bouncing against his ribs, McGill pawed the emptiness. The medicine man took his hand. "Keep your head down," he said, "this is a low tunnel."

He could feel the mountain's weight on his back, feel it through the darkness as his vertebrae brushed damp rock. On hands and knees, protecting his blistered chest, he crawled after the Thread-Splicer, and almost ran up his calves when he stopped. "Are we here?"

"Yes, but I must find—" Wood creaked as he pressed a lever. Stone rasped on stone; light broke through a horizontal slit and brightened as the slit widened into a meter-tall aperture.

He studied their vantage point. At its mouth, the tunnel spread into a two-meter-wide shelf. The ceiling still hung too low, maybe ninety centimeters above the floor. Snow blew through the window and began to accumulate in the corners. Involuntarily, he shivered, and wriggled up to peer out.

The mountainside fell away before his eyes, down, down, down into the rock-dotted drifts of the alley. Shadows lay sharp and black on the slope; the wind tossed snow into the air where it gleamed like flung diamonds. Nothing else moved. "Can you see them?" he asked, in the whisper the situation seemed to call for.

"No." The shaman shifted his weight to make himself more comfortable. "Nothing— wait. Down there, to the left. Do you see it?"

Without lifting the strap from his neck, he brought the binoculars to his eyes. Spotting a blur of white, he adjusted the focus. A monster leaped into clarity: short, squat, accordioned trunk— he kicked himself. It was a Terran disguised by a gas mask. As he watched, half a dozen others emerged from concealment to trudge up the slope. All were bundled into obesity against the cold; all wore breathers. Making no attempt at stealth, they came straight on. "It's the first wave," he said. "Would you like to use these?" He offered the field glass to the medicine man.

"No, thank you. Horrible-looking beings; what world are they from?"

He explained about the masks. "They probably have a gas-grenade launcher down there somewhere, I don't see canisters in their belts or anything. Which means—" A puff of smoke from the far side of the valley cut him off. "That might be it there." While he tried to locate the artillerymen, metal rang as it slammed into stone. "That should tip them off."

Indeed, the leader of the squad was detaching a radio from his belt. Eyeing the hillside, he spoke into it, nodded, and rehooked it.

In quick succession came a *broomph* from the valley and a *WHAHOOM!* from immediately below. Their ledge trembled as if to shake them off. "That's the explosive," he said.

The attackers were starting to run. Stumbling up the hillside toward the bazooka-d tunnel mouth, several unslung weapons from their backs. Through the glasses, they looked like 5000-round automatic rifles.

"Now!" barked the Thread-Splicer into a hollow by his head.

McGill said, "What?"

"My speaking tube, to the guards on the— ah, see for yourself."

A solitary boulder skipped down the hillside. McGill was disappointed; Hafala had done better. But then tumbled another, and another. The gunmen were stopping, starting to turn. Nature growled. A sheet of snow broke loose and sledded down. Rocks ricocheted over, and into it. One invader disappeared, possibly Flung back to safety by Crafioni. Snow clouds fountained along a hundred-meter front. In the valley, men ran from hiding places at the foot of the hill. The avalanche rumbled on, stripping the slope bare. It splashed over one man, then another. A second *PING*ed out of harm's way; McGill had felt his Talent twinge that time. A flying stone caught the fifth man in the neck and dropped him in his tracks. The avalanche buried him at the same time it caught his comrade.

"Four down," said McGill. "God knows how many to go."

Broomph snorted the bazooka; *WHAHOOM!* bellowed the shell. Again the living rock shook with the impact.

A tear-gas canister bounced off McGill's head and hissed

on the ledge before him. Reeling with dizziness, he stretched out his hand and pushed it into emptiness. It burst as it fell, and spewed its stench harmlessly.

"Did they cast that?" asked Rothono.

"Uh-huh." He'd just realized his miscalculation: since he was between Rothono, the Anchor, and Crafioni, Crafioni could Fling directly to him. "Why don't you crawl up here with us?" he suggested, sidling into the shaman's shoulder. "They cast anything else, it'll stop in front of you, and if you're right at the edge—"

Rothono obliged not a moment too soon. A man appeared, leveling a dart gun. Gravity caught him before he could fire. He had plenty of time to scream, though, before he smashed into the hillside and found silence.

They watched his body roll loosely down to the path. "A near thing," said the medicine man. "What's that?"

He'd heard it, too: a ratcheting clatter that rose in pitch and suddenly loudened as its source clawed up from behind a windswept knoll. "It's the helicopter."

"Awesome."

"Yeah." The machine was circling to the northwest; he figured their strategy would be to stay farther from him than the Anchor was, until an outjutting escarpment eclipsed them from his sight. Then they could skim in to the top of his mountain, unload the men and their weapons, and never risk tangling with his Talent. He couldn't allow it. Picking out a likely sized rock on the slope below, he visualized—felt—knew—

PING

Wherever the stone disappeared to, it did not touch the chopper. He had to assume that the Anchor was sitting on it, by now. But that gave him an idea—

"Ratatatatatatatat!" stuttered a machine gun.

"TWIing! TWiing!" echoed in McGill's ears. Rock dust swirled before his eyes. Powdered glass drifted onto the back of his hands and neck. The Thread-Splicer grunted.

He looked to his right. The shaman lay limp, eyes closed, mouth open. The tranquilizer dart that had put him to sleep dangled from his left ear. "Dammit!" He wriggled backward, propelling himself with his elbows. "Rothono, get back here!" he shouted. He grabbed the medicine man's ankles and hauled him to safety. "Those'll knock you out!"

As the machine gun fell silent, Rothono started to obey. Then he growled, loud and angry.

McGill looked up. Crafioni crouched on the ledge, an automatic in each hand. One barked as he dove inside.

Rothono screamed; the bullet tore through his back and spattered gore on the bare walls. Yet he drew his legs beneath him. Wood cracked as his fingers tightened on the spear. Moaning, impelled by the last shudder of his dying body, he rose to all fours and hurled himself forward.

The speartip bit into Crafioni's throat. Astonishment gaped his blue eyes. The spear's haft was a matchstick in his hands. Automatics clattered onto the floor. Gurgling, he straightened. And winked at McGill.

Rothono's legs still pushed, still shoved his half-dead body forward. His hand would not release the spear.

The two went out together. Crafioni fell backward, hands wrapped around the length of wood, his back arched, his eyes now wide and dull. Rothono followed him down.

"No!" screamed McGill. "OH GOD NO!!!" He wanted to shout, to kick, to cry. So much had been inflicted on these people who had loved him . . . it wasn't right . . . more would die, because of him; their camp would be destroyed, because of him . . . he could do nothing to stop them because the Anchor was still down in the valley, jamming him—

Wait. The idea that had almost come to him. He picked up Crafioni's gun, turned it over, and checked the safety. It was ready to fire.

The chopper was three minutes from invisibility; he didn't have time to waste. He aimed the gun out the aperture, steadied it, took a deep breath, concentrated—visualized—felt—knew—

PI—"KAPOW!"—NG
"KA—*PING*—POW!"
PI—"KAPOW!"—NG

Then he snaked forward. The helicopter was a fuselage length away from safety. His Talent rebelled at being forced to Fling with such little rest. His eyes found the right rocks, but could barely keep their lids up. Fatigue had turned his extremities to noodles. He concentrated—visualized—felt—knew—

PING

As he passed out, he saw the chopper explode.

▪ Chapter XXVI ▪

The telepath lay in a semitrance on the couch that Hommroummy had had brought into his office. Bony wrist across her eyes, mouth slack, she arched her back off the cushions every time she reached between the stars. "Umm." She sighed as she relaxed, "I can't get their attention."

"Then transmit more loudly," ordered Hommroummy.

She lifted her forearm to peer at him through bright green eyes. "I already have," she stated firmly. "But if they're concentrating on—"

"Just do it."

"Yes, sir." She hyperventilated in preparation, then stiffened, spine bowing, supporting herself on her heels and the nape of her neck. Suddenly she cried out, and twisted off the couch to fall heavily on all fours. Her face was flushed. She could not speak for gasping.

"What is it?"

"Death." She panted. Her eyes were unfocused, like a prizefighter's when his trainers lift him from the canvas. "Many—much—all . . ." She swung her head from side to side. "Pain and hate before silence . . . deep dark cold silence . . . no one left."

Only his caution kept her alive. "Is Feighan gone?"

Her wince proclaimed her reluctance, but his freezing glance drove her to the search. After a moment, she said, "No . . . no."

He slammed his fist into his palm. "But Gryll is, isn't it?"

"Oh, no, sir," she said, without even looking, "only your people died. Gryll is alive—and will see you shortly." And she grinned.

· Chapter XXVII ·

"So then what happened?" McGill sat in the kitchen with half a dozen blood smeared warriors. Drinking frindrin wine and shoveling down tyty stew, they exuded an air of weary satisfaction.

"Well," said Lolono between mouthfuls, "we crept out of the tunnel behind their position a few minutes after that machine had flown away. Six of them were still there: five stiff-ears, including your enemy, and one female Timili sitting on a rock, holding her head. Two of the men knelt by this thing—" He waved a black-furred hand at the bazooka propped up against the archway. "—and the other two at that." He pointed to the other spoil of war. "What did you call it?"

"A machine gun," he said, resorting to English because Throngornian had no ready equivalent. "Ma-chine gun."

"Ma Shing Gone," repeated the guard dubiously. "Anyway. Ma Shing Gone made much noise, and shook like a tree in a storm. The Big Stick there was silent. Your enemy waved his hand. Ma Shing Gone stopped shouting. Your enemy disappeared. We did not know what to do and besides, one of the men by the Big Stick was looking in our direction. He did not see us of course, but we knew that if we charged then, he would sound the alarm. So we waited a bit longer. We saw bodies fall—"

"Rothono had just killed my enemy," McGill explained to the woozy Thread-Splicer. "But my enemy had already shot Rothono; they both fell."

"Rothono was my nephew," said Lolono, "but even so I praise his courage. We saw him fall. Then from the Timili female's voice rattled death, and from her chest spurted her life-blood. The four men ran to her. They said many things in very loud voices, but—" He shrugged his apology. "—their tongue was strange to us, and we did not understand. We did rise in preparation for the assault when suddenly, the flying machine became silent. Their stiff-eared heads jerked to watch it, just as fire and smoke and thunder rose into the sky. We attacked them, then. They died quickly."

"And there were no others?"

"None. We searched the area well, hunting for the tracks of any who might have fled, but there were no footprints." He scratched his head; his silver-trimmed ears drooped forward. "What puzzles me is their manner of arrival: there were no footprints leading *to* the valley, either."

The shaman laughed, "Are your brains as mangy as your fur? The machine carried them here. Stiff-ears don't walk."

"Ours did," retorted Lolono.

"Ours is a Timili, now, no matter how stiff his ears are." He winked at McGill. "Are you not?"

He inclined his head. "Thank you. I am honored."

Gamana, Rothono's castle-building sister, raced into the kitchen. Her ears and voice twittered with excitement. "They are ready!" she shouted. "The parents have descended the hill and they are ready! Hurry!"

The group quieted, and filed into the corridor. The flap at the entrance was open, and would remain so during the ceremony, in order that Rothono's spirit could freely collect memories from the caves and caverns and chambers of his clan's winter camp. They passed through it, and stood solemn on the ledge above the valley. Below, Rothono's parents, made minuscule by distance, bowed to the assembled clan and commenced the funeral ceremony. Enveloped in their wingcapes, the observers maintained a respectful silence.

Rothono's father slung the body over his shoulder and began to climb a thirty-meter tree. The lower half was branchless; he had to pry finger- and toeholds out of its thick, wrinkled bark. Steadily he mounted, oblivious to the wind that fluffed his fur and waved his son's dangling ears. Higher he went, reaching the branched part of the trunk and moving quickly now that his grips were more secure. The tree started to sway.

While the watchers held their breath, he picked his way through the tangle of limbs.

Up he clambered, until his weight and that of his burden tipped the treetop well to one side. Then he stopped, and with deft movements lashed the corpse to the trunk. It faced the camp. The head slumped onto one shoulder, which the father ignored, but he tucked the loose, floppy wingcape tightly around his son's lifeless chest. He touched the forehead, the nose, the mouth. And began to descend.

The watchers flared their capes until he again stood next to his wife.

The Thread-Splicer cleared his throat. Softly, he said, "Sun Spearer—you were closest to Rothono in his final days. Would you care to say a few words?"

Startled, he snapped his head up and looked around the cluster of quiet Timili. Every face encouraged him: some nodded, a few smiled, others ear-wagged their approval. "Now?"

"Yes." Correctly interpreting McGill's downward glance, he added, "His parents have said farewell in their way; now we say it in ours. Please."

He pinned his gaze to the clouds that gathered in the south. There was discomfort in him, and embarrassment, too, but he set them aside. "Rothono . . ." He had to blink; the world had gotten unexpectedly misty. "Rothono was the first alien ever to become my friend. Before I met him, I . . . I was nervous, and frightened, when I was with beings not of my species. But he showed me—he taught me—that the spirit means more than the body that shelters it. He also taught me how to endure hardship, how to face danger, how t-t-to . . . to die. He saved my life, but that is not all. I— my parents are dead, but because of Rothono, I am not an orphan. I do have a family, now. Here, on Throngorn. You are my family, and for this, I thank my friend." Bringing his eyes down to the valley, down to the crisscross branches of the swaying tree, he lowered his head.

Behind him, the clan dispersed, but not before each mourner paused by his side to pat him on the shoulder, or lay a palm atop his hair.

When all had left, the medicine man approached. "Sun Spearer," he said, "you became the person you are to talk to me. Now is the time."

With difficulty, he wrenched his thoughts away from Rothono. A bird's harsh cry rang down the slope, and a cloud diffused the sun. His own quest seemed less important, now, than it had when he started out. "Many years ago," he began, "another alien came here, a large ochre being with no particular form. I understand you spoke to it, and I am curious about what was said. You see, after that being left Throngorn, it went to Sol III. I had just been born. It seized me, swallowed me, and held me for four days. Then, after excreting me, it departed with no word of explanation. This has troubled my life ever since. I have tried to find this being, but I can not. I don't know where to look. Do you?"

"No." The shaman took his arm and guided him to a rock large enough to seat both of them.

"Did it tell you where it came from?" asked McGill.

"Yes. It came here from—" Tilting back his head, he searched the clouds, as if the answer had condensed in their midst. "—a place called Delurc. I do not, however, believe that that was its home. It spoke as though it had merely visited there— yes, yes, definitely, I remember that it wished it could have spent more time there. As I recall, that was the only placename it offered."

McGill hunched over, elbows on his knees. Suddenly the wind cut more deeply. He shivered. "Did it say anything about the Far Being Retzglaran?"

"I do not recall the name. Would that have been its employer?"

"Yes!"

"Ah . . . of its employer, it said . . . 'a wise being, older than some of the worlds I have visited. I make no effort to understand it because it is much too complex. I am an errand thing, and I do what it commands.' It said no more about its employer."

"Bapasa said you spoke to it every night."

"Yes, I did. Mostly I answered its questions about Kuturu, about the animals and the plants and the best way to build walls."

"Did it say why it was traveling?"

"Yes, yes." He nodded gravely. "Its employer had rewarded it for something it was about to do—perhaps you were the something."

"Yeah . . . you don't know the name of its home planet?"

"No. I asked, but it said that its employer had forbidden it to answer that question."

"Damn." Chin in hands, he fought with acute disappointment, trying to think of anything else he could ask. "Did it talk about its home?"

"No, not at all. Again, it had been forbidden to."

"What about its destinations after this?"

"Sol III, it said, and beyond that—" He shrugged. "—it said that when it finished there, it would know where it should go next. That is all." His hand patted McGill's knee. "I am sorry."

"What a waste." Standing, he drove a pebble into the frozen ground with his heel. "All this effort, for nothing. I walked my legs off. I shamed a Rhanghan. I killed maybe twenty people. And I killed Rothono." Huddled in his coat, he glared out at the mountains. Clouds played tricks with the nearest peaks, and obscured those farther away. "Dammit, what a waste!"

"Was it really?"

"Rothono—"

"—might well have died without the life-totem your friend gave him." He smiled gently. "Yes, I know about that. There's no shame to it; he told me about it. A spear is a spear, and it made him a man." Pausing, he studied McGill's sorrow. "And it made you a man," he added.

He could only nod.

"There is more, you know."

"There is?"

"Of course. You told us that here, you have found a family to replace, in some small way, the one you lost. This is fine and good, is it not? But it is greater even than that. The clan of casters has smoothed star-paths from world to world, yet such paths can be used two ways: to promote good, or to cause harm. It is easy to hurt those one does not know. Consider the Timili boys, who flood to the sea every autumn to steal Rhanghan life-totems. They think it wonderful sport, and those who return boast of their feats—until, eventually, they come to trade with the Rhanghan, and learn to know them as friends. You, Sun Spearer, when you return to your world, will never think of us in quite the same way that you did before. When you hear the name Throngorn, you will see not the letters of your language, not a list of numbers in a book, not even a picture of Lufu rampant. Rather, you will see my face or Rothono's, or will tenderly finger the ritual scars on your chest. This world has become real to you, and my people and yours will be richer for it." He sighed. "It is one thread linking our peoples. In time, perhaps, there will be many, many more...you are, I think, ready to leave?"

"Yes." Stamping his feet, he shook snow off his pants and coat. "I— Thread-Splicer, I thank you. Will you offer my farewells to the clan?"

"Of course. And they would want me to wish you fortune. You are a clan brother, now, to all of us, and we hope you will return to Kuturu soon."

"Thank you."

They embraced, then, the tall, broad-shouldered Terran and the taller, golden Throngornian. Beard rubbed fur and pelt rustled against nylon. They separated, and cleared their throats. "Farewell," they said as one.

PING

His first breath evoked the snake house at the Cleveland Zoo, and he almost looked around for Jose. The presence of a friendly Talent was strong in the den. He relaxed. "Sahaang!"

"McGill!" The voice floated in through the open door. "Sit, be comfortable. I shall join you promptly."

He slid out of his coat and laid it on the floor. Then he sprawled on a folded blanket under a reading lamp. Scrolls were scattered next to his feet; he ran his eyes along their title-shells, but decided that trying to read one would be too much effort. Instead, he reached past them to take a guitarlike instrument from the shelf. Its neck was wider than his hand could easily span, and its fretting was peculiar, but he fingered out a chord and strummed the strings lightly. It sounded like he'd dropped a sack of empty tin cans. Wincing, he returned it to its place.

Feet shuffled in the tunnel. After a moment, Sahaang entered. Behind her came the nurse, her neuter-mate, who peered anxiously into the room over her shoulder. "Don't be silly," said the Flinger, "this is the same one who was here before."

The nurse nodded, but scampered to the diagonal corner and hid behind its flute.

"Sso, young warmblood." Sahaang smiled, as she eased herself onto the couch facing his, "it is good to see that you have recovered from our doctoring."

"Oh, the arm?" He lifted it, flapping it like a wing. "You did a great job—many thanks. Without you, I might have lost it."

"Yes, the doctor said as much." Her eyelids nictitated as

she studied him. "What brings you back so soon?"

"Three things." Unbuttoning his shirt, he reached inside and withdrew the hide-wrapped egg. "First, I forgot to ask: when this hatches, what will the youngster eat?" He hefted the bundle, puzzled by a difference in it.

"Are insects common on Sol III?"

"Oh, sure." He peeled back the layers of hide to examine the egg. Something wasn't the same. "All kinds, all shapes, all sizes. What's best?"

"One that is perhaps half the length of your littlest finger. Alive. Put it into the hatchling's container—"

"Container?" He snapped his fingers. "Hey, this has grown, hasn't it?"

"Of course it has. It will stretch to the size of your head before it hatches—did I not tell you?"

"Not that I remember. And what's this about a container?" There was something faintly repulsive about the notion of raising an intelligent being in an aquarium.

"It's not essential, of course, but the hatchlings are stupid, curious, and annoyingly mobile. We find it best to confine them for their own protection—otherwise they would go outside to explore and die." She raised a scaled finger. "As it grows, feed it larger and larger insects, not more and more, but larger and larger. It will sleep when it has eaten its fill."

"It's hard to get them much bigger than—" His fingers demonstrated the size of a giant cockroach. "What do I do then?"

"Small mammals. Again, one at a time. It does not require privacy while it eats, but you might wish to leave the room. As infants, Rhanghan are savage—and messy—diners." She chuckled. "Next summer, during feeding hours, our nursery will sound like a torture chamber."

"Will it eat only live food?" He prodded the shell with an experimental finger; the material gave way, but filled out as soon as he removed it.

"Oh, no. When it is perhaps—" She held her hand at knee height. "—this tall, you can start to feed it raw meat. Or raw fish. After a while, try cooked meat. Once it comes to accept that, you can start offering it vegetables and starches and the like . . . although it may be three or four years before it develops a taste for them."

"When will it start talking?"

"It will start listening about the time you run out of insects. Speech comes more slowly. Perhaps a year? Two years? It varies. Once it starts, though, it will be loath to stop. Consider yourself warned."

"Thank you." Covering the egg again, he slipped it back into his shirt.

"You said three things," reminded Sahaang.

"Yes, I did. The entire time I've been here, you've been really helpful and friendly. I'm grateful for that—you saved my life, literally—but I am curious. You didn't owe me anything. You didn't take me into your clan, like the Timili did. Why?"

Her leathery lips parted in a toothy smile. "Could it be, McGill Feighan, that I accord you the courtesy I accord every honest Flinger? Could our Talents not forge a link between us tighter than the link between our worlds?"

"I— I'd never thought of it like that before."

"I did not say that was the answer." She leaned back. Her forest-green eyes glittered with unreadable emotions. "Could it be that I am a meddler? That, seeing you opposed by forces unknown to you, I could not resist interfering for the purpose of balancing the scales?"

He blinked. "It could be," he admitted, sensing now how she wanted to enact the scene.

"Could it not also be that aliens and warmbloods both intrigue me, and that I did what I did to bring you closer to me, so that I could learn some of your ways, some of your thought processes?"

"Sure, it could be." He nodded.

"Could it not be that as Senior Flinger on Throngorn, I have a duty to ensure that corruption touches us not?"

"Y—es," he agreed.

"Finally, could it not be that by aiding you, an enemy of The Organization, which is my enemy, I have strengthened my position at little or no cost to myself?"

"It's certainly plausible," he said. "But which is it?"

She laughed. "You warmbloods never have learned to appreciate subtlety and ambiguity, have you? I think I choose not to answer. I have been as definite as I care."

He had to shake his head. "All right." It seemed like the older he got, the more confusing were the motivations of the people who interacted with him. "I guess I'll have to live with uncertainty. I want you to know, though, that I did—that I do—appreciate everything you've done for me."

She dismissed her assistance with a wave of her hand. Lamplight shimmered on her scales. "And the third thing?"

"I'm going home, now. I wanted to say goodbye."

"'Goodbye' or 'until we meet again'?"

"I thought you were the one who liked ambiguity."

She threw back her head, and laughed loudly enough to startle the nurse. "I deserved that, McGill Feighan. You are welcome here any time. And I hope that on Delurc you will find the answer to your questions."

He gawked at her. "How did you know?"

"I am Sahaang, young warmblood. Come back sometime, and I will evade your questions on that subject, as well. Goodbye."

"Goodbye."

PING

Strangely bland to his nostrils was the filtered, dried, cooled, and machine-blown air of the New York City Flinger Building. He looked around the room he knew so well. Small, low-ceilinged, cinderblocked, yellow paint peeling off in long strips—he was home. As usual, Greystein was bent over his desk, concentrating so furiously on a circuit chip that he hadn't noticed McGill's arrival. He crept up behind him, and in his ear whispered, "Boo!"

"Jesus!" The chip bounced off the acoustic panels of the ceiling. "Dammit, Feighan, you scared the shit out of me, but it's good to have you back, quite a suntan you picked up, and the beard is definitely rancid, it must go as soon as possible, and what the devil is that?"

The exposed egg wobbled on the desktop. "It's my next roommate, a Rhanghan from Throngorn. Think you can build me an incubator?"

"No problem." Picking it up, he held it to the light. "Damn, there *is* something in there. Body temperature all right?"

He shrugged. "I guess so. Look, can you fix it so it runs off both electricity and solar-rechargeable batteries?"

"With a thermostat to keep the temperature from varying more than half a degree either way, it'll be a cinch. Tomorrow? I'm going to charge you for it, you know, now that you've inherited that trust fund the amoeba set up for you."

"I'd forgotten all about that. Damn. I'm a rich ol' bastard

now, huh?" He wondered where he could buy twenty good knives... "Whatever it costs. And tomorrow's superb."

"How big does this grow?"

"The egg or the Rhanghan?"

"Oh, the egg grows too? How much, I'll leave room."

"About the size of my head. And the Rhanghan— big. Very big." He dropped onto his bed and bounced a time or two to remind himself of all he'd missed. The springs squeaked. It felt good.

"Why the solar-power bit?" asked Greystein, swaddling the egg in the hide again. "Expecting generator trouble?"

"Uh-uh." He took the bundle, tucked it inside his shirt, and lay down on the mattress. Memory claimed it was lumpy. Body said it was the smoothest, softest surface he'd slept on in ages. "No, not trouble, just travel."

Greystein frowned. "Is the FNC shipping you out, or what?"

"No, I picked up a lead to another place the gastropod stopped at on its way here."

His roommate's frown became a wince. "I thought they would have told you."

"No, I Flung right— told me what?" He raised his head from the pillow and supported himself on his elbows. "Told me *what?*"

Greystein spun a chair around and straddled it, draping his forearms over its back. "McGill, I—" Half-closing his eyes, he made a visible attempt to conjure up the best, the most comforting words. "It came here while you were gone, and—"

"The gastropod? Here?" He leaped to his feet. "Why didn't you say so sooner? Where is it, I've got to—"

He put his hand on Feighan's stomach and gently eased him back onto the edge of the bed. "McGill, it arrived and it died."

The news blackjacked him. Dazed, he rubbed the nape of his neck and shook his head. "Died?" The word emerged as a squeak. It couldn't have; it was almost his third parent and for it to pass away without him in attendance was a betrayal. "Dead? But—" Looking into his friend's eyes, he found sorrow and compassion—both of which annoyed him. He didn't want them. They were no help. Still the eyes, clear and sad and compelling, swelled in his vision; the walls unfocused. He heard himself ask through a fog, "H-how?"

"Nobody knows. It just— died." He shrugged his help-lessness.

"Did it— did it say anything, or—"

Greystein took a breath. "Yes," he said slowly, "yes, it did, just before— I mean, it wasn't sick or didn't seem so; it didn't complain, it just— it said something, and then collapsed. It lost its shape and flowed outwards, spreading like an ochre pool, and—"

"What did it say?" He clenched his jaws. Two-thirds an orphan before, he was now fully alone—and it hurt. His whole body was rigid; he could practically hear his tendons snapping from the strain. "What. Did. It. Say?"

He touched McGill's arm as if to offer aid. "Its last words were, 'Feighan—must expiate self for twisting otherwise straight life—caused I you to dwell in lie—did it I on a lark. A lark.'"

"A lark?" he whispered out of stunned disbelief. No, it couldn't have, it was his— no, for a parent so to deceive its— *Oh God the pain!*

"A lark," repeated Greystein, while sympathy softened his face. "McGill—I'm sorry."

"Yeah," he mumbled, falling back onto his pillow and, eyes open, not seeing the ceiling, "yeah, so'm I."

▪ Chapter XXVIII ▪

The curtains rustled away from their midline; the tank glowed blue and gold. The swirls were paler than they had been before Throngorn II, as if the expedition had exhausted Gryll. They were more agitated, too, more convoluted. They looped upon themselves in a webwork so intricate as to be hullucinatory. "Hommroummy," staticked the speakers.

"Gryll!" he exclaimed, feigning heartiness. "Thank God you survived the ambush."

"Discuss ambush later. Feighan on Earth."

"Yes, I know." He indicated his computers. "The report just arrived."

"Capture."

"Of course. I shall assign—"

"Yourself."

"Sir?" Eyebrows arched, but face impassive, he cocked his head as he peered into the tumbling gases. "I am to capture him myself?"

"Relieved of all other duties. Re-evaluated after capture."

Somewhat unsteadily, Hommroummy made his way to a chair and sank into it. He didn't have a chance of catching and holding a Flinger. The assignment was a sentence to lifelong frustration. "May I— may I ask why, sir?"

For a moment the tank brightened, as if with pleasure. "Punishment. Lenient punishment. Rebels usually die."

And the curtains closed on Hommroummy's shock.

▪ **Chapter XXIX** ▪

The opening door poured light across the darkened room. McGill closed his eyes and turned his head away, not caring who padded through the dimness toward him. What did it matter, now? Dishes rattled; coffee awakened his nose, if not his interest. A hand prodded his shoulder. "McGill."

"What?" he slurred, pretending to a sleepiness he didn't feel.

"I brought you breakfast." Greystein grated the tray on the grit of the desktop. He fumbled for the lamp switch. "Since you missed dinner—"

Blinking, shielding his face, he said, "I'm not hungry." And he wasn't. He was mourning. A dull disquiet knotted his stomach, but it was as much nausea as hunger. He'd gag if anything crossed his tongue, gag and heave it right out again. "Go away."

"Oh, and I put the egg in the incubator, which is working perfectly fine, as is usual with my creations." He sat on the edge of the mattress.

Starting to slide down the slope made by his roommate's weight, McGill braced himself with his left hand. He felt sticky and smelly—and hoped he was repulsive enough to drive the other away. He didn't want concern, or friendship, or affection—he wanted silence, blackness, oblivion: a quiet time and a private place for his bitter grief. "Leave me alone, will you?"

"I talked to the boss." His voice was warm and soft. "You've got a month of leave time coming, which he said you might as well take to relax, lie in the sun for a while—"

Greystein's proximity was an irritant, like an anthill beside a picnic blanket. His worry oozed from his skin to fill the room with a sickening stench. McGill knew that at any moment he would jump up and grab him by his collar, then throw him out, maybe after bashing his head against the wall, maybe after breaking his arm, but he would do it. His presence was a buzzing fluorescent, an untuned engine, a sander shoved against his side and rasping through his ribs. "Get out of here."

"—and once you're back in shape, you can start work."

"Uh-uh."

"Pardon?"

"I'm not going to."

Greystein cleared his throat. "You're not going to do what?"

"Work. Why should I?"

"Well, there's your living to earn—"

"The trust fund'll take care of me."

"—your Talent to use—"

"Shit on that."

"—the Network to maintain—"

"Screw it."

"Look, McGill, you can't just—"

"Out!" he shouted. He rolled onto his stomach, then pushed himself to all fours. "Get out. Now."

Greystein stood. "Hey, listen—"

"Did you hear me, fuckhead?" bellowed McGill. "I said get out! Take your shitty face and then get the hell out of my goddam room—" He was pounding the mattress with both hands. Raising them above his head, he slammed them down with all the force in his body. "—and stay the hell out or I will take you by the scruff of your neck and ram your jewboy nose so far up your ass that it'll come out your ears now GET THE HELL OUT NOW!"

Greystein paused long enough to open his fists, untense his body, and exhale loudly. "Yeah," he said at last. "I'll go. Before I do, though—I know you're under a lot of pressure, and you didn't mean what you said, and—and anytime you need me, give me a holler, okay?" He turned, then, and walked quickly to the hall.

"I meant it all!" Tears streamed down his face. "All of it,

every word, do you hear, every goddam motherfucking w-w-word—" The door closed, quietly. Salt water spattered his wrists. He turned, and hurled his face into the pillow.

A joke, he thought, muffling his sobs. *My whole life ruined for a joke.* He kicked his feet against the sheets and rubbed his face on the pillowcase, back and forth, harsh and quick, back and forth, scrape and shave, rubbing it as though to file away his features and obliterate his being.

He couldn't believe that the gastropod had died. It wasn't right; it wasn't fair. And that it had so betrayed him, twice—that was incredible. He hated it. And he loved it. All he was, he owed to it—and yet he wasn't what he was, because it had lied, so he owed it nothing . . . he was torn, and tortured, and grief throbbed in his emptiness like a wound bleeding into vacuum. He couldn't stop mourning its death, no matter how he tried to despise its life, because it had always been an integral part of him, like a seafaring father, or a starbound brother. He cried. Half the tears were for himself—the rest he wept for it.

A joke, a joke, a goddam joke . . . the refrain had run through his mind for almost twenty-four hours, now, pulsing like a heart, as unshakable as a shadow, *a joke, a joke, a goddam joke* . . . realer than the world, louder than a war, *a joke, a joke, a goddam joke* . . .

He felt hollow inside, eviscerated almost, as though his soul or nature or identity had been definite only so long as the gastropod served the Far Being Retzglaran. It had been a lie, though, a balloon, and the needle of revelation had punctured it. The air had hissed out, emptying him. But he'd already shaped himself around it, contouring his character into congruence with its curves and planes, its awkward angles and asymmetrical solids. It had informed him; it had been the skeleton of his spirit. Now that it was gone, and no longer supported him, he was crumbling, sagging, slumping into an amorphous nonentity that bore no relation to the McGill Feighan who would have been had the alien not swallowed him, or to the McGill Feighan who would have been had its initial explanation been true. Lost between the two divergent could-have-beens, bereft of himself, he melted like a sun-washed ice sculpture, and longed for death.

For he'd brought that to the others: to his mountainous father and softeyed mother, to spry old Schwedeker and ear-cocked

Rothono, to innocent bystanders and deadly enemies alike . . . *for a joke, for a joke* . . . the face swam up before him and maggots crawled in their mouths, multiplied in their moaning, moribund mouths . . . because of him, because of who he'd thought he was, because of a goddam goddam joke . . .

A jest, a jape, a joke, a jibe, a jeer . . . the world was jeering him, billions and billions of nameless faces crowded together in laughing, pointing, mocking masses. "Feighan the fool," they cackled, "Feighan the infecter . . ." They saw, while he writhed humiliated on a rumpled bed in a darkened room, how he'd gone deluded through life—worn a mask that he'd palmed off as his visage—woven a fantasy out of a hoax and in its tangled, lethal threads strangled those closest to him . . .

The gastropod was dead, and he was not who he'd thought he was. All the separate facets of his former being fell away from the false framework, burst out like the shrapnel of a bomb, glittered briefly as the sun hit their once-protected undersides, and disappeared.

He was nothing.

PING

Tumbling across time-smoothed tiles, head over heels over ass over shoulder, he had time to gasp "Wha—?" before a wall broke his nose. It was a clear wall, transparent, but the light within and the dark waters without made it a mirror that reflected his shock-stretched features. Blood gushed from his nostrils to mat his beard. His fingers shook. "Who— who did that?" It took three tries to pull his handkerchief from his hip pocket and press it to his upper lip. "Who— fuck it," he mumbled through the sodden cloth. His mind whirled, losing him in time as thoroughly as it had lost him in space. "Mom, I'm sorry! Dad— Dad—" And the dome echoed back, "—reee, Da-a-aad, dead . . ." And the pain, oh God the *two* pains and the hate and the swelling nose and the rage at being thrown into the light, thrown sloppily into the glare and the gleaming white tiles and a voice full of surprise asked, "Sir Sky Swimmer. Be you well?"

He whirled, and leveled a trembling finger at the ceiling-mounted speakers. "Do I look well, asshole? My goddam nose is goddam broken and where the *hell* am I?"

"Delurc, Sir Sky Swimmer, Delurc of the deep and the dreams. Forgive my poor speech; the Terran talker sleeps. What currents bear you to our reefs, may I ask?"

He stamped his foot as if to drive his boot through the floor. "Bring me the Far Being Retzglaran!"

"There be no such being here, as I know it. Perhaps another may have answer to your question. But first the formalities demand satiation." A panel slid into the wall at the far end of the Flop Booth; beyond it extended a glassed-in walkway around which fish swam and seaweed twined. "Customs be that way; please experience them."

"I want the Far Being!" His voice cracked as the vibration of his vocal cords twanged his septum.

"Sir Sky Swimmer," said the Delu, now audibly impatient, "a shipment of sportsrips be due here now, and though they be frisky delights to adult Delu, their teeth chew Terran flesh and relish the gnash of bone. Please, Customs await you."

His rage was diminishing, now, as the cold dampness of the Flop Booth seeped through his skin. He shuffled across the large room, seeing his image bounce off the curved walls like ball lightning trying to escape. His tunic was flaring brighter than ever before, but he was too discouraged to care. He trudged into the corridor. The door whisked shut almost before he was clear of its path. Instantly, the room behind him filled with snapping, twisting, ten-meter monsters—the great white sharks the Delu imported as pets. The being in charge at once began to flood the chamber to keep them alive.

In a cubicle ahead sat a Terran, a middle-aged female of paper-pallid skin and sequoia girth. She wore a metal cap, and wires ran from its top to the water-side wall of her booth. Outside, an eight-finned fish wore a similar, linked cap. She was its translater. "Passchip," she said in a voice as hollow as an air bubble.

"Tell the Far Being I'm here."

"Passchip."

"I'm a Flinger, I can go anywhere, it would save a lot of trouble if the Far Being would just come to—"

"Purpose of visit."

Lights awoke in the other cubicles as Delu, aroused by the commotion, slipped into their translators. "You must show your passchip," said one. "Tell us the purpose of your visit," cross-spoke another. "Name rank and serial number," called a third.

"Are you the Far Being?" he screamed. "Give me the Far Being, I must see it, I'll search-Fling-ping-pong till it shows,

bring it to me, I don't want *you, it* must, *I* want, bring, give—"
And he slithered to his knees, crying aloud, while the blood
dripped from his nose and the interrogators babbled on. It was
hopeless, useless; he'd never find the Far Being. It didn't exist.
There had been a slug, but it was a phony. It was dead, now,
dead and decomposing and strangely enough that hurt so very
much that he had to remind himself that it had swallowed him
for a joke and destroyed his life. He was alone on Delurc where
fish called for his name but he could not answer because he
had no name. Orphaned again, he was no one, he was nothing . . .

PING

Sulfur burned his eyes while he tumbled helplessly across
cinder-strewn tiles. The ceiling speakers made a noise like a
gasp but he didn't hear, he was confused by the pains of his
nose and abraded back and shattered soul. He staggered to his
feet. "Who *did* that to me?" he wailed, swinging his arms and
jerking around as though to confront an attacker, an enemy,
but there was nothing within the white box except wisps of
acrid smoke. His antagonist, who'd thrown him here to Actu,
world of volcanic fire and flame, had already fled, so he would
follow. He ran to the door, coughing in the bad air. "Where
is he, let me at him—" beating on the metal portal while
grieving, *thought I was special to the Far Being, thought I'd
grow up and it'd summon me, we'd prolly sit and talk, be like
bullshooting with God, it'd make me see myself, it's the wisest
creature alive and answering just one of its questions'd teach
me more about myself than,* but it was a lie, "LET ME AT
HIM!" thudding fists on the aloof door and a voice up above
going "Please calm yourself, sir. You will avail yourself nothing by such behavior. Please, sir, self-control is all. We see
that you sadly lack it, but please, gentle with the equipment."

He was ranting in his mind, raving while his energy dwindled and dragged him down an emotional spiral staircase to
the bottom, to the slower, lower rageless bottom, to the lair
of despair, but he was descending with reluctance, screaming,
"LET ME AT HIM!" while thinking, *Me, McGill Feighan,
could have known myself like no man ever has, should have,
would have, won't 'cause the slug lied, the bug died, oh my
lost father, I'll never look into that infinite mirror now, or ever
fulfill myself,* "LET ME OUT OF HERE!" *all my life wanted
to meet the Far Being, say, 'I'm McGill Feighan, the one you*

had your gastropod eat, and I've always been curious, why me?' but the slug for a joke for a goddam the slug lied wasn't orders, wasn't singling me out for anything but a hoax and I'm not special, it meant nothing, I'm not anybody, nobody, nothing...

PING

This Flop Booth had an untiled floor because the Rii—edsch were proud of their topsoil. Six feet deep in the shallow spots and so full of life that farms were unnecessary—what grew wild was enough—it balled rich and black and spongy in a squeezing hand, like good chocolate cake.

McGill went face first into it and dug a furrow with his jaw that ran the length of the room. Stonefree, it slashed no gashes in his chin, but it packed his mouth and ran up his nose and fluffed his beard with its humus. Retching, spitting, he pushed himself to his feet. "WHO DID THAT TO ME?" he bellowed when his tongue was free. "WHY ARE YOU TORTURING ME, can't you SEE I hurt enough?" He wiped his face. Blood slicked his hand, blood from his nose and tears from his eyes. He stumbled to the exit door, which portcullised up before he could reach it.

In the corridor beyond stood a twelve-legged marsupial with shifty eyes and a nervous tail. McGill ignored it, McGill pushed past it—for out the far door slipped a gray man clutching a ratty tattered coat around an energy tunic. "Jose! JOSE!" He was halfway down the hallway before the marsupial caught him from behind.

"Aren't you Feighan?" it asked in Terran.

Turning bewildered to address it, he said, "Huh?"

"Are you—" It consulted a memo-com. "—McGill Feighan?"

"Never heard of him."

"Bushwa." It drew a laser. "We're looking for you, and—"

"AAARRRGGGHHH!" he screamed in frustration, and noticed absently that its eyes popped as he Flung it into the heart of Sol. Then he pivoted again, and began to walk toward the vine-framed doorway a hundred meters away. *The Organization*, he thought, *still after me, still chasing me, why the hell, whyn't they just leave me alone, go away, prolly think...dunno what they think, whyn't they just...*

It was almost more than he could bear, that The Organization was still pursuing him, even though he wasn't the quarry they'd thought . . . the Far Being Retzglaran had had nothing to do with him, and it was the Far Being which had always seemed to interest them. Now that the gastropod had admitted its hoax, he'd have thought that they would leave him alone.

But they wouldn't, that was the problem, and the irony. They would never believe that the Far Being hadn't ordered his ingestion. Liars themselves, they would never accept his story as the truth. Their entire mental outlook would convince them that he was lying just to avoid a confrontation. The irony: he was mad, but they were crazy.

So they'd continue to pursue him, dogging him night and day, from planet to planet, star to star—no matter where he went, the local arm of The Organization would have been warned to watch for him, as it had been here, on Rii—edsch, a world he hadn't even known he was traveling to until he was already on it. Everywhere in the universe, cold beings would seek him out to deliver him to their masters.

And why? For a goddam joke . . . oh, he didn't deceive himself, he knew he had a Talent that they might find useful, but thousands of other beings had similar talents and *they* weren't being hounded, no, just him, McGill Feighan. The Organization would take him, and it would break him to bare the secret of his association with the Far Being, and, exposing nothing, would settle for making him its tool, as it had with Crafioni . . .

And he would be helpless to resist because he wouldn't know where the attacks would come from, the manner they would take, the time of day, the point of the compass, anything . . . his life would be one of constant wariness, constant alertness . . . for when the moment came, if he weren't ready, he would be impotent . . . and he would be consumed, ingested, digested . . . and he would again be no one, nobody, nothing . . .

*PI—

This time, in the instantaneous eternity of the Fling, he caught his assailant: himself. His subconscious. His Talent itself had been teleporting him to random planets to wake him up, to free him from his lunatic prison, to shock him back to sanity.

—NG*

An openwork wicker floor skinned his knees as he hit too fast and rolled like a hard-stroked cue ball. The air was chill, and stroboscopic upward glimpses showed a cloudless green sky. A voice whistled, "WARE!"

He hit a light, feathery body.

Which yelped.

Shredding wicker walls shrieked dryly as the being into whom McGill had collided hurtled through them.

Momentum transferred, he stopped. On his back, he gathered his breath and studied that emerald sky. Then he knew, with a pang, and a pain like a dagger had breached his ribcage, that he was on Rehma, a world of intelligent avians. That the Flop Booth where he trembled was woven onto a tree branch a hundred meters above the ground. That the being he'd propelled through the walls had emerged in open air, with nothing below its feet but those hundred vertical meters... "No!" He scrambled erect and ran to the gaping hole in the wall. "No!"

"More luck have you than a fortune moth, Flinger of Terra," tweeted the Flop Booth operator through its speakers. "The being stricken by you ope'd its wings wide, and averted calamity by the length of a beak."

"It saved itself?" he asked, hardly daring to believe it.

"That's what I said," replied the Rehmal.

"Thank God." His legs were weak; slowly, they shrugged off their responsibility and eased him to the floor. *Jeez, could have killed it*... for a moment his anger surfaced and seared his soul, *dumbshit fool Flinging around like that blasting into innocent bystanders oughta throw you outta the Network, cool you off in a prison somewhere, teach you not to—* but he recognized the start of another cycle. Knowing that if he didn't break free it would carry him off to despair and ruin, he struggled mightly to tame his rage.

But it was hard. His teeth ground together; his hands fisted again and again. Shallow and harsh rasped his breath, while his heart beat like a war drum. *Dammit, you fool!* His biceps flexed, and the muscles across his chest drew tight. *Idiot!* Quivering with pent-up fury, he almost gave way to a mindless explosion—

And caught himself just before leaping to his feet. *No.* He forced his fingers to open, to spread. *Easy.* Deliberately, he inhaled his lungs to pained fullness—and then sucked in a bit more. *Relax.* He pried his jaws apart and willed his head into a loose loll on his shoulders. *Calm and easy and relax, man...that's better, much better.*

Anger wouldn't help—

Nothing will help, called a part of his mind.

—he had to gain control of himself—

How can you control what you don't know, what doesn't exist?

"By being calm, breathing easy, and staying cool."

Why?

"'cause I could hurt somebody," he muttered.

So what?

"Can't go around hurting people, it's not right."

That's all you do is hurt; you never help. You can't. You don't have the ability to help.

"It's not true, I do."

Uh-uh. You thought you did, when you thought the slug was the Far Being's, but now that you know it's not—

"Whatever it was doesn't change what I am."

What are you?

"I—"

Human? Eetie? Half-n-half?

"I—"

You'll never know, will you?

That was the worst of it. Regardless of whose the gastropod had been, it had swallowed him. It had held him for four days. It had, somehow, changed him.

But how?

He would never know. Never. It wasn't around to tell him. It was dead, and whatever changes it may have wrought might as well be dead themselves, because they wouldn't have anyone to explain them, to instruct him in their use...what did he have in himself, in his soul or in his cells, that the slug had put there? How would he ever find out? He couldn't...no, there *had* to be a way. The talents, the gifts, the whatever—they couldn't lie dormant till the end of time, just because the gastropod was dead...someone, somewhere in the galaxy knew what it had done, and...

But you don't have them now, and without them, you're nothing.

"Y— No! I—"

Nothing.

Weariness washed over him, yet a distant part of his soul shouted through its muffling thickness not to succumb, *resist!* "No," he slurred, "no . . ."

Nothing!

"No, you're wrong, no . . . go away, will you? . . . can't be nothing, I'm a Flinger, huh? I'm something else, too, something I'll maybe never find out . . . but if I don't, I'm still a Flinger . . . me . . ." He shook his head, and winched as his scrapes and bruises complained. Picking a seed out of his teeth, he dropped it through the floor.

Curiously, he felt almost peaceful. Sad, yet at ease. He'd lost a very special, very precious attribute—but one which, seen from his new and rather precarious vantage point, had only insulated him from himself. Instead of enchancing the true McGill Feighan, it had suppressed him . . . forced to assume its configuration, he'd been a bonsai tree: unique and eye-catching, yet unnaturally stunted. Because of it, he hadn't grown the way he should have.

He flushed with shame, and leaned his head back against the wall. The cold breeze dried his sweat and took his excess heat. *What an obnoxious little bastard I must have been*, he thought, *making that eetie's prank into the only important event of my life . . .*

But you'll never know, whispered that tempter.

"So?" He shrugged, and the movement hurt. His battered body was beginning to stiffen. "So?" What difference did it make? He wasn't a rock, a fossil, frozen at one point in time and afterward unable to adapt. He was a human, a man, and to a man, the past is no more than prologue. Like skiing: the top of the slope imparts a direction and a velocity, but one is not bound to them—one can change them—if one wills it.

But the mystery! insisted that seducer.

He made a rude noise. That didn't matter as much as he'd once thought. If he never learned the reason for the gastropod's behavior—so what? He'd probably encounter clues anyway, and trace them . . . but everyone's birth is a mystery, everyone's! People don't know why *they* and not others were brought into being. They just take it for granted that their lives did commence—their lives, not others'—and they proceed from there. It would be stunningly audacious of him to refuse to fulfill himself until he'd unraveled the secret of his birth . . .

And immature, too, he realized ruefully.

He had a lot going for him: a Talent, an education, a job . . . health, wealth, and a certain degree of fame . . . good looks, an affable if dwarfed personality, friends . . . he blushed again as he remembered his abuse of Greystein. He'd have to apologize when he got back.

Because he was going back. He'd do his job, develop his real self, explore the areas he'd ignored throughout the gastropod quest—*like girls,* he thought wryly, *they ought to be much more fun* . . . he'd learn to become McGill Feighan, and he'd enjoy every step of the way.

"O Flinger of Terra," called the Rehmal from its perch high above his head, "broken still is the wall. Are you skillful at caning?"

"My deepest regrets," he said, looking up. "I haven't the craft to fix it, but it is my responsibility. My name is McGill Feighan. If you'll send me a bill—?"

"Assuredly we will."

"Thank you."

He pulled himself to his feet and leaned against the quick-bulging wicker for support. He shook his head.

Greystein materialized directly in front of him. "The Rehmal told us—"

Startled, McGill raised his hand—and lost his balance. He fell.

Greystein shouted, "Are you okay? Do you need—"

He chuckled, quietly at first, but then more loudly. Unsteadiness cackled the sound.

The other looked worried. "McGill—what is it? What's wrong?"

He made an effort to sober up, but laughter punctuated his explanation: "You know," he said, "this is the very first time that somebody who's come to help me has gotten here after I've already helped myself?"

He was still puzzled. "But—"

McGill stood, and fought off a wave of embarrassment. "Greystein, I—"

"Hey, no need to say it." He waved his hand in dismissing forgiveness.

"No. I do need to say it. You offered me friendship, and I threw it in the dirt. I'm sorry, so sorry I don't have words for it. And I called you some things that I'd like to cut my tongue out for having said. I know I can't take 'em back, but maybe I can make up for them, if you'll let me try." He held out his hand.

Greystein took it and, without a word, shook it solemnly.

"Come on," McGill said, slapping his friend on the shoulder. "Let's get home. I've got a lot to do before my leave time's up—and say, how's the egg?"

PING

MS READ-a-thon— a simple way to start youngsters reading

Boys and girls between 6 and 14 can join the MS READ-a-thon and help find a cure for Multiple Sclerosis by reading books. And they get two rewards — the enjoyment of reading, and the great feeling that comes from helping others.

Parents and educators: For complete information call your local MS chapter. Or mail the coupon below.

Kids can help, too!